... is ... bestselling and award-winning author of twenty-nine novels and one work of non-fiction. From his teens he wanted to be a novelist but first tried his hand at a real job, studying and working in architecture before turning to English literature, spending five years at a newspaper and obtaining an MA and PhD in literature.

The ex-CIA character of Jed Walker was first introduced in *The Spy*, which was followed by *The Hunted*, *Kill Switch*, *Dark Heart* and *The Agency*.

James has also written five titles in the Lachlan Fox thriller series, and the Alone trilogy of young adult post-apocalyptic novels. A full-time novelist since the age of twenty-five, he spends his time writing thrilling stories and travelling the world to talk about them.

To find out more about James and his books,
visit www.jamesphelan.com

Follow and interact with James

www.facebook.com/realjamesphelan
www.twitter.com/realjamesphelan
www.instagram.com/realjamesphelan

BY JAMES PHELAN

The Lachlan Fox books
Fox Hunt
Patriot Act
Blood Oil
Liquid Gold
Red Ice

The Jed Walker books
The Spy
The Hunted
Kill Switch
Dark Heart
The Agency

The Alone series
Chasers
Survivor
Quarantine

James
Phelan

Fox
Hunt

CONSTABLE

CONSTABLE

First published in Australia and New Zealand in 2006 by Hodder Australia,
an imprint of Hachette Livre Australia Pty Limited.

First published in eBook in Great Britain in 2018 by Constable

This paperback edition published in Great Britain in 2019 by Constable

1 3 5 7 9 10 8 6 4 2

Copyright © James Phelan, 2006

The moral right of the author has been asserted.

A CIP catalogue record for this book
is available from the British Library.

ISBN: 978-1-47212-926-0

Typeset in Simoncini Garamond by Bookhouse, Sydney
Printed and bound in Great Britain by CPI Group (UK), Croydon CRO 4YY

Papers used by Constable are from well-managed forests
and other responsible sources.

MIX
Paper from
responsible sources
FSC® C104740

Constable
An imprint of
Little, Brown Book Group
Carmelite House
50 Victoria Embankment
London EC4Y 0DZ

An Hachette UK Company
www.hachette.co.uk

www.littlebrown.co.uk

For Nicole

Sydney Evening Times

21 August 2005

AUSTRALIAN NAVY OFFICER DISCHARGED, CHARGES DROPPED

By P. Masson

Yesterday morning Lieutenant Lachlan C. Fox of the Royal Australian Navy was dismissed from service. The decorated veteran will never serve in the Australian Defence Force again. It took six months for a military tribunal to reach the guilty verdict.

Lt Fox was charged with seven military crimes, including 'Leaving a post' and 'Imperilling the success of operations'. 'Gross negligence in command', the one charge that could have brought prison time for Lt Fox, was dismissed. The death of Leading Seaman John Birmingham under Lt Fox's command has now been classified 'Killed in Action' by the Navy. LS Birmingham has been posthumously awarded the Commendation for Gallantry.

Lt Fox's record was a mitigating factor. Graduating from the Defence Academy near the top of his class, Lt Fox transferred from Defence Intelligence to the hands-on Special Forces, where he led a Clearance Diver Team – Australia's equivalent to the US Navy SEALs and Britain's Special Boat Service. He saw active service in the liberation of East Timor in 2000, and later in Afghanistan and Iraq.

While on peacekeeping duty, Lt Fox led members of his CD team into Indonesian-controlled West Timor without authorisation. LS Birmingham was shot and killed in an exchange with Indonesian troops and militia while attempting to release captured East Timorese nationals from a makeshift detention camp.

Lt Fox is still undergoing rehabilitation due to serious injuries sustained during his unauthorised mission.

Outside military court in Canberra, Lt Fox was asked if he thought the findings of the tribunal were fair. He replied with a quote from Theodore Roosevelt: '"The credit belongs to the man who is actually in the arena, whose face is marred by dust and sweat and blood…who, at the worst, if he fails, at least he fails while daring greatly."'

Lt Fox added that 'Today's finding was a tribute to the good that John Birmingham did for his country and those in need. But it also shows what kind of bureaucratic world we live in – those East Timorese captives died because of the UN's continued inactivity and there's no inquiry into that. It just proves the old adage: war is never black and white.' Asked what he would do now, Lt Fox said: 'Get as far away from here as possible and lead a quiet life.' ■

PROLOGUE

WAHABAD DESERT CAVES, IRAN

'This is incredible,' Alissa Truscott muttered to herself for the hundredth time that day. With almost every bone perfectly in place, it was the most exciting archaeological find any of them had ever come across. Alissa knew that soon, when the secrecy of the expedition was lifted, their discovery would stun the world.

Just as incredible as the preserved skeleton was the surrounding earth, which contained fragments of assorted flora, suggesting the figure had been buried ceremoniously. The emphasis on the rituals of death at such an early prehistoric period was an amazing revelation, made even more so by crude stone pictographs cut into the tomb walls, hinting at the life once lived and a belief that it could be carried on after death.

'How are you going there, Alissa?' inquired a deep, resonating voice. Richard O'Brien was a diehard Irishman with a large soup-straining moustache that made up for the lack of hair on his head. He had barely managed to squeeze his girth through the crawl space into the tomb itself, a small antechamber to the main cave system. The process had resembled a walrus moving across the ground.

'Fine, thanks, Professor O'Brien,' replied Alissa in her southern US way, richly articulated unlike the stereotypical drawl. She had six years at Princeton to thank for that.

'Magnificent,' O'Brien said, taking in the fully exposed skeleton. 'Shall we discuss our impending fame over lunch? The *National Geographic* photographer has arrived.'

Alissa wiped her thick cotton sleeve across her brow; it came away with a dirty smudge. 'Remind me to freshen up if a camera gets pointed my way.' She offered O'Brien her hand and he took it in his, pulling her slender frame to her feet. 'I'll leave my workbook here and finish up after lunch.'

The other members of the dig were already in the mess tent, exchanging the data they had uncovered during the morning in their separate areas of the cave system. On the table were several varieties of preserved vegetables, some dried meat and fish, a large bowl of yellow dip and a mountain of fresh flat bread. A decanter of one of O'Brien's reds was being passed around to add to the merry atmosphere and a small CD player was playing in one corner.

'Alissa, come sit down,' called Christian, a Danish student studying with her. He was holding an open sandwich in one of his long tanned hands; the other held a tin cup of wine. He scooted across the pine bench and made space for her shapely behind; it had become open knowledge that the two had begun an affair shortly after their arrival in Iran. The twenty-three-year-old Alissa would admit to no one, especially her new casual lover, that he was the first man she had slept with. She was a little disappointed that he was a bit clumsy but, admittedly, it wasn't a bad way to spend the cold nights of the desert winter.

Towards the end of their lunch, O'Brien, who had ended up beside Alissa, turned to whisper to her while the others were busy laughing at a story the *National Geographic* photographer was telling.

'I forgot to mention it earlier—last night I was preparing our material for the photo shoot and I noticed some of the excavated material is missing.' The soft smell of wine was evident on O'Brien's whispered words.

Alissa, fearing the worst, felt her stomach turn. 'Not the organic material, or the tool fragments—'

O'Brien cut her off: 'Shhh, not so loud.' He looked around to check everyone was still preoccupied. 'Nothing that important, but puzzling nonetheless. It's the rock trays, the mineral samples.'

Alissa looked from O'Brien to the others in the room. 'The mineral samples? You're sure someone's not running tests on them?' She knew the answer though: O'Brien ran a very tight ship.

'They'd have to clear it with me and sign them out.' O'Brien had a distant look on his face, trying to grasp a reasoning that he was sure was out there somewhere.

'It wouldn't surprise me if Orakov didn't bide by your rules,' Alissa said. 'He's given me the creeps since day one.'

O'Brien cocked an eyebrow, considering the comment. 'Before we figure out who, we have to ask ourselves why,' he said eventually.

The CD player stopped mid-track, hardly a rare occurrence due to its state. Christian, who had been humming along to the tune, got up to check and quickly saw it had no power at all.

'That bloody Russian hasn't fuelled the generator again!' he shouted, interrupting the photographer's current anecdote.

The tent went silent and all nodded agreement that the generator had gone off.

'I'll fix it myself,' Christian mumbled as he donned his parka and made for the door. He was only halfway to it when something came rolling through the doorway. Every eye in the tent stared uncomprehendingly at the small metal object as it tumbled across the floor.

An intense light and tremendous thunderclap rocked the tent and Alissa was thrown backwards onto the sand-covered floor. The last thing she saw through a smoky haze was the unshaven face of Dimitry Orakov staring down at her, an automatic pistol comfortably gripped in his hand.

GROZNY, CHECHNYA

The parade attracted a fanfare the like of which had never before been seen along the main streets of Grozny. State-funded vendors supplied hot foods to the crowd, while thousands of soldiers and police in dress uniform kept any citizens from flowing onto the sanctioned-off parade area. Every able body in the city had turned out despite the cold. Steam rose from the masses, giving physicality to their vocal jubilance. Independence had taken almost ten thousand military and civilian lives to achieve. Not only lives, but also years of hardship and misery for all concerned. Almost all.

The towering broad-shouldered man dressed in a long cashmere coat, Italian suit and shirt had not felt such pains. He had spent the past four years travelling between Grozny and a luxurious secret retreat, all the while maintaining true control over his semi-autonomous country through Russian-friendly rulers. Disposable men.

Now the time had come to take the reins himself.

President Sergei Ivanovich of the Republic of Chechnya stood on the decorated back of a flat-bed army truck—against the advice of his personal security chief—resplendent in the glory of the moment. For too long he had stayed in the shadows. Now he was the centrepiece of the procession, a convoy of over two hundred military vehicles. No one would dare make an attempt on his life today. In death he would become a martyr, creating even bigger problems for Mother Russia. And the local bands of rebels knew how ruthless he could be—a botched assassination attempt and the capture of the perpetrators had proven that point.

The people loved the show. Not that they really knew much about Ivanovich, besides his stellar career trajectory in the KGB and subsequent position as special military aide to the old Politburo, the former USSR's governing body. Being labelled by Putin as one of the most dangerous men in the world had guaranteed his prominence to the Chechen masses. They knew he looked like a leader, spoke like a leader.

Leading ran in the Ivanovich family. Ivanovich was old-school Soviet; his lineage had all been officers in the Soviet army and his younger brother was the current Vice–President of Azerbaijan, Chechnya's neighbour on the Caspian Sea. Already that alliance had reaped mutual benefits: free trade, dual citizenship, a combined military force.

Ivanovich waved to the masses, a collective of exiles driven to the region over the past two centuries. He had made it clear that their lives and futures were entwined, destined for greatness: a nation which would be heard on the world stage.

A security officer walked over to the float and passed up a folded note, which Ivanovich opened and glanced at quickly. He smiled. He waved. He threw his fists into the air and shook his arms to display the emotions he felt.

Yes, he thought, *yes! Now we will have real power!*

•

High above, death loomed. Orbiting slowly and silently, unknown to almost all in the world.

PART ONE

1

CHRISTMAS ISLAND

The day was windy and bright. Clouds whispered through the sky and an aeroplane soared overhead. It was a time of peace and quiet on the beach; too early for most tourists but too late for the morning anglers. Only one figure disturbed the serenity, his large feet splashing in the warm tropical water of the Indian Ocean. For Lachlan Fox this was the most peaceful place on earth, a sanctuary from the real world.

Every morning for the past few months this had been his ritual: a seven o'clock run along the beach for five kilometres and a swim back.

Fox paused at the end of his run and stretched out against the lone lifesaving tower that marked his distance. The paint flaked beneath his hands as he worked the tension out of his thighs. He couldn't help but laugh as the tower moaned against his weight, his own body protesting against the force. Every movement of his legs was a chore, but thankfully getting easier with each day of rehab. The swimming was therapy.

Five minutes and several routines later, he walked into the water. Every few seconds one of the soft breakers that rolled through the mouth of the cove sprayed against him, the waves remaining upright in the offshore breeze. The wind carried the noises of a small town rising.

Fox could see movement atop the far headland, mainly kids and their dogs running from house to house in search of whatever entertainment was on offer inside, getting as much as they could out of their morning before school. Fox looked at his house in the distance and saw the specks of kids playing cricket in the street.

For a wonderful moment his mind was free of purpose. Just the water and sky and murmurs of life.

The lapping water against his waist brought him back. The bay went deep fast, and there was no standing still in the shallows as the gradient of loose sand lured swimmers out.

With the sea calling, Fox duck-dived under a fresh set of waves and broke the surface with a practised freestyle.

•

Almost back where he'd started, Fox climbed the weathered wooden stairs leading up the steep cliff face of the northern headland of Flying Fish Cove.

The island's only port, and the township of Christmas Island, grew around the cove's arc like a crust. Most beach-view houses were original settlements, dating from the island's early days as a phosphate mine for the British Empire.

Fox's house was a never-ending renovation job, already with six months' worth of his own blood and sweat. Inside it looked like a bookstore, with barely a piece of wall in view. Stacks of *The Islander*, the local newspaper that Fox had created and edited each month, were piled like skyscrapers in one corner.

Fox entered, picking up the mail behind the door and flicking through it. The letters from the mainland he tossed on the unopened heap near the coffee table, the familiar handwriting of friends and family among the official correspondence.

He walked to the bathroom on autopilot and let the warm shower from rooftop solar pipes engulf him, the water removing both the sand and salt from his tanned skin. It had been a couple of days since he'd shaved and he lathered up whilst still in the shower, shaving with the speed and precision of someone who'd never used an electric razor.

Towelling off in front of the mirror, he decided to pick up the pace of his current exercise regime. Not that his six foot two, ninety-kilogram frame wasn't toned—it was merely something else to set his mind to.

He brushed his wet hair out of his eyes and left the room and its mirror, no longer noticing the pink scars that carried so many memories.

•

At ten o'clock that evening, Fox emerged from a pub and started walking home. It was balmy and the wind had picked up strength; bits of foliage were flying about. Cyclone Catherine, which was meant to skirt the island the next day, was closer than predicted. He pulled his collar up around his neck to shield himself against the sea spray—a futile gesture. The fine mist soon soaked him through.

Walking through the town's small botanical garden, Fox thought he heard a cry. He stopped to listen, but with the wind so strong it was impossible to pinpoint. Branches scraping metal roofs and loose items knocking about created a symphony of chaos. A few more paces around a bend and he came across three burly men, the type of merchant seamen who frequented the island's casino. They were blocking his path, and that of two young women headed in the opposite direction. The pair clung to each other for support, fear in their faces.

'Evening, boys,' Fox said as his danger sensors lit up.

'Fuck off—this ain't your business,' replied one of the men in a deep, heavily-accented Afrikaans voice. Two more figures emerged from the bushes to Fox's right.

'How do you know what kind of business I'm in?' asked Fox, buying himself time to weigh up his opponents. 'Why don't you boys leave those girls alone—I'm sure you can find something you like at the casino.' The casino was a notorious spot for Thai prostitutes.

'Piss off, mate, last chance.' This came from a mountain of a man to Fox's right.

Fox took a few more steps towards the five beefy men surrounding him. 'You see,' he began in a low, calm voice, 'there's the problem.' His blue eyes came alive and gleamed before the threat in front of him.

The first two sailors looked at each other in bemusement.

'Last chance, boys . . . how about I spot you a couple hundred for a good time some place else?' Fox continued in the same crisp voice. His days in the navy had included being at the pointy end of enough conflicts to know what he could handle. This situation was borderline. *Have to catch them off guard if it blows up . . .*

Of the two men to Fox's right, the largest, apparently the leader, gave a laugh.

In a lightning move that none expected and barely saw, Fox knocked two of the thugs to the ground. They dropped with cries of agony, whilst in seemingly the same passage of motion Fox's leg spun to his right with perfect timing. The resulting crunch was sickening. The man on the receiving end fell to the ground clutching his throat, barely able to breathe after the gracefully savage blow.

Fox was now facing the last two standing, the leader being one of them. His look of fright and disbelief turned to rage and he gestured his remaining henchman forward.

Fox let him approach. When the man produced a long curved blade, the two women—until now stunned into silence—let out shrill cries.

The two men mirrored each other's movements in a circular motion, much like a battle of wits between a matador and a near-defeated bull. The thug made his blunder when he got tired of sending jabs at Fox, which were expertly parried, and made an angry slash at his opponent. Fox jumped back a little to let the swipe go by, then caught the beam-like arm of the man and broke it like a twig across his upcoming knee, following with an elbow in the man's face.

Fox turned to where the leader stood, but was a second too late. Another cry came from the women, this time in warning, as Fox moved around, but a blow to the side of his head, accompanied by the shattering of glass, ended all motion.

Fox's eyes were still open when he hit the ground in a heap. The last thing he remembered passing through his blurred vision was a pair of feet moving towards him.

2

WASHINGTON, DC

Bill McCorkell, National Security Advisor to the President of the United States, had just finished his morning run. He shook his running partner's hand and the pair went their separate ways. McCorkell turned and strolled back towards the White House. As he ambled along in the light snow covering the ground of the Constitution Gardens, he looked about at the few early morning joggers game enough to brave the elements. Some ten paces away, his Secret Service agent jogged on the spot to keep warm. *Bet he wishes he'd been assigned to one of the fat cabinet members*, McCorkell thought.

A young family, southern tourists by the sound of their accents, were preparing to take a photo with the White House as the backdrop. McCorkell considered the scene—the white snow like a blanket of cottonwool hiding the city grime with a layer of freshness, and the young nuclear family proudly admiring the seat of their government and capturing it for posterity. The white snow was the purest thing in Washington, but even it would eventually succumb to the dirt beneath.

On reaching the Reflecting Pool, whose long expanse ran between the Washington and Lincoln monuments, McCorkell selected a position near the middle to pause and gaze in. The face of a weary man who'd had too little good sleep looked back at him, but he stared past the image into the dark stone. He enjoyed a full minute of nothingness before turning back to the House.

•

With the winter just past being one of the coldest on record, the temperature in the Oval Office at 8 a.m. seemed little above that outside to the six men gathered there.

A large TV screen on a portable stand was set up against a wall, showing file footage. McCorkell sped up the film to a point that showed tens of thousands of jubilant Chechens rugged up against the cold of last December's National Day, cheering President Ivanovich as he waved from the back of an army truck. After UN arbitration, the former Russian state had successfully achieved independence, promising peace in the region for the first time in decades.

'Mr President.' McCorkell began the daily Intel Meeting. On the early side of his fifties, McCorkell bore an uncanny resemblance to Napoleon Bonaparte—who was indeed a relative far removed. There was an edge in his voice as he spoke that the President rarely heard and doubted anyone else in the room detected. The pair went back many years, through many a crisis and many more bottles of scotch. What no one in the room knew was that this was the second such discussion McCorkell had conducted that morning.

'Last night at 11 p.m. our time, there was a huge explosion in Iran's portside city of Bandar-e Anzali.' McCorkell flicked the TV remote to show footage from an Iranian news station. 'Bandar-e Anzali is Iran's only military naval yard and main oil repository on the Caspian Sea. The Iranian government is selling this as an earthquake, but our sources are indicating otherwise. What caused the devastation is still unknown, but forty minutes ago the intent of this action was made clear. Chechnya are claiming responsibility.'

McCorkell reached into his attaché case and retrieved five folders, which were passed around the room to the members of the Security Council present: the President, CIA Director Robert Boxcell, Secretary of State Adam Baker, Secretary of Defence Peter Larter, and Tom Fullop, the White House Chief of Staff.

'Still fresh in our minds are the breakaway Caucasus oblasts—'

'Oblasts?' Fullop said.

'States,' McCorkell continued, 'of Russia forming an independent alliance with Azerbaijan, giving them a shared border with Iran and access to the Middle East and the Caspian Sea. The catalyst for this new collaboration was the election and international recognition of an autonomous Chechnya last December.' McCorkell gestured to the TV screen, now showing a close-up of Sergei Ivanovich, president of the world's newest nation, waving his fists at the cheering masses along the main avenue through Grozny.

'While most of the world's intel resources have been tied up in Afghanistan and Iraq combating global terrorism,

Chechnya has just stood up to tell everybody it wants to be noticed.'

'Hell of a way to go about it,' Larter said as he flicked through his folder.

'We are all aware of the military might of this nation—a force augmented by passionate and war-hardened personnel, and suspected to harbour many Afghanis and Iraqis after those regimes fell. The economy is propped up by extensive oil and natural gas reserves, and the country has shown a willingness to open trading channels with its neighbours and anyone else prepared to inject hard currency.' McCorkell took a sip of water as he held everybody's attention.

'And the attack on this port?' the President asked.

'The attack on Bandar-e Anzali left virtually nothing standing in the blast zone, which was almost a kilometre in diameter. Beyond that, fires and debris stretch throughout the suburban city.' McCorkell looked up from his notes.

'What could have caused the blast?' inquired Tom Fullop, genuine curiousity written all over his pointy face.

'Peter?' The President's National Security Advisor palmed off the question.

'Mr President, let's look at two things,' Larter said. 'One, the capabilities that Chechnya has. Two, what we can learn from the impact zone.' He produced a map and several A3-sized glossy photographs. 'The devastation caused could not have been produced by any known weapon in the Chechens' arsenal. From the size of the blast area, the easiest view to take would be that it was a small nuke or an incredible amount of explosives—which not only seems unlikely, but if you look at the photographs closely, there is no visible sign of a blast crater whatsoever. Even a daisy-cutter or an MOAB leaves a decent dent in the landscape.'

McCorkell, having been briefed on all the intel prior to the meeting, watched as the rest of the room took their time scrutinising the series of high-altitude images. The various magnifications of what was left of Bandar-e Anzali were as ambiguous to the others as to him. It was mass destruction with no telltale remnants of cause.

'Our analysts are going to need a bit more time nutting this one out,' Larter admitted.

Even the Secretary of Defence, responsible for the world's most formidable armed forces, has his limitations, McCorkell mused. Larter's parted blond hair showed the beginnings of grey and had thinned out over the past year of office; bags under his eyes augmented the lines on his lean face.

'Has this attack prompted any movement across the border?' the President asked his advisors.

'No,' Larter said flatly. 'The majority of Chechnya's troops have amassed along the Azerbaijan southern border, but this has been mirrored in force by the Iranians. Iran is still moving assets to the scene whilst calling up substantial numbers of reservists.'

'How's the projected outcome looking?' McCorkell asked the Secretary of Defence.

'The front line is going to be a tough call,' Larter said. 'Assuming Chechnya wins, how they hope to march all the way to the Gulf is beyond the Joint Chiefs and all our strategists. The Chechens barely have a quarter of the number of Iran's forces and their supply lines could easily be cut off.' Larter shifted in his seat before adding, 'Our Warfighter II satellite picked up something interesting overnight.'

McCorkell gave the Secretary of Defence a sideways look. *Withholding information? That's interesting . . .*

'Chechnya has sent its small fleet of heavy-lift aircraft to a suspected insurgent camp in northern Iraq about two hundred kilometres from the Iranian border. So they could, potentially, reach into Iran and back up their forces, but it's a damn small force—and that's if they can get over the border.'

'A small but important force,' McCorkell said. 'Chechnya only has one battalion of airborne armour.'

The room was silent for a moment as each man dwelled on the escalating situation.

'What the hell are the Chechens doing in Iraq?' asked Adam Baker, the youngest Secretary of State ever. His question was directed more to himself than anyone else, since overseas relations with and between countries fell within his realm of responsibility. He cracked his knuckles distractedly, then fidgeted his hands on his growing paunch. 'That's what we need to find out—'

'All right,' the President cut in, looking at his watch. 'By this time tomorrow I want answers. What the hell was used on Bandar-e Anzali, and what are those Chechens doing in Iraq?'

He pointed to Larter. 'Get the damn Iraqi Army ready to kick them out. And move in whatever assets we have nearby that can handle them, ready to move on my order.'

'The 11th Armoured are on standby outside Baghdad—I'm talking with the Joint Chiefs about scenarios this morning,' Larter said.

'Good. Bill, you mentioned that we have some idea why the Chechens targeted Bandar-e Anzali,' the President reminded his National Security Advisor.

'Yes, Mr President, here's the crunch.' McCorkell cleared his throat. 'The President of Chechnya, Sergei Ivanovich, has given Iran an ultimatum: if they do not secede everything west of the Fiftieth Longitude down to the Gulf, Chechnya will wipe Tehran off the map.' McCorkell felt the dynamic in the room change; the tension in the air was palpable. 'They have threatened a seven-day ultimatum, which started ticking at eleven o'clock last night.'

'This Chechen alliance is barely half the size of Iran, with a respectively proportioned armed force,' Larter said. 'Those Arabs will wipe them off the face of the earth within six days!' The Secretary of Defence was noticeably red in the face.

'Calm down, Pete.'

Larter took a sip of his black coffee in response to the President's words.

'Go on, Bill,' said the President, looking at the A3 photos of Bandar-e Anzali with a worried frown.

'Despite high oil prices, Iran is in the greatest economic lull it has ever experienced, with opposing sections of the country's Muslim populace creating havoc on the streets—particularly in the western provinces, where extremist militia have been causing hell for years.

'Late last year Chechnya and Azerbaijan offered millions to Iran for access to the Gulf, but Iran refused the offer.

'Now the Chechens are loading every naval and merchant vessel afloat in the Caspian Sea with military personnel and hardware. They seem intent on landing on Iranian soil. Iran hasn't responded to the attack yet. They are still dealing with the shock of the port's destruction, and are in the process of diverting army units from the growing northern front to evacuate the injured and recover the dead.'

'Adam, I don't care what you have to do to make it happen, but get an audience with the Ayatollah and President of Iran. Today.'

'Yes, Mr President,' Baker said.

'We've got just over six days to avert this mess,' the President said to his staff, all true and trusted men of sound judgement.

Each man paused, waiting for someone else to begin the debate.

'Well?' the President asked, his temper rising.

McCorkell took the cue, flicking through his notes as he spoke. 'Let's have another look at what assets we have on hand . . .'

3

WEST TIMOR, MARCH 2005

Fox lay in a pool of mud, the rain cutting visibility to a few metres. To his left was Leading Seaman John Birmingham, covered in blood from a gouge across his brow.

'They've got us pegged, Lieutenant,' Birmingham said as he loaded another high-explosive round into his M203 grenade launcher.

'Looks that way, JB,' Fox said, using a small mirror to look above the rim of the trench they had taken cover in. If they didn't move in a few minutes, they'd be fully submerged in the torrential downpour. Fox felt the mud sucking him down and shifted his weight to compensate. His fatigues were heavy with rainwater. Not that the Royal Australian Navy's Clearance Divers minded getting wet. Especially CDT4, specialists in shore assaults and the most active unit in the Australian military.

'Try to get the others on the blower again,' Fox said, as a spray of heavy calibre automatic gunfire tore into the trees around them.

'Damn if these are bloody militia!' Birmingham said, trying the satellite phone again.

'Indonesian Army, you reckon?' Fox wiped down his Austeyr assault rifle, wishing he had one of the SAS's new M4s—much better in the wet.

Several more shots rang out, splinters of wood showering them, before Birmingham answered.

'They're M16s, boss—and they're gettin' closer. No answer on the sat-tel.'

Fox looked across at the confident face of Birmingham and was glad he had chosen him for this recon. There was supposed to be a prison camp of East Timorese refugees nearby, and the man next to him had seen more combat than anyone else in CDT4. Birmingham's cool head under live fire was invaluable, especially since they were well outside the mandated security zone and no one knew where they were.

'Ideas, JB?' Fox asked.

Birmingham looked about him; the visibility was unchanged. 'Fire a couple of HE rounds and bolt, or wait here for a full company of bad guys to show up.' He took a couple of jelly babies from his top pocket and passed one over.

'Hmmm, tough call,' Fox said.

'That's why you're paid the big bucks, sir,' Birmingham said, cocking his M203 ready for fire.

'Okay, let's do it. We'll hump it north, exactly a kay from here, if we get separated,' Fox said, inserting a round into his grenade launcher.

'On three,' Fox said, getting ready to move.

'One,' Birmingham said, moving into position.

'Two,' Fox said, doing the same.

'Three!' In unison the pair raised to one knee, brought their grenade launchers up . . .

. . . and came face to face with thirty rifle barrels, topped by the camouflaged faces of Indonesian Special Forces and the unpainted faces of the local militia.

4

CHRISTMAS ISLAND

Fox awoke slowly, opening one eye first, groggily followed by the other. The smell of coffee immediately aroused his senses. He certainly wasn't in Timor—he'd managed to separate those dreams now. He sat up in bed, but went instantly back down as a searing pain shot through his head. He let out a groan and fingered the egg-sized lump on the back of his skull.

'Good morning.' A woman wearing one of his cotton shirts entered the room carrying a tray. Fox closed his eyes tightly, trying to remember exactly what had happened the previous night.

'How did I get—wait, who are you?'

Fox looked at the tray she placed next to him, picked up the glass of aspirin and downed it in two gulps. Slowly, fragments of the night before and the five guys came back. He also realised that the howling sound he could hear wasn't inside his head, but was the promised cyclone belting down on his little house.

'My name's Sarah. My friend and I took your dive course last week. And then you saved us last night,' the woman said with a grin. 'And it seems you have a guardian angel.'

Fox sat up again and pulled a strip of bacon off the full plate of breakfast Sarah had prepared for him. Things were starting to fall into place, but he still couldn't work out how he'd ended up in his own bed.

'Morning, Jackie Chan, how's the noggin?' Alister Gammaldi entered, Fox's best friend since high school. 'I've always been more of a Rocky myself,' he added with a grin that his friend had not seen in months.

'Al!' This time Fox ignored the throb of his head and jumped out of bed to give his mate a huge bear hug. He realised who Sarah had meant by his guardian angel—not that Al looked like one. At five four, with more muscles and hair than a silver-back gorilla, Gammaldi had held up his end in many a bar-room brawl during their navy days.

'So you came to the rescue last night?' Fox said.

'Aw, it was nothing. After all, there was only one left standing. Still looking for trouble outside bars, I see. I thought you moved out here to relax for a while.' Al gave his best friend a sly grin and a poke in the ribs.

'Yeah, yeah. But what the hell are you doing here?'

Fox put on a bathrobe over his shorts and they moved downstairs to the living area where Sarah's friend was lying on one of the soft leather couches intently reading a copy of *The Islander*.

Fox glanced outside at the blustery conditions and was thankful he'd put storm shutters on most of the windows. The mercury had fallen rapidly within the past day and the extreme low-pressure system was battering the island.

'If you ever bothered to open your mail,' Gammaldi said with a nod towards the pile on the table, 'you'd have known I was coming. I've taken my long service leave from the navy— something you were close to being able to do.'

They sank into the comfortable lounge suites and for a moment all was silent.

'Thought I'd spend a week or two in this sunny, tranquil, tropical paradise,' Al added lazily.

Fox fingered the swelling lump on his head again and figured that it could have been worse. Sarah, on the couch next to him, leaned over and had a look and feel of her own.

'It's a beauty all right,' she said. 'Do you have an icepack?'

'Yeah, in the freezer, keeping the vodka cool,' he replied with a Machiavellian smile. He watched intently as her lithe body moved swiftly towards his kitchen.

'So, aside from saving lives, what have you been up to?' asked Gammaldi with a grin.

'Just taking it easy, mate. Built this little number.' Fox gestured at his house with a wave of a hand.

'You built this yourself? It's fabulous!' said the other girl. Fox smiled at her as Sarah applied the icepack to the back of his head. *What was her name again? Rachel? Sonya?*

'Thanks,' he said.

'Not too bad if I say so myself,' Gammaldi offered. 'But if you like this, Rebecca, you'd love the homestead that I've restored outside of Sydney. Not a detail overlooked.'

Rebecca, aha! Fox knew his friend had slipped her name in for his sake, picking up on his frailty in the telepathic way only best friends and twins seemed to share.

'Yeah, but you should see the mess it's in!' he quickly chided his friend, who was trying to impress Rebecca. Not that it seemed he needed to—the girl was stealing glimpses of Gammaldi's bulging biceps whenever she could.

'Hey, I happen to like clutter, okay? It's not normal to live in such orderliness.'

The two women giggled at the pair's banter.

'The only reason you don't clean is because you're lazy and you know your mother will come around and do it for you once a week!' Fox said with a broad grin and the room filled with laughter.

'Why I stopped that thug from mashing your melon last night I'll never know,' Gammaldi retorted.

•

By the next day the cyclone had passed over. Apart from a few powerlines taken out by trees and some of the older roofs lifted off houses, there was little damage.

Fox and Gammaldi were cleaning up the eastern beach of Flying Fish Cove, where masses of seaweed and manmade trash were strewn across the pristine whiteness of the fine sand.

'They were nice,' offered Gammaldi, breaking the silence the two had shared since dropping the girls off at the airport an hour and a half ago.

'Yeah,' said Fox, his voice raspy with the morning's exertions. He reached into the cabin of the two-tonne truck, borrowed from the local council's collection, and produced a couple of water bottles from an icebox.

As they gulped down the cool water and took in their morning's work, Fox studied his friend. Sweat was seeping from every pore in the naval pilot's skin and streaming off his pronounced Roman nose. His proportions were immense in their own compact way: wide shoulders, barrel chest, washboard stomach and short beam-like arms and legs.

Fox smiled to himself and took another long pull on the water bottle. 'Well, are we going to just stand around here all day or do you need a rest, old friend?' he baited.

In reply Gammaldi looked at the bottle of water in his hand and then over to his mate's. They both had about a third left and Fox knew what was coming. Gammaldi lifted his bottle to his lips competitively and Fox followed suit. It was a dead heat as they threw the bottles in the back of the truck, deftly picked up their shovels and began vigorously filling the cargo tray with more refuse from the beach.

•

At five in the afternoon they were on Fox's catamaran and on their way to the northern part of the island. Whilst Fox was relaxing at the helm, the craft humming along at a lazy fifteen knots under his fingertips, Gammaldi was making the final preparations to their dive gear.

Fox slowed the vessel as they neared a small outcrop of rocks and coral about eight hundred metres from shore. This small satellite of Christmas Island had been formed over thousands of years as an underground volcano attached to the larger chain that formed the island proper. Fox had brought his friend here to see the lava tubes that mazed under the water. The almost perfectly circular tubes, which had once channelled the molten rock, were now filled with amazing marine life.

'So this is how you spend your days now?' Gammaldi said as the pair donned their diving equipment.

'Taking tourists like you out diving? Writing a local rag about refugees, diminishing fish stocks and drunk sailors tearing up the town? Sure beats diving for the navy, mate. Mind you, I miss the sixty thousand dollar re-breathers we got to play with. But there's fewer people trying to kill me and no bureaucrats waiting at home to crucify me, so it's a fair exchange.' Fox donned his goggles.

'Yeah, not that I'd know from piloting helicopters, huh? Closest I got to action in Timor was picking your sorry arse out of the water once or twice.'

'And that's why you're the fat one,' Fox said. 'Ready?'

Gammaldi grinned and followed his friend off the lower aft deck into the turquoise water.

Since the onslaught of the cyclone the sea had lost much of its usual crystal-clear quality, though most of the debris and sediment churned up had settled to the sea floor once again. The pair swam down to six metres and then slid over a coral shoal, the sea undulating to a rocky bottom created by the volcano long ago. Schools of fish darted by in playful bliss like great flocks of birds, only to be herded off by a trio of juvenile reef sharks.

The two friends followed a river of igneous rock to a giant cave opening that lay partially curtained with seaweed. Inside, the cylindrical cave measured about fifteen metres and was pretty much devoid of sea life, bar a few whiting passing through. The light at the other end of the space filtered dimly towards them as they swam the distance, heading on a slight downward angle.

On exiting it was clear why the cave was short in length. The next section had collapsed in on itself for about thirty metres. Fox led back around the side of their cave and pointed to a large coral-encrusted object ahead.

After close inspection, Gammaldi signalled his opinion to Fox—it was a Boomerang fighter, an Australian-built World War II aircraft. Her port wing was blown off, the canopy open and empty. The aluminium craft was otherwise in incredible condition, with only a few crustaceans inside who had claimed it as home.

While Gammaldi was busy scrutinising the open cockpit, Fox noticed a large object, darker than anything else in the surrounding waters, some fifteen metres away.

His adrenaline began pumping as he swam towards the unknown object. At touching distance, it measured close to two metres in length and a third that in diameter. It lay deep within a coral reef, partially buried lengthways. It was evident why no one had discovered it before. The cyclone, however, had split away a large section of the coral, which must have been weakened years before by the object's impact.

Fox felt a presence near him. In a lightning move he somer-saulted in the water and produced his dive knife, only to confront a startled Gammaldi.

Relieved, he motioned to his friend to surface with him and with several swift kicks they broke into the afternoon sun.

'What the hell is that thing?' Gammaldi said.

'My guess would be a mine or maybe an underwater detection device. I've never seen anything like it. No markings, no protrusions, nothing. And what's more, it's so damned deep in the coral.'

'Well?' Gammaldi flushed his goggles in the water. 'Let's not forget that we came out here to catch some lunch too.'

Fox patted his mate's shoulder. 'Al, you're a genius sometimes.'

Alister Gammaldi smiled a big toothy grin and his thick brow danced in confusion. 'What'd I say?' he mocked dopily.

•

It soon became clear to Gammaldi what his reminder of fishing for lunch had in common with the black object on the sea floor. Fox wrapped an eighteen-millimetre thick steel cable around the 'pod', as they now referred to it, which in turn was attached to a small derrick atop the catamaran's stern.

Gammaldi slowly let the twin three-hundred-horsepower diesel engines bite into the water and took the catamaran on a straight heading, reaching a cruising speed of barely four knots. Fox watched as the one hundred metres of cable splayed out on the aft deck became taut. He felt the catamaran shudder slightly under his feet as it fought to free the inert object from its coral cocoon.

In the wheelhouse, Gammaldi altered course slightly to a point marked on one of Fox's maps.

'What a great way to check if it's a mine. Drag it along, bumping into things,' he said to himself.

From the stern, Fox watched expectantly for the large explosion—but none came.

Gammaldi notched the engines' rev down and the craft slowed to a drift eighty metres past the wrecked hulk of an old phosphate transporter, which had been scuttled to form a new reef a few years ago. The inertia carried the pod a little farther under water until it clanged none too gently against the steel hull lying in ten metres of water. Again nothing happened.

Fox, his mild suspicions of the object being a mine put to rest, ordered Gammaldi to bring the catamaran back around to where the pod lay next to the sunken ship. As they passed over the targeted area, Fox worked with the three-tonne winch on the derrick, and, with a mixture of sweat, cursing and downright determination, the pod was brought back to Flying Fish Cove within an hour.

•

'Tell me again why the wise old Fox knows this thing isn't a mine? Maybe it's just broken, ready to explode any second.' It was amazing that Gammaldi did not lose any of the hamburger that was bulging from his talkative mouth.

'It didn't look like a conventional mine,' Fox said thoughtfully. 'So then I thought it might have been a hunter mine.' He paused to take a swig of water.

'Hunter mine?' Gammaldi almost paused, but then continued chewing thoughtfully.

'A hunter mine is basically an encased torpedo that is engaged when something large and metallic passes by.'

'Aha! That's why we dragged it up to that old boat.'

'Exactly. You know, it's not true what they say about you.' The only retort was the further scoffing of food.

Fox got up from the deckchair on the boat and walked over to the pod sitting on the stern deck. There were no apparent fissures or openings anywhere to be seen, so he took out his dive blade and began freeing the object of the marine growth that had claimed it over the years.

The task proved easier than he first thought, and with Gammaldi's grumbling help the job was over in less than half an hour. The clean-up revealed a seam running along the length of the pod, yet there was still no indication of how it might be opened, nor markings of any kind. Fox left the conundrum to his pal for a moment, but soon reappeared with a solution and a grin.

'Well, if it isn't my favourite tool,' remarked Gammaldi, referring to the crowbar Fox was brandishing.

'Stand back and observe a master at work, mate.'

Gammaldi did so, and after ten frustrating minutes it became his turn to attack. Unlike Fox, who had tried to pry open the seam from numerous vantages, the stocky Italian took station a pace away from his target, raised the bar above his head and swung down with every ounce of strength he could muster.

Fox was laughing even before the collision occurred, and even louder once he saw the enormous vibrations tremor up the steel bar and along Gammaldi's trunk-like arms to rattle his teeth. His laughter stopped when he noticed the small crack appearing along the seam, and then the pod slowly creaked open with a hydraulic hiss.

5

DRAGON CONTROL ROOM, GROZNY

The cursor on the screen had been blinking for almost an hour before the sweating technician in a cheap polyester suit noticed it. It took him a further half hour to realise what the message and coordinates meant. Once the information was passed along the chain of command, he became even sweatier, until finally, almost four hours after initially finding the signal, he was standing before his President and the war cabinet in a farmhouse north of the city.

'I believe you have good news for us . . . Popov.' President Ivanovich had to check the notes in front of him.

'Yes, Mr President.' Popov put his hands in his pockets to stop them from trembling, for there was good news and bad. And Ivanovich was known for his explosive temper. One of the KGB's favourite sons, he had risen to colonel in their Bureau of Interrogation and Persuasion, after leaving many a corpse on the Gulag floor.

'The homing beacon onboard one of our Dragon pods has been activated, so somebody must have found it—'

'Is your conclusion based on evidence, Popov, or are you just guessing?' inquired Mishka, the country's Chief of Intelligence. He was a slender man with a thin rat-like beard and squinting eyes—Popov immediately disliked him.

'Sir, as you know, the Soviet rocket carrying the two pods exploded during flight just over twenty years ago. Numerous attempts to trace them failed and it was assumed they lay deep on the Indian Ocean floor. The tracking devices could not be homed in on underwater—a grave error of my predecessors, I might add.' Popov allowed himself a little comfort in making it clear where the blame lay.

'According to your report,' the Chief of the Air Force held up a three-page document faxed through prior to Popov's arrival, 'only one pod has been located.'

'Yes, comrade, one of the two.' Popov hastily unrolled a well-used map of the Indian Ocean. 'Right here,' he pointed, 'in the Australian Territory of Christmas Island.'

For a full minute no one spoke. Every mind in the room appeared to be focusing on solutions to the scenario. Naturally it was President Ivanovich who broke the thoughtful silence.

'Thank you, comrade Popov, your work here has not gone unnoticed. You may yet prove a hero of the nation.'

Popov stood a little straighter and the corners of his mouth lifted in the hint of a smile.

'You are now chief technician on the Dragon re-arming project,' Ivanovich said, before turning away to Mishka.

'Organise a team to retrieve the pod,' he ordered. 'Find out who discovered it and how, then track down the other one. But our first priority is to get this pod back. That will buy us time to conduct a full search later. This changes everything, my friends, and proves God is on our side in this. Why, just yesterday our best hope was waging war against Iran for long enough to mine the element and reload the Dragon to attack. Now we can wipe out Tehran within days!' Ivanovich pounded a fist on the table.

He rose and made for the door—then turned to face his war cabinet.

'You have less than seventy-two hours.'

6

CHRISTMAS ISLAND

The plane touched down at six-thirty in the evening and five men got out. The first four figures were burly and rugged, their military crew cuts matching their alert postures. The last to emerge was Popov, unshaven and gaunt, his large dark eyes like a nocturnal animal's. His knowledge of the target meant his services had been involuntarily volunteered on this assignment. He also suspected that he was dispensable to those warmongers back home. But then again, he consoled himself, the retrieval of the pod was of the utmost importance to his nation and the men who controlled it. Success on this mission would set him up for life.

The group entered the small airport terminal, picked up the two hire vehicles that had been arranged and sped off in the direction of Flying Fish Cove.

•

Gammaldi noticed them first. He was lounging in a hammock on Fox's veranda and groggily opened his eyes after an hour's siesta. They certainly weren't the usual breed of tourist by their size and stance; even at a distance and in diminishing light, it looked as if four of them were clones. That, and the way they were snooping around the jetty near his friend's boat, made him suspicious.

'Hey, Lachlan!' Gammaldi called as he swung to his feet and stretched out his stiffness.

After a couple of minutes with no reply, he tried again. 'Lach, you about?' he called into the house this time. He found Fox at the computer, just finishing an email to an old investigative journalist friend with some digital photos and measurements of the pod.

'Yeah, just sending this. What's up, sleepyhead?'

'Did you forget to make the payments on that pretty boat of yours?'

'What are you talking about?' Fox watched as the email sped off into cyberspace.

'There's some burly guys checking out the boats tied to your jetty, and—' Gammaldi looked over his shoulder out the open door '—right now they're boarding yours.'

Fox jumped up and made for the door in a lightning dash.

'Now this is what holidays are for!' Gammaldi said, following just as fast.

•

It took less than five minutes for Fox and Gammaldi to reach the jetty, coming to a screeching halt in Fox's lovingly restored open-top Land Rover. There was no sign of the men now, but Fox was off in a dash towards his mooring.

It was all too evident what they had been after. The aft deck lay empty, the pod taken from its place under a green tarpaulin.

The humming of a small outboard came from behind a couple of yachts and Fox ran down the jetty towards it.

'Did you see some guys hanging around here a few minutes ago?' he called out to a returning angler in a small tin dinghy.

'What was that you said, mate?' the fisherman asked, killing the engine. He was on the other side of his eighties, a salty old sea dog with a white Van Dyke beard.

'Did you see four or five men on this pier a few minutes ago, boarding my catamaran?'

'Yeah, they loaded some gear into the back of a van and headed towards town. You missed your friends, mate?'

Fox didn't respond, just jumped back into the idling Land Rover and took off. Seconds later, an ear-shattering thunder-clap ripped through the air. BOOM! Fox stomped on the brakes as the explosion echoed around the bay and off the island's mountain ranges. He closed his eyes—he knew exactly what had happened.

A glance back at the jetty revealed the charred mess of the twin catamaran hulls, oily flames licking out in every direction. Other boats nearby had been devastated by the blast, and the torn-apart stern of the little tin dinghy floated lifelessly in the churning sea.

'Jesus!' exclaimed Gammaldi. 'Those bastards could have killed us!'

Fox was silent. Gammaldi looked at his friend knowingly, and a moment later the four-wheel drive's big diesel engine revved up. The tyres chewed up the gravel road and the Land Rover took off in a cloud of dust.

•

They soon found their quarry cruising towards the airport—the fastest way off the island.

There were two vehicles: a small four-cylinder sedan and a van whose back axle was riding low due to the weight of the pod. Fox's Land Rover easily won the contest in weight, but was under-classed in acceleration compared to the two newer, better-geared hire cars. The van's load was limiting their speed though, so the convoy was only travelling at around ninety kilometres per hour.

'We've got about ten minutes before we get to the airport. You'd better buckle up.'

Gammaldi didn't need any further prompting and pulled his seatbelt tighter.

'Have you got any weapons in this rig?' Al was anxiously measuring out the closing five hundred metres or so between the vehicles.

'Nothing but a toolbox under your seat.'

Gammaldi reached underneath and produced the toolbox in all its glory. Aside from a hammer and a few wrenches, nothing else looked like it would do any damage.

'Great. If you can get us close enough to take their cars apart undetected, I think we may just stand a chance,' he said with deadpan seriousness.

'Did you have to speak so soon?'

The distance between the vehicles was a hundred metres and closing rapidly when two burly torsos leaned out of the back of the sedan and started firing at the Land Rover. Thankfully, due to the winding road and Fox's quick evasive manoeuvres, few of the nine-millimetre pistol slugs met the thick aluminium skin of the four-wheel drive. Not so lucky was Gammaldi's side of the partitioned windscreen, which disintegrated from a direct hit.

'Should I ask if you have a plan, or shouldn't I speak any more?' Gammaldi said as he spat out some blood streaming into his mouth from a gash on his eyebrow.

'Since when do I plan ahead?' Fox said.

Slipping the Land Rover's big rebuilt engine down a gear produced a surge in speed and the next volley of fire went sailing behind them. The cars were pulling parallel and Fox yelled at Gammaldi over his redlining engine: 'Take out the driver!'

Gammaldi, hammer in hand, readied himself.

Fox used the superior weight of his vehicle to nudge the rear of the sedan and send it careening off the road. In the same movement one of the gun-toting thugs, leaning out the window, was crushed between the vehicles. The driver of the car overcorrected and set himself on a collision course with the Land Rover, only this time Gammaldi rose up and threw the hammer through the open window.

The result was spectacular. The driver suddenly slumped unconscious over the wheel and the out-of-control car rammed into a Moreton Bay fig tree and disintegrated.

Gammaldi let out a hoot. Fox couldn't help but share the moment: they'd just taken out three armed assailants in a high-speed car chase with a grimy old hammer. But the split second he looked over his shoulder to admire their triumph spelled disaster.

The rear door of the van ahead opened to reveal a man sitting on the tied-down pod. It was the device he was aiming at them that made Fox gasp, slam on the accelerator and spin the steering wheel.

A Soviet-made rocket-propelled grenade slammed into the bitumen below and to the left of the two-tonne Land Rover and exploded into a devastating ball of flaming shrapnel. The vehicle and its occupants were sent cartwheeling end over end until they finally came to rest upside down in the thickly treed national park that bordered the road.

•

Gammaldi looked across at his mate. Fox hung unconscious in his seat, his legs cut up from shrapnel that had torn through the floor, his face a bloody mess from the shattered windscreen. Gammaldi reached over and put two fingers to Fox's neck—he was still alive.

Gammaldi checked himself over. Apart from a few minor abrasions and bruises, and a pounding in his head, he felt remarkably fine. *Thank god*, he thought, they were going to be okay.

Then he saw the van pull up beside him and heard footsteps marching in his direction. His door was yanked open, and he closed his eyes as a pistol pressed against his forehead.

7

THE WHITE HOUSE,
FIVE DAYS TO GO . . .

Usually Bill McCorkell began the 0800 briefing. The first official part of the day for the President of the United States of America was a half-hour rundown on the world's hot spots and specific risks to the nation's security by his National Security Advisor. Lately, the meetings had been running overtime and included most of the executive members of the Security Council. Today Peter Larter, the Secretary of Defence, began.

'Gentlemen, I believe we've found our mystery weapon,' he told the men seated around the room as they scanned the photos of strange-looking equipment laid out on the low coffee table between them.

'Oh, boy, Pushkin was right . . .' the CIA's Robert Boxcell murmured with an incredulous look on his face.

'Who the hell is Pushkin and what is this . . . "coilgun"?' demanded the President, reading the name from a sketch on the table.

'A coilgun, Mr President, is basically an electronic gun,' McCorkell said. 'Think of a cannon that uses rails and an electric current instead of a barrel and gunpowder.'

'Mr President, the sketch you're looking at was made by a Soviet scientist who defected to us in the eighties.' The Secretary of Defence swallowed hard, McCorkell noted. 'It was part of the Soviet counter-effort to create a Star Wars system of their own, in response to Reagan's Strategic Defence Initiative—the precursor of our current National Missile Defence system.

'Rather than imitating our research into particle beams, railguns and missile-killing missiles etc to shoot down incoming ICBMs, the Soviets concentrated their efforts into a very small area of space-based weapons. Like us, they saw the benefit of having NMD systems in space which would be hard to detect and destroy. But they took it one step further.'

'Peter, are you telling me that they put weapons of mass destruction—this coilgun—into space?' asked a shocked Fullop. The Chief of Staff was the administration's most vocal proponent of space-based weapons. 'Greatest defence we could have—' McCorkell had heard Fullop's favourite phrase a hundred times.

'It's the only explanation we have, Tom. My team has gone over this all night,' Larter said.

'Robert?' McCorkell prompted, bringing the CIA chief out of his mindful reverie.

Boxcell looked up from the diagrams of the coilgun, glanced around the room and settled on the President.

'Mr President, there may be cause to take this assumption seriously. In 1985 Vladimir Pushkin defected across at our West German Embassy. We knew him as a senior physicist working for the Soviets in their Bureau for Strategic Research and

Development. We ended up gaining little useful information, as most of our systems then were well ahead of the Soviets'.' A pause. 'He did claim, however, to have worked on a counter-version of our own Star Wars program. Apparently, due to limited funding, they concentrated on one design only—railgun technology.

'Pushkin claimed the years of testing proved the railgun was unable to destroy one ballistic missile, let alone hundreds or even thousands in an all-out nuclear war. But what grew out of that failure was a coilgun, a variation on the railgun theme and potentially much more powerful—an electric current would surround the projectile and shoot it out at phenomenal speeds, much faster than conventional ballistics.'

At Larter's signal a military aide switched on a digital projector.

McCorkell leaned forward, taking in the first image: more detailed hand-drawn diagrams of the coilgun.

'Bandar-e Anzali after impact,' Larter said, nodding to the aide who switched images.

The next shot showed the devastated area they had seen the previous day in greater size and detail.

'Our computers have been able to place a contour map over the blast area to within centimetre accuracy.' Onscreen, a green spider-web-like grid mapped out the gradient of the blast area.

'The gradient measurement is in *centi*metres?' McCorkell asked.

'That's right,' Larter confirmed. 'What you see on the screen here is in fifty-metre intervals. From the epicentre of the blast there is a slope of around one centimetre for every six metres. This equates to the centre being only 1.2 metres below the edge of the blast. No explosive we know of could create this damage and not leave a deep impact crater at detonation point. Moreover, notice the shape of the contours?' All the men strained their eyes to notice something they apparently should have. 'It is close to a perfect circle. Not from something fired at an angle, but from directly above.'

'My God,' muttered the President. 'The Russians—no, the Chechens have this capability and this is how we find out about it? Do we have anything this advanced?'

'Sir,' began Larter. The other men in the room were silent. 'We are not saying that this attack is definitely the result of so-called Star Wars technology. We have yet to implement this sort of offensive technology into space ourselves—but our own research has led to the development of railguns for our military. It is the next stage of ballistic weaponry. But I think this vindicates the good life we set up for Pushkin.'

'I think you're forgetting a couple of things,' Boxcell said to the Secretary of Defence. 'Firstly, Pushkin died in an "accident" within weeks of defecting—using a knife to get bread out of a toaster. This was in a temporary safe house in Virginia, and it just so happened his security detail was found by the next shift commander watching MTV in an outbuilding. Forensics found high-voltage burn marks under Pushkin's arms and tyre tracks in the driveway that weren't from an Agency vehicle.'

McCorkell watched everyone in the room straighten a little.

'Are you this well briefed on all Agency files?' Larter asked with a mocking grin.

'I was that next shift leader,' Boxcell retorted.

McCorkell cringed at the exchange—although all men present were friends, their professional rivalry was the same as in any high-powered boardroom.

Boxcell went on. 'The last thing Pushkin managed to document of the coilgun project—the Dragon, as the Soviets termed it—was that the projectiles were made from an extremely rare element . . . theterion I think it was called.'

'Theterium,' Larter corrected. 'A new element discovered in Tunguska, Siberia, early last century.'

'A new element?' asked the President.

'Mr President, there are apparently quite a few combined or totally different elements to be found in meteorites and so on,' McCorkell said, getting nods from Larter and Boxcell to affirm his explanation. 'It stands to reason that such elements could be potentially much stronger than those on Earth if they were, say, from a binary or tri star system, due to the extra gravity.'

Larter had another image brought up on the projector: grainy black and white shots of rural destruction.

'So . . . a relatively small amount of this theterium could be made into a projectile for a coilgun small enough to be launched into space,' McCorkell added, cottoning on to the idea that was becoming a much more realistic hypothesis.

'Exactly,' Larter said. 'What you are seeing here are images taken in 1908 of what has become known as the Tunguska Event. These fallen trees spiral outward from the centre point for up to half a kilometre. Devastation was wreaked close to a thousand-mile radius from the blast point—equivalent to a three-hundred-megaton nuclear blast,' Larter brought up an aerial photograph. 'And as you can see using the same contour grid, there was absolutely no blast crater whatsoever.'

There was thoughtful silence in the room as each man took in the information.

'How many of these weapons did Pushkin say he developed?' the President asked.

'Pushkin claimed they had built one Dragon prototype and had enough of the element to manufacture three projectiles, which could be reloaded one at a time in space,' Larter said.

'And the weapon takes time to recharge in between firing?' McCorkell asked.

'Yes, but the time frame was never specified by Pushkin,' Boxcell answered. 'Could be the Chechens' seven-day timetable though.'

'And we're down to five days now,' McCorkell said. The comment hung in the air for a moment.

'So it is possible there are at least two more weapons in space,' the President stated with raised eyebrows. 'Able to be fired on anywhere on the globe . . .'

'There was one major hole in this coilgun theory,' Larter interjected. 'The size of the Dragon, as documented in sketches by Pushkin, made it too bulky to be put into space intact. Pushkin himself said it would have taken at least two, probably three flights, and then tens of hours of labour in space to assemble the pieces. There was no way the Soviets could have launched this under our noses, and their Salyut space stations couldn't have accommodated the hours of space-walking to put the sections together. Our predecessors considered Pushkin was unreliable in these fantastic claims, which is why they did not pursue his information—'

McCorkell interrupted the Secretary of Defence mid-sentence. 'Tell me, did our predecessors disregard Pushkin's claims before or after the Soviets launched and assembled the Mir Space Station?'

8

WEST TIMOR, MARCH 2005

Through the thin sheet of corrugated iron Fox could hear the life being beaten out of Birmingham. He'd been through such an ordeal himself the day before and was certain his left leg was fractured below the knee. Now, two days after being taken captive, he sat behind one of the bamboo-framed huts near the cage he'd been kept in. The militia guards had fallen asleep after smoking dope all day and he'd managed to pop the lock on his cell. Armed with an ancient AK-47, Fox surveyed the area for threats. The main force of militia and Indonesian Army had moved off the night before, and for the first time that week the rain was easing.

He was faced with two tasks. Around fifty East Timorese sat captive in the centre of the camp, surrounded by rings of razor wire and half a dozen stoned guards sitting under a tin roof. And there was Birmingham, on the other side of the wall behind him, on the receiving end of hell. If it were like his torture session, there'd be two Indonesian soldiers and the local militia leader inside.

It was a difficult choice. He had a duty to his soldier, his countryman, his friend. He also had a duty to save the people he and his friend had come here to protect.

He knew he could take out the prison guards with about half a mag of ammo to spare. The prisoners could flee while he took on Birmingham's captors. Either or both Australians would probably die, but it was what the navy soldiers were paid to do.

He leaned his head against the wall and closed his eyes. He was far past exhausted. He'd been stripped to his underwear, hadn't eaten since they'd been dropped off some fifty hours prior, and he could no longer tell where his blood stopped and the mud began.

Inside, the gasping screams of his friend were now accompanied by a whipping sound. He knew they were lashing Birmingham with wire, as he himself had been lashed. Fox made up his mind.

Crawling around the corner of the hut, he peered through a gap in the door. Three targets. He shouldered the door open quietly and took a couple of quick steps in, crashing the militia chief in the back of the head with the rifle and quickly bringing the barrel up eye-level with the Indonesian commanding officer.

'*Merdeka dia! Merdeka dia!*' Fox said. *Free him!*

The Indonesian soldier looked down the AK-47 barrel and slowly took out his pistol and put it on the floor.

'You too!' Fox said to the officer who was still holding the whip. The pair locked eyes, and Fox could read the man's defiance. He dropped the whip reluctantly and joined his comrade on his knees.

'John?' Fox said, taking a step forward and unlooping his leading seaman's hands from the bar he was bent over.

'Thanks,' Birmingham said through a mouthful of blood.

'Hands on head!' Fox said in Indonesian. The young soldier obeyed, but the officer just stared at him. Fox glanced at Birmingham as he struggled to stand up. His face was a pulp, his eyes puffy slits.

'Shit—can you see?' Fox asked.

'No.'

'Shit.' He held the gun trained on the Indonesians and had a quick look around the room for a rag or something. He heard Birmingham grunt behind him.

'*Menanamkan itu bedil turun!*' the Indonesian officer said.

Fox turned and saw the officer was pointing a small revolver against Birmingham's head. He took a moment to translate. *Put the gun down.*

For a few seconds there was silence. No one dared make the next move.

'Fuckin' pop him, Lachlan,' Birmingham said, swaying on his feet.

The officer and Fox held each other's gaze.

'You go now—leave,' the officer said.

'You have to let my friend go—and the other people,' Fox said, starting to shake from the effort of holding the AK-47 steady.

'They are my people,' the officer said, digging the revolver into Birmingham's cheek.

'Pop the fucker!' Birmingham repeated.

Silence.

Before Fox could do or say anything else, Birmingham lunged to his left, taking the officer crashing down as a shot rang out and the gun clattered across the floor.

Fox squeezed a single shot off at the other soldier as he dived for his pistol, and leapt over the man's falling body to help Birmingham—only to discover a neat hole bored through his friend's temple. He tried to fire at the officer but his gun jammed, so he smashed the AK-47 into the other man's head. Losing strength but pumped with adrenaline, Fox grappled with the officer in a hand-to-hand struggle. He managed to grip his hands around the officer's neck and pushed down with all his weight, but the officer fought back, clawing at Fox's eyes and face.

Fox could hear more hostiles approaching the hut. He scrambled off the now lifeless officer, picked up the revolver and fired a shot through the chest of the guard who opened the door. Another shot and he grabbed at Birmingham, dragging his dead comrade across the dirt floor to the back of the hut, where he kicked the tin wall loose. The safety of the jungle was only metres away.

An ear-shattering wave of automatic gunfire ripped through the hut and a bullet tore into Fox's forearm.

He dropped the pistol and tried to support the dead weight of Birmingham with one arm. 'Come on, mate, come on.' He fell to the ground, sliding backwards in the direction of the jungle. 'Come on!' he yelled again, heaving to his feet and pulling at the fallen soldier.

Another wave of bullets crashed over him and tore into Birmingham, spraying blood. With a pat on his mate's head, Fox left him and scrambled into the jungle . . .

9

GROZNY

'Yes?' Ivanovich said, waving silence to the assembly of military chiefs.

'We have the pod, Mr President,' Popov said over the satellite phone. 'It is operational and we are on schedule.'

'Excellent work, Popov. Any problems?' Ivanovich motioned a security officer to pour vodka for his war cabinet.

'Nothing much, sir,' Popov said. 'We took a hostage—one of the two men who found the pod.'

Ivanovich stopped before taking a sip of his vodka. 'And the other man?'

Popov hesitated. He'd seen the other man covered in blood in a car wrapped around a tree. He'd stopped one of the commando thugs from setting the smashed car alight when he'd seen a bus of tourists coming up the road, but surely the man had perished from his injuries.

'He's dead, sir,' Popov said.

'Well done. It seems I am getting quite a collection of Western prisoners,' Ivanovich said with a smile. His generals shared a laugh.

'When you have succeeded with the next part of your mission, I will reward you beyond your dreams,' Ivanovich said. A wicked smile crossed his lips. 'You may even choose a woman of your own from our political prisoners.'

'Thank you, Mr President,' Popov said, but the phone had already been disconnected at the other end. The chief technician allowed himself a smile at his day's luck.

10

CHRISTMAS ISLAND

The ceiling was the whitest white Fox had ever seen, accentuated by a bank of stark fluorescent lights. His bloodshot blue eyes blinked at the harsh environment; he felt like someone who was seeing the world for the first time. He thanked the darkness his eyelids provided, and for a moment the clouds of drowsiness cleared enough for him to wonder where he was and what he was doing there. Before he could ascertain any answers on his own, a soft feminine voice caressed his ringing ears.

'Good morning, sailor.'

A friendly face above a white nurse's uniform came into view, and departed before Fox could say anything.

His world became a condensed nightmare of confusion for the next few minutes. Time and reality were spinning backwards to the last time he was in this situation, a nauseous sense of déjà vu mimicking reality. It was all he could do not to pass back into the safety and silence the dark cloud of unconsciousness was offering him. He blinked the cloudiness away and, one by one, each of his senses came back online. He wasn't in the military hospital in Timor—this place felt different. The room was a lot smaller, the air drier.

'Ah, Mr Fox, glad to see you've awoken.'

The doctor was young, only a few years older than himself. He checked Fox's vital signs and made some adjustments to the file tucked under his arm.

'Where am I?' Fox asked hoarsely, his mouth and throat dry.

'Christmas Island Hospital, Mr Fox. You were involved in a serious car accident and have been comatose the past four hours.'

The doctor whispered to the nurse who was at his side and she left the room again with a purpose.

'You have sustained some bruising to the ribs,' he went on, 'plus some lacerations to your legs, and we've sutured a lesion above your right eyebrow. According to the paramedics who attended the scene, you're damn lucky to come out alive.'

Fox was trying to piece together the events, but things were still too foggy, too incoherent to make sense. Car accident— hospital? *Gammaldi* . . .

'Where's Al?' he asked.

'I'm sorry, Mr Fox?' The doctor continued making notes on the medical chart.

'My friend, in the car . . .'

Fox lost his fight to stay conscious and slowly closed his eyes, barely noticing the tall figure that entered his peripheral vision and stood there for a moment.

Ten minutes later Fox opened his eyes again. He felt a small device in his palm, the size of a cigarette lighter. It had a button on the top . . . morphine. Fox considered pushing the button, which would have released five mls intravenously—but he'd been down that road before.

It was then he felt the presence in the room. Someone was there, watching him. He was unable to turn his head because of the cautionary brace on his neck. There was an uneasy silence during which Fox felt he was being appraised.

'Nurse?' he said, hoarser than before.

It took every ounce of strength and willpower to raise and tilt his head towards the person. A puzzled look replaced the frown of pain on his face, and he opened his mouth to speak but only a gargle came out.

She was a striking woman, tall and athletic, with a straight posture that made her seem even more impressive. Her hair was long and thick but she had it wrapped into a tight bun, the flaming red set off by the green in her eyes.

'You have a rather impressive record of escaping serious injury—and death for that matter, Mr Fox.'

Faith Williams sat on the edge of the bed and took a good look at the man she had learnt so much about during the flight from New York. The few photos contained in his military and intelligence records certainly didn't do him justice. Even when he was lying back with bandages covering various parts of his body, sapped of energy and practically motionless, she could feel his allure—not because of his good looks, but simply the natural assuredness he exuded. A presence. It caught her off guard.

'My name is Faith Williams, Mr Fox. Are you feeling comfortable? Shall I call for the doctor?' She pulled her attention back to her task, her words coming in a crisp Ivy League accent.

Fox blinked up at her and appeared to think. He winced a little when he moved, some badly broken ribs clearly causing stabs of pain, but she could tell he wasn't going to let on.

'Water?' he asked.

She held a cup of water to his lips, tipping small amounts into his mouth.

'Thanks.'

She saw the pain on his face as he tried to sit more upright in bed. 'You from my health insurance or something?' he joked.

'Not exactly. Did you need something for the pain?' She gestured to the self-medicating morphine button by his side.

'No, can't stand the stuff.' He pushed it even further away as the temptation became greater.

'Mr Fox—'

'Lachlan.'

'Lachlan. I've seen your service records, they're very impressive.' Faith paused, testing the water. 'One question has been intriguing me for hours though . . .'

Fox lifted his eyebrows.

'Your actions in Timor, which led to the death of Leading Seaman John Birmingham . . . Do you regret them?'

Fox appeared to look at Faith in a different way now.

'Who—'

'Did you know that during your rescue attempt, three families of East Timorese managed to escape?' She could see by Fox's face that he hadn't known this bit of news. 'Fourteen of the forty-seven prisoners escaped during your firefight with the militia.'

'How do you know that?' Fox said. The Indonesian government had reported them killed, 'caught in the crossfire' of Fox's unauthorised incursion. 'Okay, Faith, you have my attention. Who the hell are you?'

The authority in Fox's tone surprised Faith—not that she let it show.

'Mr Fox, I represent an organisation that would like to acquire your services—pressingly so because of what you found on the sea floor near here. It happens to be part of a weapons system of mass destruction.'

Faith paused to make sure he was listening.

'There is only one party in the world with the means and inclination to use such a thing, and several hours ago they took it—and your friend.'

PART TWO

11

THE WHITE HOUSE,
FOUR DAYS TO GO . . .

The Situation Room in the White House was located in a basement level of the West Wing. The oak-panelled walls were hidden behind plasma televisions, maps, screens and other technical necessities of modern military intelligence. Behind those walls lay a metre of reinforced concrete encapsulating the entire room. This was the command centre for medium-level 'situations', when more resources and security were required than the Oval Office or Cabinet Room could accommodate.

Bill McCorkell nodded to two marines in dress uniform guarding the entrance and almost tripped over a miniature castle propped up beside the double doors. He shook his head with a wry smile: the President was starting to take his golfing obsession way too far. As he entered the Situation Room, late for the morning briefing, the conversation between the others died down.

'Morning, Bill, glad you could make it,' the President greeted him good-humouredly from the head of the table. Peter Larter and Robert Boxcell sat to the President's left; both nodded a silent greeting. Baker, the Secretary of State, was not present, nor was Chief of Staff Fullop.

'Sorry I'm late, Mr President,' McCorkell said as he took his position to the right of the President. He nodded to the two Joint Chiefs of Staff present: the appointed Chairman, currently a naval admiral, and the head of the Marine Corps. As the JCS was the highest body for planning and coordinating the armed forces, they brought with them a myriad of aides—always in full dress uniform—who scurried around the room talking on phones, working on computers and scrutinising data.

'Okay, gentlemen.' The President officially opened a new day in the White House.

'Mr President, two major pieces of intelligence came across last night,' Boxcell began. 'We now have solid confirmation that the Dragon exists. This comes from Moscow and a British MI6 agent in Grozny.'

'And the confirmed number of projectiles?' the President asked with raised eyebrows.

'The only good news, Mr President,' the CIA chief continued. 'Initially, the Dragon was loaded with one projectile. Another two were launched in '85 but failed and splashed down in the Indian Ocean. The Soviets called off their search during Gorbachev's time, as he ended many military programs to demonstrate goodwill.'

'There's no chance they could have found these pods?' McCorkell asked. It was a question he already knew the answer to.

'No chance. The Soviets never caught a whiff of the downed pods in years of searching with a dedicated armada. Chechnya has no such search capabilities.'

'How many of these projectiles could they have on hand?' the President asked.

'Mr President, the projectile is made up of one of the rarest elements on Earth—theterium,' Boxcell reminded the President. 'So rare, in fact, that we know of no substantial deposits outside of what was found in Tunguska. To cause the destruction wreaked on Iran two days ago, the Chechens must have used the one remaining projectile and the last of the theterium.'

'Then we're in the clear and the Chechens are bluffing.'

'Not quite, Mr President.' The Secretary of Defence entered the exchange. 'A substantial reward for any discovery of theterium was offered in all Eastern Bloc geology periodical literature—funded by a body with links to Sergei Ivanovich. The reward offer was withdrawn shortly after Christmas—the same time we picked up troop movements in Chechnya.'

'So . . . theterium has been found in Iran,' the President said, making the connection.

'Based on reasoning, yes, sir. And this must be the mother lode, since the Chechens are staking everything for the claim,' McCorkell answered. 'How close are we to finding the location?' he continued.

Larter turned to the JCS Chairman, who in turn referred to an aide—it all took two seconds and a couple of head shakes in the negative.

'It may take minutes; seventeen hours at the longest,' the Admiral said.

'We can have men on the ground the moment it's found—including the Resourcer Regiment,' added Larter, with a confirming nod from the marines boss.

'US forces in Iran!' The President raised his voice so loudly that all the aides in the room stopped still for a second.

'Are you telling me or asking me, Pete?' The President's face was becoming red.

'Mr President, I don't think I can stress enough the importance that this theterium not get into the hands of the Chechens—or anyone else in the world for that matter. Our resourcers conduct this sort of operation all the—'

'You won't have to deal with the press and public of this country when they find out our boys have died in Iran!' The President slammed his palm on the solid table.

'Mr President, with all due respect, a few more dead US soldiers in the Middle East is a damn easier news item to deal with than a space weapon taking out the cities and people of this nation that those servicemen are sworn to protect—sir.' Larter was looking the President square in the eye and the President conceded the point.

McCorkell let the President take his time to digest the argument. He took in the others around the room and settled his gaze on Boxcell, who was sitting pensively, watching the exchange with detached interest. He could just imagine the chief of the world's most capable spy network filing the observation away in his memory banks: the President could be pushed.

McCorkell watched as the President bit his lip in thought; he could tell the leader understod little of the reasoning. To save face he turned to the man whose sole job it was to advise him on matters of national security.

'Bill, how do you see it?'

'Mr President,' McCorkell began slowly. He knew exactly how to work the man he had known for most of his adult life. 'We have a few options but the bottom line is this: if anyone gets their hands on this element, it must be us. If not, it must be destroyed beyond all useful purposes.

'Consider what is occurring. The clock is ticking for the threatened destruction of Tehran. Whilst all our intelligence points to the Dragon having only one projectile, we cannot take that as gospel. Iran sure as hell won't call the Chechens' bluff and instigate the battle along their border.

'Right now, every expert we have is using satellites to look for heat signatures in Iran, west of the Fiftieth Longitude. If the theterium is down there, we will find it before the deadline.' McCorkell paused. 'And what then? We either go after it and blow the site, or we launch from a boomer in the Gulf and wipe the site from the map so no one can have it.'

McCorkell looked away from the President to the others around the table for confirmation of his summary. They nodded back in the affirmative.

'Well, let me know as soon as we find the damn stuff.' With that, the President stood from his chair and walked from the room, picking up a putter that was leaning against the wall as he exited.

For all the thickness of the reinforced concrete, McCorkell swore he could hear the golf club striking a wall in the outer corridor.

12

NEW YORK

The Gulfstream X touched down at JFK International Airport. Fox was glad to be rocked awake by the landing as his dreams were starting to turn bad. Faith Williams moved past him up the aisle as the aircraft taxied to a private terminal.

Waiting on the tarmac for the two passengers was a black V12 S650 Mercedes, its windows almost as dark as the duco.

Faith ushered Fox into the soft leather seat of the Mercedes limousine, and went around the car to the other rear seat.

As the driver took off at a reasonable pace, Fox looked back and took in the Gulfstream's radical design. The sleek jet aircraft had been moved to a hangar where an identical jet was being serviced. The Gulfstream X was ultra fast and manoeuvrable, yet radically angular and not very aesthetic in conventional design terms. Only a handful had been made to order so far, and with a price tag in the same echelon as the cost of a large commercial airliner, numbers were likely to remain low.

For the first time Fox noticed the light grey stencilled signage on the aircraft's fuselage. It was so light he had to focus hard through the dark window and the dim light of the New York evening to decipher the company name: GSR.

Fox was glad for the silence Faith offered and used the time to gather his thoughts. He had many questions he wanted answers for.

13

ITALY

On the other side of the world, Gammaldi was being treated far less cordially. He had endured a long flight bound in the cargo hold of a twin-engine jet. During the trip, he had managed to wriggle his feet free and had spent the rest of the journey rubbing the tough plastic straps that clasped his hands together behind his back and through his belt against the small metal handle on the inside of the cargo door. His desperation had heightened when the handle broke off and his hand binds proved inescapable.

They had stopped once to refuel, and afterwards he'd had to spend every other ten minutes breathing near a hissing gap close to the small cargo door to prevent the nauseating jet fuel vapours overwhelming him.

The final landing was rough and Gammaldi guessed it was a corrugated gravel runway—something he loathed landing on when he flew himself. He moved to a darkened corner of the tight cargo hold and nestled next to the pod container, ready to pounce at his captors once the chance presented itself. He had not slept at all during the flight, which he'd calculated to be fifteen hours according to the hourly beeps on his watch, and it was all he could do not to topple over as he waited.

The muffled sound of voices outside the door alerted his senses. It was some sort of Eastern European dialect but he couldn't work out anything beyond that.

With a gush of heavily salted air, the cargo door opened. Gammaldi took a welcome gulp and held on to it, waiting for his chance. It was fairly dark outside and two heavy flashlights shone into the small cargo hold; the guards obviously expected their quarry to be lying where they had left his immobilised body. It was the break he needed.

Two shaved heads came into view through the open hatch and Gammaldi lashed out with his boot, kicking the first square in the face and sending the man reeling backwards, sputtering blood. His cohort's head spun around—in time to see the blow but failing to dodge its bone-crushing force. The heel of Gammaldi's boot clipped the man's nose, breaking it with a muffled crunch. He, too, fell to the ground in pain, clutching at his face as Gammaldi jumped onto the tarmac and bolted past his kidnappers.

He ran awkwardly towards a thin tree line, wrists still bound behind his back. He found himself thanking his trainers at the Escape and Evasion Centre, where he'd done a training course for military pilots in case they came down in enemy territory. During that training he had run five kilometres blindfolded with his hands tied behind his back.

Gammaldi grunted as he ran, squinting, through the line of trees, which proved to be spindly and scratchy. He came up short against a tall wire cyclone fence and was faced with a decision: left or right. It was a decision hastened by voices shouting behind him in the same dialect he had heard before. *Russians*, Gammaldi thought as he sped off to his right into the cover of trees again, welcoming the darkness ahead.

After about a minute, he came into a large clearing of well-manicured lawn, and five hundred metres away was a gap in the tall fence—what appeared to be a boom gate lit dimly by an old greasy street lamp. To his right was a small cluster of buildings that he took to be a farmhouse and outbuildings.

The muffled voices behind him became louder and were joined by the deep bark of a dog. Then another. *Why is it always dogs?* Gammaldi resigned himself to it, pulling a thin but sturdy wooden stake from the ground and bolting towards the gate.

Four hundred metres. His hamstrings stung from the restrained sprint.

Three hundred. The shouting was getting closer.

Two hundred. His lungs and legs were on fire. There was excited shouting from behind him, then the sound of the dogs running for him.

One hundred metres. Ahead, the gate was clear, but to his dismay there was nothing beyond but an open plain and a wall of tall pines on the blackening horizon. He could see the dogs— a pair of angry-looking Alsatians. Always an advocate of animal rights, Gammaldi's compassion went out the window as he wished for a substantial weapon of some sort. If it weren't for the dogs he might have a chance of escape.

Twenty metres from the gate he spun and stood his ground. The sight of bared, snarling teeth greeted him almost instantly. The first dog sprang from the ground, aiming its ferocious canines at Gammaldi's jugular. With a ducking spin he swiped the stake across the dog's head with a blow that sent it flying through the air sideways. It rolled around on the ground yelping, put out of the attack with an injured snout.

The second Alsatian was still snarling but reared back at the sight of its companion's injury.

The throaty sound of two-stroke engines roared to life from the direction of the farmhouse. Gammaldi gave up all precautions for safety, turned, and ran. Ran for his life in a last, desperate dash to the relative safety of the trees in the distance.

Two spotlights pierced the twilight, moving in his direction, and he could see that the engines he'd heard were a pair of four-wheeled motorcycles. Their riders hadn't yet spotted him; his immediate threat was the bloodthirsty dog hot on his heels. Kicking out at it had no effect; it kept lunging for his legs. Only the continual chopping of the stake kept the vicious fangs from his flesh.

He had about a kilometre to go before reaching the trees when gunfire whipped at either side of him, carving up the knee-high open pasture. Gammaldi knew he was beaten. Turning himself in now and escaping later was better than certain death right here, right now.

'Down, boy,' he mocked the dog as he stopped and faced his captors. He was surrendering. For now.

14

NEW YORK

It was the second time Fox had been to New York City. The first was a distant memory from childhood, when he'd accompanied his father on a business trip. He remembered walking through knee-high snow in Central Park and hand-feeding walnuts to squirrels.

Faith Williams broke his brief reminiscence with the business-like tone that New Yorkers did so well. 'The drive is about twenty minutes or so. Why don't you read over these and ask questions on the way in? Dr Wallace will have you on another flight within an hour.'

Sure, I'd love to read while my friend is being held hostage, Fox thought. He took the Apple notebook computer that Faith produced from a Louis Vuitton satchel. *They certainly aren't tight for cash*, he thought: one of the world's most expensive corporate jets, this top-of-the-range Mercedes limousine, and the finer details such as the custom fittings inside the aircraft. Then there was Faith herself: the pinstripe suit she wore that screamed Milan fashion house, the hair that looked as though it required a salary of its own to maintain, and, of course, the Louis Vuitton accessories.

The computer came to life as soon as Fox opened it and the screen filled with the company name, Global Syndicate of Reporters Consortium of Investigative Journalists, along with worldwide addresses and a US telephone number: 1800 GSR HQ.

'Just click on the screen and it will give you an overview and company profile—'

Fox could stand his restrained demeanour no more and cut Faith off. 'Look, lady, all I give a damn about is saving Al—a task you said this mysterious GSR would help facilitate. I'm certainly not coming here to conduct a business meeting with some delusional old—'

'Mr Fox,' Faith began with sharp calmness, 'I'll save you the time then of looking over our formal company outline. I assumed from your profile that you would want such assuredness of faith in us.' She paused for a perfectly timed beat. 'The Global Syndicate of Reporters, or GSR, comprises the greatest collection of investigative reporters and photojournalists in the world. For almost twenty years, GSR has worked as an independent news source, going where other media agencies don't dare, reporting the truth as it unfolds.'

Fox opened his mouth to again inquire how the company could help with his friend's disappearance, but he timed it wrong—she had not finished.

'Dr Tasman Wallace is GSR's founder and chairman, and he has noticed the work you have done on Christmas Island investigating people-smuggling.'

This time Fox was ready and interrupted the pause.

'This is all great, Faith, it really is,' he said, with just the right amount of sarcasm. 'I just don't get why my friend was taken. Are we in the middle of some GSR investigation to do with that pod? I mean, we—Al and I—really know nothing about it.'

'GSR is conducting an ongoing investigation that ties in with the pod you discovered—that's really all I know about the situation,' Faith replied. 'As for your friend's abduction, we are tracking the flight and have a rescue team prepping. We would like to propose this, though: we need each other's help in retrieving both your friend and the pod.'

Fox looked blankly out the window as the speeding car overtook a traffic jam by hammering down the emergency lane. Whatever the hell was going on, he gave GSR credit for one thing—they certainly weren't wasting any time.

•

The Seagram building was beautiful in its simplicity. Fox gazed up at the facade, a tower of dark amber glass that reached to the sky between hundreds of bronze columns. The backlit GSR sign shone in stark grey illumination over the expansive granite-paved plaza; no other corporate logos were evident.

In the elevator there were no buttons to access the top five floors, just the numbers themselves: 34 through 38.

Fox watched curiously as Faith stood at eye-level with one of the segmented mirror panels and said, 'Access thirty-eight'. A vivid green line waved across her eyes, side to side.

The lift rose with an electric hum at a speed that sent the blood to Fox's feet. The elevator door suddenly opened to a lift lobby with carpet so thick Fox lost an inch in height as his feet sank into the plush charcoal wool. The white walls were stark and the ceiling was well beyond reach. No light fixtures were apparent but somehow the room was lit without shadows. A long desk splayed across one side of the room, made from a great slab of stone and supported by sheets of frosted glass. A huge hand-blown glass vase held metre-long stems of Asian lilies, yet the scent in the foyer was far more precious than that.

The woman behind the desk greeted them in a refined accent. 'Good evening, Ms Williams. Glad to see you in good health, Mr Fox.'

Her elocution teacher should be proud, Fox thought. He took her remark in his stride and added it to the growing list of peculiarities.

'Good evening, Emily,' Faith said, walking towards the only door in sight, made from heavy stainless steel and set to the right of the desk.

The door slid away as they neared. The carpeting flowed into a small anteroom, then halted and gave way to dark stone flooring. This next room was not as simple in décor. Instead of stark whiteness, warm timber panelling covered its walls. Book-lined shelves ran along one wall, ending at an illuminated display case housing various Scottish and Norman antiquities. The floors were a rippling dark marble, with Persian rugs adding colour to the room. To one side were windows over-looking the bustle of Park Avenue, which juxtaposed with the tranquil quiet of the plant-filled, soundproofed office.

'Hello there,' a man welcomed them. Standing up behind his desk, Dr Tasman Wallace proved to be a match for Fox in physical stature, if not slightly shorter due to a stooping posture. Although fifty-four and with a birthday approaching, Wallace could easily have passed for mid-forties. The only indicator otherwise was the mane of thick white hair.

'Thanks for coming,' he said.

Fox looked the older man squarely in the eyes as they firmly shook hands, sizing each other up.

'I didn't have much choice,' Fox said.

'We are preparing a Gulfstream as we speak and it will be ready within the hour for take-off. Please, have a seat.' Wallace gestured to a group of soft leather armchairs around an ornate timber coffee table.

'Thanks.' Fox sank into the nearest chair and Wallace into the one opposite. Emily brought a tray of coffee and tea to the table.

'Thank you, Emily.'

Fox could not place Wallace's accent. It was as if Wallace had no accent at all; he enunciated his English as clearly as his secretary did, minus the old-English twangs.

'Faith, if you could check on the team, please?' Wallace waited for her to leave the room before speaking again.

'You must want a lot of questions answered, Mr Fox. I can only try to imagine what you are thinking about all this.' Wallace leaned towards the table between them and poured two coffees, adding a dash of milk.

'I read about your organisation on the way over,' Fox said. 'Under different circumstances I'd be handing you my resumé.'

Wallace smiled and nodded. 'I read the piece on people-smugglers in Southeast Asia you had published in the *Washington Post* last year,' he said. 'Your interviews with asylum-seekers led to authorities breaking a big smuggling outfit in Malaysia.'

'Yeah, well, I got sick of my country labelling the innocents "boat people", locking them up and deporting them, while the guys making money from it all went untouched.' Fox put his coffee back on the table without drinking. 'Look, Dr Wallace, how can you help me find my friend?'

'I'm able to help you find your friend because his disappearance is linked to something we have been investigating.'

'The pod we discovered?'

'Yes, that's a part of it.' Wallace looked at Fox closely. 'I just want to say: what you are getting into may be very dangerous.'

'That doesn't bother me,' Fox said.

'Yes, I'd expected as much.'

'So you help me find Al, and what is it I'm doing for you?'

'I'm hoping you can finish a job for me,' Wallace said. He stood up and paced the room.

'Lachlan, three months ago an archaeological expedition which I helped finance went missing in Iran. I sent two of my best investigative journalists to discover their whereabouts. After weeks of tracking the archaeologists' moves, they too went missing. Recently their bodies were found washed ashore in a lake near the expedition site.'

Wallace took a folder from his desk and passed it to Fox. 'In there is what they had managed to find out about the dig.'

He paused while Fox flipped through maps and aerial photos of the site.

'Two days ago you found a pod on the sea floor near Christmas Island. I know this because you sent this email—' Wallace held up a printout '—to a friend of yours, a man who also works for us on defence news stories.'

Fox's answer was a blank look as he briefly thought back to the day he and Al had brought the pod up from the sea floor. *If only we'd left it down there . . .*

'Allow me to paint a very brief picture for you, Lachlan, of the events leading to your attack on Christmas Island. I assume you've heard about the threatening conflict in the Middle East at the moment?'

A resigned nod from Fox as he sat further back into his chair to listen to what Wallace had to say.

'The mass media is—strangely for them—downplaying the whole affair, but if they knew the reason for the looming invasion of Iran, it would certainly occupy the front pages and prime-time broadcasts with all sorts of sensationalised headlines.'

'I've read a little about the situation—Chechnya is threatening Iran with invasion. All over a bunch of oil and access to the Gulf,' Fox said with deliberate haste.

'That is precisely what the world has been led to believe, and the newly formed nation of the Republic of Chechnya is rallying behind their President with hope for a mighty future for all.' Wallace paused to finish his coffee.

'In December last year, Chechnya secretly offered Iran a hundred million dollars per year for access to the Persian Gulf. Iran's leaders emphatically rejected all offers, hence the military build-up. What they are unaware of is that Chechnya wants access not for oil or land. They're after something specific, something far more valuable.'

'More valuable than oil?' Fox had trouble conceiving what that could possibly be in that region.

'Superpower status. Or put more correctly in their case, superterror status. The idea of superpowers holding nuclear weapons in order to deter potential conflicts such as a world war has been redundant for years; too many nations have the capacity to use or obtain these devices. Even terrorist groups or individuals can get their hands on working nukes if they have deep enough pockets. Look at the United States. Are they still seen as a superpower?'

'Well, if you classify a superpower as a nation with the greatest economic might and still boasting the world's most advanced weaponry, then, yes, I think the consensus is that they're still the sole title holders,' Fox said.

'And there you have said it perfectly. Economically, the US seems the powerhouse, yet it has more debt and foreign ownership than economists care to publicly admit.' Wallace paused for effect. 'What if I told you that the newest and most aggressive nation on earth now has the most destructive weapon the world can envisage?' Wallace looked over his cup, apparently watching for a reaction.

Fox raised his eyebrows. 'Chechnya?'

'That's right. The weapon used on the city of Bandar-e Anzali was something that could propel this new Chechen alliance into superpower status as we begin this century. Since the fall of the Soviet Union, national cohesion has proven fragile among the Caspian states. Already Chechnya has Azerbaijan as a completely integrated ally, and they are leaning on other neighbours to join the fold. Potentially, the region could be pulled into an alliance with a conjoined land mass the size of western Europe, a population of over a hundred million, and enough revenue in oil and natural gas to enter the G8.'

The look on Fox's face as Wallace spoke was one of wonder. *What the hell am I getting into here?* he thought.

'And all this comes back to that pod?'

'Remember the Star Wars program undertaken by the US government in the eighties?' Wallace asked.

'Of course: the theory of putting weapons in space for missile defence systems. The US spent billions of dollars and got little or no use out of it.' Fox had written his honours paper on the Cold War political and economic climates, in which the Star Wars program featured heavily.

'Well, there was a similar program run in the USSR, only due to their more limited finances they decided, rather wisely as it turned out, to concentrate in one main area of research: railguns. After a couple of years of experimenting, the Soviets found, as we did, that the feasibility of such weapons was not real. The power and size required by a railgun in space to shoot a projectile fast enough to knock down a missile in flight is unfeasible. They did discover one thing though: a weapon that showed its destructive force three days ago and which Moscow has now confirmed.

'It seems instead of making a weapon to shoot down ballistic missiles, they found that a similar weapon to a railgun—a coilgun—in space could fire a special projectile down to Earth with enough force to annihilate a mid-sized city.'

Wallace watched as the news sank in.

'How did Chechnya get their hands on this weapon?' Fox asked after a moment of disbelief.

'Lachlan, have you ever wondered why Moscow wanted to hold onto the Chechen provinces so badly? Oil? A stop-gap to Middle East aggressors? Attempting to stop a domino effect of small states seeking independence? No.' Wallace leaned back in his chair. 'The controls for the weapon lie in a secret location in Grozny, so secret it remains unknown to all but a few of the surviving Politburo members. Men whose directives were to cling to Chechnya as the battle played itself out—with either side's forces ignorant of the true objective for well over the past decade.'

'Why the hell wouldn't the old Politburo have moved the controls of these weapons into Russian territory well before the break-up?'

'Weapon, Lachlan, singular. That is the first piece of good news. Sergei Ivanovich, the man who ran the program, was the only surviving person to know the controls' location. Ivanovich bided his time until Chechnya was close to gaining independence before assuming power.' Wallace paused. 'Our other good piece of news is this: as it had to fit in the Soviet space rockets of the time, the size of the weapon was limited to carry only one projectile at a time.'

'The pod we found had two spheres . . .' Fox said. He looked at the printout of the email he'd sent his contact. The attached photos were printed in colour and showed exterior shots of the pod, then of the inside. One sphere was the size of a basketball and a metallic grey. The other was the size of a grapefruit, in swirly shades of red and orange.

'The smaller sphere is made from theterium,' Wallace said, 'an element originally found only at a comet impact crater in Siberia. Indeed, due to this element originating from what is thought to be the tri star system Theterion, it is comprehensively denser than anything found on Earth. The other, larger sphere would be a depleted uranium counterweight to be jettisoned from the opposite end of the coilgun when fired so as to keep the satellite in orbit—to balance the recoil.'

'So apart from the sphere they now have, they can't make any more?' Fox did not see how this could be a large-scale threat if the element was so rare. *How could Ivanovich possibly hope to cause a serious threat with just one more projectile?*

'Lachlan, the attack on and pending invasion of Iran is not merely to seize land and oil and gain access to the Persian Gulf.'

Wallace cleared his throat and let Fox hang for a second. As Wallace went to speak again, a light went on in Fox's head and he made the connection. He knew what the next sentence would be before it was spoken, word for word.

'More theterium has been found—in Iran.'

15

THE ADRIATIC SEA

Popov and his trusted team of technicians had just completed their work. The makeshift lab sat on the deck of a Sicilian-registered twelve-thousand-tonne transporter with four modified shipping containers on the deck joining to form a large useable space. The captain and crew of the *Scarpa* were used to hiring out their vessel for large cash sums and had the innate ability not to ask questions or even bat an eyelid at their cargoes or destinations.

The recovered spheres had been transferred into a shiny new pod, fifty of which had been stored in various secure locations since the mid-1980s, in the hope of finding more theterium to be machined into projectiles. After making sure all calibrations were correct for the loading procedure, Popov gave the theterium sphere a last look. The mirror-smooth finish of the crimson red and orange swirls looked positively spectacular, and he felt a little sad knowing such a magnificent specimen would disintegrate on impact in just a couple of days' time. Indeed not just disintegrate, but turn into a white-hot fireball, leaving only death and destruction behind.

He closed the pod by switching on a magnet at the rear end—the loading doors sealed together with a hydraulic hiss.

That was all he had to do. For Popov it was now a waiting game for whatever came first: finding the other downed pod, or mining raw theterium from the site in Iran and machining more spheres. He was eagerly looking forward to the challenge of the latter.

16

ITALY

From the airfield at the farmhouse, Gammaldi was led to a timber jetty where two speedboats were tied up. His captors were taking no chances this time: Gammaldi was bound, gagged, blindfolded, and a beefy hand clamped either arm.

The boat ride was short and fast, no more than twenty minutes, and zigzagged in places. When the boat came to a stop and the party left the craft, Gammaldi smelled the pungent odours of a stagnant sea—a shoreline littered with dead sea life from a slow-moving tide.

From the dock, he was led down a stone staircase, the steps the shortest in length he had ever negotiated. It was pitch dark and his bindings limited movement so he continually fell forwards onto the beefy kidnappers in front, only to be pushed back again to bump into the wall of unaccommodating men behind him.

Gammaldi's final destination proved to be a damp-smelling room. He was pushed inside and the heavy door slammed behind him. In the dim light he could see he was alone in the bare room. It was cold now. They had descended to what must be two or three levels below the sea. The only sounds he heard were trickling water in a distant corner and the squeaks of nesting rats that he had just intruded upon. The room smelled like rotten vegetation and excrement.

At least my lodgings are improving, he thought.

17

NEW YORK

The Mercedes ML 320 SUV roared over the Brooklyn Bridge at break-neck speed late in the evening. Fox sat in the passenger seat, getting to know the man next to him.

'Sure beats working for the government,' Sefreid said.

'What service?' Fox asked, pegging him as an army boy. The haircut, the bulk, the manner.

'West Point 1980,' Sefreid said. 'Eight years of airborne, then eleven in the rangers. I came on board as GSR's security chief four years ago, after a brief stint in 'Stan working alongside some SAS boys huntin' in the mountains. Mind you, when I started out in the private security sector, it wasn't the popular choice it is now, what with Iraq and all. Man, there's some hack cowboys over there. Way too much money and not nearly enough brains.'

'I know what you're talking about,' Fox said, recalling some of the jocks he'd served with. There was a cowboy in every squad, especially Special Forces.

'Not that I'm complaining about the pay—it's embarrassing, actually, to think what some of my friends still in the service are getting to put their necks on the line for their country.' Sefreid shifted the Mercedes down a gear as he crossed lanes and took the turnpike to JFK. 'You'll meet my team at the plane—an eclectic bunch. We'll wait till we're airborne to go over the mission and get you kitted up.'

He honked his horn to get a cab to make way. 'I think it was a damn fine job you did in Timor,' he added. 'I experienced a similar thing in Mogadishu. Shit going down right in front of you and we, as UN personnel, were powerless to intervene unless fired upon. God knows, only a soldier understands what it's like on the front line.'

It didn't surprise Fox that Sefreid knew his past, just as the other two GSR people had, and he found himself put at ease by the man's understanding.

He allowed himself a half smile. GSR was puzzling him. Yes, private soldiers were prolific in the days of globalisation and war on terror. More hot spots, more money to be made, more companies needing protection abroad for their executives. Considering what he knew about GSR's clandestine operations—a private company with an armed force meddling in the affairs of other nations, albeit with seemingly 'good' intentions—he felt confident that the resources were good enough to find Gammaldi.

'Thanks, mate,' was all he said to Sefreid though, and they rode the rest of the way to the airport in silence.

18

VIESTE, ITALY

It was the last time Popov was to see the pod. He watched as it was carefully hoisted up to the tip of the Italian Legion VI rocket. Regarded as one of the best high-orbit deployment transports, the rocket's sleek eighty-metre tall frame was a classically designed piece of Italian art. Three bulbous external rockets ran halfway up the sides, partially moulded into the main rocket for a more streamlined effect.

Apart from aesthetics, the true reason the Legion VI rocket was so successful and popular was that it was very cheap. This was thanks to the recycle capacity of the components; the main rocket body on this occasion was to set a record—its thirteenth use.

'God speed, comrade,' Popov called as he took his last close look at the Legion VI. He would spend the next three hours until launch in the mess area, bluffing his way through conversations with the Italian space technicians. He'd done a fine job so far and was actually beginning to enjoy the deception. No longer was he merely sitting in a room lit by flickering neon lights, dealing with technical data; he was practically an agent now.

It had been surprisingly easy to switch the communications satellite his country had booked for launching with the Italian space agency with the far more lethal pod. Whilst the pod was smaller in size than the com satellite, it was over twice as heavy. This meant recalibrating the Legion VI's rockets to burn at their maximum rate and hold a respective fuel payload—moves that were counteracted by the changed orbit conditions. The rocket was now destined to travel less than half the distance.

In the mess, a small man with thick glasses met Popov at the espresso machine. He asked a question about the new weather satellite to be launched, seemingly fascinated by its total encapsulation.

Popov took a deep breath and turned to the man, showing his crooked teeth in a smile before answering.

19

HIGH ABOVE
THE ATLANTIC

The mood aboard the Gulfstream X was electric. The jet flew through the starry night over the Atlantic at phenomenal speed, its flight crew thanking their lucky stars for the job they held. The hours were often erratic and they were seldom given advance notice about which destinations they travelled to, but it sure beat flying a 747 bus or being a Fed-Ex courier.

Fox concluded this must be the other of the Gulfstream pair he had seen back at JFK airport. Inside, the plush leather seats and stylish interior furnishings had been removed to make way for a veritable mountain of assault gear. Fox got to know the seven-member GSR security detail and liked them all instantly. That and the thought that he was going to rescue his best friend filled him with a satisfaction he had not felt since his navy days, and—whilst he tried to deny it—it was a feeling he welcomed.

'This is the coilgun,' Sefreid said, passing over a folder.

'The Dragon,' Fox said dramatically. 'This thing can wipe out cities? Looks like an ordinary satellite.'

'I'd believe it,' Sefreid said. 'I've seen a railgun in action at the Anchorage naval base. Looked like an ordinary destroyer gun battery, only instead of an eighteen centimetre barrel, this thing had a long slender rail. Shot a titanium arrowhead through a *metre* of reinforced concrete.'

'Jesus,' Fox said, flipping though the folder as he listened. 'And if this element is as powerful as they say . . .'

'And rare,' Sefreid added. 'Rumour is there's a second pod like the one you discovered somewhere in the sea off Christmas Island—they must think your mate Gammaldi knows where it is.'

'Stubborn bugger won't be helping them in a hurry,' Fox said, allowing himself a smile.

'Military pilots are good at that,' Sefreid added to lighten the mood. He passed over another folder and turned serious. 'This guy is one tough nut though,' he said.

Fox looked at the photos of Sergei Ivanovich. The face could have belonged to any middle-aged Eastern European guy, but the eyes gave him away. They had the same expression as those of men seen on trial at The Hague.

'And with all the troop activity along the Iran border, he's going for broke,' Sefreid said. 'The scariest thing with these nutters is their hair-trigger willingness to die.'

'I know the kind,' Fox said, switching into gear. 'Okay, how are we doing this?'

'When we're over the drop zone, we free fall for ten seconds exactly, then deploy our 'chutes,' Sefreid said happily. Fox could tell he was raring to get back into some action.

'Now, here's the target area.' Sefreid took the large map of Italy off the card table set up in the centre of the cabin and revealed a huge glossy photo of the Italian farmhouse.

'Damn good resolution,' remarked Fox as he studied the black and white image. It was obviously zoomed in from a very high altitude, and showed a small cluster of buildings, a short dirt runway and a boundary fence. At the edges of the photograph were thick tree plantations, with only one road leading out. To the east were the muddy banks of an inlet with a small timber jetty.

'It was taken from a Warfighter II sat—the latest used by the National Reconnaissance Office.' The explanation came from Ben Beasley, the team's signals expert. He looked more like a librarian than a Special Forces team member, stooped over his notebook computer. 'The old Keyhole sats could read newspapers, but these mean machines can tell you what ink was used to print them. Practically infinite pixels at any magnification. The Warfighters can pick the pigment differences between a tank hiding under camouflage netting and tree canopies, the difference between a crop of barley and wheat—nothing hides from those babies.'

'What's the NRO's role in this?' Fox asked Sefreid, but Beasley answered immediately.

'Well, so long as it's not my brother in the JAG Corps asking . . . We have a couple of friends at Langley who help us out occasionally—they don't care what we ask of them so long as it's within range of one of the three Warfighters. Apparently retasking one of those things requires presidential approval. Hey, remember the time they sent us the shots of the Playboy Mansion? Man, those—'

'Thanks, Ben.' Sefreid brought the young man with the sandy-coloured mop of hair back on track. 'We'll drop in two teams of four,' Sefreid continued, marking on the photo with a coloured pen where each team would land. 'I'll take team one: Goldsmith, Ridge and Pepper, you'll be with me. We do the first drop by the road and come in through the front door.'

Sefreid's team all nodded, acknowledging the task at hand. 'I always wanted to go to Italy,' Goldsmith commented.

'Fox is going to head up team two, which will drop at the far end of the landing strip and secure the southern section of the compound. From there we'll meet in the middle and take the main buildings from two sides.' Sefreid concluded with a description of how they were to enter the farmhouse.

•

The two teams separated and went through their respective planning. Fox led his three team members to the rear of the cabin. They crouched down in a huddle and he laid out another photograph of the target area between them and transferred the drop zone coordinates with a coloured marker.

'Okay. Gibbs and Beasley, when we hit the deck, you two flank out to the northeast to this transmission tower and provide cover fire.'

Fox looked at Beasley. 'And whilst you're there, you might as well see if you can shut that tower down—quietly.'

'No problemo,' replied Beasley, studying the small building with an assortment of antennae sprouting from the roof.

Fox turned to the third member of the team and pointed at him with a strained look.

'Eyal Geiger, sir, ex-Marine Force Recon.'

'Sorry, Geiger, I'm shocking with names. You and I will head double-time to the hangar, under Gibbs's cover fire.' Fox looked closely at the image. 'From the hangar we'll head straight for the guard box, and wait there for the assault on the main house. When we do, I want you—' Fox looked up from the photo to Beasley '—to take up our post at the guard box and cover Geiger and me. And mop up anything that gets past us.'

'No problemo,' Beasley repeated with gusto. Fox knew it had been a few years since Beasley had left the FBI as a Special Agent in the Comms Division at their Baltimore office and he was clearly looking forward to the task at hand.

'Any comments?' Fox asked of the three people dressed in black fatigues crouched alongside him. He was assuming his role as commander as though he had never left the profession.

They all took in the photo and the coloured marker lines delineating their prescribed movements. They added up the tally of men to deal with, as calculated when the Warfighter sat had passed over in the dead hours of the morning before: zero estimated to be in the transmission tower; ditto in the hangar; two in the guard box; and zero again in the motorbike garage. Beyond that lay the main house, kennels, gatehouse and a small building, probably a toilet. These added up to another four men, with Gammaldi assumed to be held in the main house. Last but by no means least was the barracks-like structure, which at 4.30 a.m. local time they hoped would be filled with nine beefy figures all sleeping like babies.

'Sounds good to me,' said Geiger with a grin, 'so long as you can keep up with the marines' record-holder over a hundred metres.'

'Yeah, what's your time?' prodded Fox.

'Ten-oh-three.' The numbers rolled off Geiger's tongue with deserved pride.

'Ha!' bellowed Sefreid as he came over to the group, a wide toothy smile under his moustache. 'That was before you started enjoying the good life and taking girls to every fancy shmancy restaurant in New York—and still he doesn't get any, I might add.'

Fox could tell Sefreid was turning on the army/marine corps rivalry for his sake—to take his mind off Gammaldi. It worked; everybody laughed—especially Gibbs, the only female member on board and a good friend of Geiger's.

'Oh, look at him . . .' Gibbs chided as she tried to grab one of the non-existent love handles under Geiger's Kevlar armour. Truth be told, every member of the GSR security force—Fox included—was as fit as ever and damn proud of it.

'Okay, okay,' said Geiger, putting his hands in the air as if surrendering. 'You're right, I'm a slow, old has-been who can't get it up.'

And with that he lunged to his right and tackled Gibbs around the waist, taking them both flying to the floor.

Fox was surprised to see how even the good-natured wrestling match turned out to be. Emma Gibbs had a small advantage in height, but was slight of frame, and Geiger managed to knock off the Yankees hat that was keeping her hair in place. He turned his attention away from the tangle of limbs after a few seconds—just as Gibbs had Geiger pinned down in a half-nelson manoeuvre—to find Sefreid standing next to him.

Sefreid produced a thermos and a couple of tin cups. 'Hot, strong coffee—the only way to plan an op.'

20

ITALY

A giant of a man, using his bare hands, had been pummelling the life out of Gammaldi for the past half hour. Dressed only in baggy pants and an eye patch, the giant looked just like a pirate, and his heavily stubbled face and huge naked torso glistening with sweat added to the perception. It was this small piece of humour in an otherwise painful situation that kept Gammaldi conscious throughout the bashing.

'What the . . .' Gammaldi tried to catch the breath that had been beaten out of him. 'What the hell do you want?'

In answer, the pirate sent his bare foot deep into Gammaldi's ribs while he was down on his hands and knees spitting out blood. Whilst a kick with a bare foot may not be thought of as painful, Gammaldi could confirm that when the foot is the size and weight of a Thanksgiving turkey, it hurt. He was sent a metre through the air and crashed into the stone wall with bone-jarring impact.

The cruellest part of this whole ordeal, Gammaldi had quickly realised, was that the pirate allowed him to regain his breath after every blow. With the short break came the registering of pain—a torrent that sent his vision into a blur.

Then it stopped.

Another figure entered the dungeon-like room. Gammaldi rolled onto his aching back to look up at the new arrival through swollen eyes. He was a much smaller man, of average height, with a dark tan and thin greying hair. He spoke to the pirate in the same Russian dialect Gammaldi had heard before from his kidnappers.

Gammaldi smiled, baring bloodied teeth, when he saw the pirate—who had to duck and walk sideways to fit through the doorframe—leaving the room. He lifted his head to call after the leaving hulk, 'Thanks, Bluebeard—it's been real.' With that, he lay back and caught his breath once again.

The new arrival looked down at Gammaldi with a rueful smile.

'Hello, my friend, I trust you are having a pleasant stay?' he asked in heavily accented English.

'I must admit,' Gammaldi groaned as he sat up and leaned his back against the cold stone wall, 'I always thought the Ritz had better rooms than this. And I'm a bit dubious about the look of your staff's uniforms—somewhat dated.' He spat out some more blood onto the floor in front of the man's boots.

'Very amusing. Allow me to introduce myself, Mr . . .' The man looked at the licence in Gammaldi's wallet. 'Gammaldi. Your name is Italian, no?'

'It is Italian, yes,' Gammaldi managed, whilst inspecting a loose molar with his tongue in his pain-filled mouth.

'An Australian citizen of Italian descent. How apt that you shall die in your motherland.'

The man gave a chuckle at his own display of humour. Gammaldi did not let his surprise at being in Italy show.

'My name is Dimitry Orakov,' continued the man, 'and I am the Chief of Security here.' He seemed very pleased to be relating his importance to Gammaldi. 'You have a few hours to relax until your next visitor arrives. He is a specialist in the field of obtaining information from . . .' Another snigger. '. . . our guests. He jumps at the chance to practise his craft.'

'I'd be happy to have a chat now,' Gammaldi prompted, in the hope of saving himself from another episode of pain.

'There is no hurry, and I wouldn't want to spoil the Doctor's fun. I hear his favourite technique is to attach electrodes to our guests' testicles.' Orakov laughed again as he made for the door.

He turned, his face red with anger, when he heard Gammaldi chuckling. 'Something funny?' he asked through pursed lips.

'Yeah,' Gammaldi said, and spat the tooth at Orakov. It flew through the air with a glob of blood and slid down the man's cheek. 'Would you mind cancelling the Doctor and making an appointment with the dentist for me?'

21

HIGH OVER EUROPE

Fox sat on a large box with his back against the rear bulkhead, looking out at the starry night. There was intermittent cloud cover below their flight path and it reflected back the dim light of the quarter moon. They were now passing over Belgium and Fox recalled that it was the only landmass discernible at night from space as it was so densely lit up—some sort of fetish with street lights, he mused to himself. It was especially bright when compared to the dark blanket of the Atlantic—a sight he had been looking at for the past half hour with nothing but a few ships' navigational lights to break the monotony.

Nearby, most of the GSR team were cleaning their weapons, more to keep themselves busy than to remove any dust particles, as Fox could see their weapons were positively gleaming. Beasley was deeply involved in a Game Boy, occasionally swearing when the small handheld computer game beat him at tennis.

Remarkably, Sefreid was sleeping in the far corner amid the pile of parachute packs, a trickle of drool from the corner of his mouth just visible against the black face paint he had already applied.

Again Fox looked out the window and into the night. The lights of Belgium were vanishing below and it was darker again. In his peripheral vision he saw a slow shooting star, just a tiny speck going upwards into the black sky. He watched it for a couple of seconds before it disappeared into the cosmos—and made a wish.

22

SPACE

The Legion VI carrying the pod jettisoned its external fuel tanks and continued on main rocket for another few seconds. Two more stages of separation occurred before the coned head of the rocket was all that was left orbiting the Earth.

The cone was the size of a station wagon and had a small booster rocket at its rear. The computer inside registered that it was time for a slight directional change to deliver its payload on the correct orbit, and twelve circular discs the size of CDs popped out and flew into space, leaving small dark holes. Within an instant a seemingly chaotic series of hissing vapours jetted out of these holes and brought the craft to a virtual standstill.

Eleven seconds elapsed and then the nose cone opened up like a blooming flower bud. With another series of hissing vapours this, too, was sent plummeting back down to Earth, where it would disintegrate upon re-entry.

The pod, bearing the stencilled flag of Chechnya, drifted slowly towards its destiny only fifty metres away. The huge magnetic force of the Dragon coilgun drew the pod towards it on a mating course. The long protruding rails, which carried the electrical circuit and directed the theterium cartridge to pinpoint accuracy, fanned outwards, as if mimicking the earlier space dance of the Legion VI's nose cone. The scene took place in the incredible slow motion and silence that only the vacuum of space could provide.

The Dragon was armed and charging.

23

NATIONAL RECONNAISSANCE OFFICE, LANGLEY

Paul Kopec's night was a welcome change from the monotonous routine of the past few months' work. The graveyard shift leader at the National Reconnaissance Office's Department of Orbital Data: Grid 3 had just started on his sixth coffee. His five-member team had been doubled tonight as they put the Middle East Warfighter II satellite through its paces.

Three of the large screens that lined the viewing wall were dedicated to the task of showing heat signatures in the targeted area, starting from Azerbaijan's border with Iran and working to the right in an eighty-kilometre square search grid pattern. After every image was taken, analysts would study it on the large screens, put filters on it, zoom in and out of different areas and doublecheck anything that looked like a possibility. By the time one team of three had analysed their grid, it would be their turn to pull down another image from the satellite. The process slowed every now and then when a heat signature was picked up and needed further investigation—but each time they came up with the same result: nothing.

24

ITALY

'Fifteen minutes to drop,' Sefreid bellowed as he emerged from the cockpit. Each member of the GSR team was making final preparations to their equipment, readying for the assault. The air of excitement and humour had left the cabin, replaced by the serious faces of highly trained professionals dedicated to the task. Fox was going through a few military rucksacks and Geiger came over.

'Need a hand?' asked the ex-Marine.

'I think I'm okay. I'm taking an MP5 and a Sig,' Fox said as he holstered the pistol.

'You chose the MP over this?' Geiger asked incredulously, brandishing his M16 assault rifle complete with M203 grenade launcher slung under the barrel.

'I prefer the quieter approach,' Fox said, screwing a long black silencer into the barrel of his submachine gun.

'That's why I carry this.' Geiger unsheathed a wicked-looking knife. It was a K-Bar standard-issue combat knife for all marines since the Vietnam War, long and razor sharp along one edge and jagged along the other. Geiger's was as shiny as the day it had received its factory polish.

'Again our preferences differ—if I have to kill someone, I prefer to be further than arm's length away,' Fox said, and began sighting his weapons.

•

'On my mark: three, two, one—go, go, go!'

At Sefreid's command, his three team members jumped out of the Gulfstream, followed by their leader. Whilst the Gulfstream was not designed for paratrooper drops, it served this purpose well.

Fox sent his team out, then followed the last out the door, which was then closed by the co-pilot, who was wearing the same breathing sets as the parachutists to prevent asphyxiation at high altitude.

Each member of the GSR team peeled off in their respective attack groups and free fell the first three thousand metres, before deploying their parachutes.

It was the first time Fox had used a Falcon parachute, although he had heard rumours about them in his navy days and knew they were used only by small elements of the US and British Special Forces, due to their enormous cost. They were the same black and charcoal camouflage as all the team's combat gear, and their rectangular design was virtually invisible in the night sky. Fox looked about him and saw a couple of vague silhouettes against the sky. His legs vanished into pure black, and he kept his arms loose by his sides. He could feel how the honeycombed layers of the Falcon made it so easy to manoeuvre; it was almost like hang-gliding.

The best part, though, was how little he had to do to keep the Falcon on course. The eight-kilogram backpack he was wearing contained GPS coordinates, including the exact height of the target landing area. All he had to do was select from several modes of operation—in this case, a quick glide into position and then a slow, quiet landing. An electric motor made up to six adjustments per second through the descent, an array of gears pulling at the thirty-six strands of Neolite cord that suspended him from the silent canopy above.

As he was blanketed in a cloud of mist, a chime sounded in Fox's earpiece. He knew it to be a warning that the ground was closing.

Sefreid's no-nonsense voice came crystal clear over the small headset each team member was wearing. 'Ten seconds to the deck. Weapons ready. Good hunting.'

The MP5 was hanging from a strap around Fox's neck. He squeezed the pistol grip with his right hand and the forward horizontal grip with his left. The butterflies that always came when a planned mission became reality turned in his stomach.

At eight seconds the sea mist cleared and the landing area came into view through the artificial light of his night goggles. Unlike ordinary night-vision devices, which brightened the viewing field with a stark green haze, the small wraparound goggles provided a light blue hue that was easier on the eyes and much more realistic. A custom-added feature of the goggles was a translucent film on the lenses, which caused the black tape securing each team member's throat mike to fluoresce.

Fox touched the ground in such a feathered landing it was as if he were suspended from stage wires. Geiger landed exactly ten metres to his left. Ten metres behind them Beasley and Gibbs landed to form a perfect square.

•

At the other end of the farmhouse, Sefreid and his team touched down in the exact same pattern. The four of them released their parachutes, which were amassed by Ridge for later retrieval. Goldsmith and Pepper disappeared into the tall pine trees that forested the surrounding area of the compound, as their first objective was two hundred metres off to their left. Sefreid and Ridge moved to a vantage point near the road that led in through the high cyclone wire fence, where a solitary guard was meant to be in the gatehouse.

•

At the southern end, Fox's team ran a gradual uphill course parallel to the dirt landing strip, using a thicket of spindly trees for cover. Once they reached the small transmission building, Gibbs was boosted up to the roof and Beasley prised open an aged window with his combat knife. Satisfied the room was empty save for some generating equipment and radio sets, he scrambled in through the small opening.

Peering around the corner in the direction of the guard box, Fox and Geiger got ready for their dash to the hangar.

•

Gibbs watched as Fox and Geiger moved quickly to the hangar building. She was lying flat on her stomach with the long, silenced Accuracy International sniper rifle resting on its titanium stand. The crouching figures of her comrades disappeared into the hangar and she switched the sight on the half a million dollar rifle to infrared. Immediately she picked up the hot-bodied outlines of Fox and the shorter Geiger through the corrugated steel walls of the hangar. The lens of the scope had the same film that, even on infrared setting, showed the bright fluorescent collars of the team members.

'Fox, Geiger, I have you clear in the hangar,' Gibbs said through their small radio earpieces. She then moved her rifle around the grounds and looked through the scope for any threats. The only other figures within the five-hundred-metre range of the infrared scope were the two targets in the guard box.

•

'Roger that, Gibbs, clear in the hangar,' Fox responded as he and Geiger visually checked the hangar for any threats. The large open space contained no plane, and had several engines, including aquatic outboard motors, in various states of repair on long benches. Having confirmed the all clear call from Gibbs, the two men moved back to the hangar door.

'Sefreid, this is Fox,' Fox called from the open doorway. He could just make out the guard box in the dim blue light of the night-vision goggles.

'Roger, Fox,' Sefreid replied.

'We have the hangar secured and report that it is empty; repeat, the hangar is empty—no aircraft to be found.'

Fox was a little disappointed at the thought that perhaps Gammaldi had been transferred from the compound—but he put it out of his mind and concentrated on the planned task.

•

'Roger that. Hangar secured and empty,' Sefreid acknowledged in a whisper. He and Ridge were only metres away from the rear of the gatehouse now and stealthily moving closer.

'All positions ready?' he called through his mike. Every member of the two teams quickly responded in the affirmative.

'Execute first objective and report in,' he ordered.

Sefreid rose from his position in the tall grass and moved towards the small timber gatehouse. It had windows looking out along the road and was open to the elements on the gate side.

Ridge took aim at the greasy old lamppost that lit the area. With a single shot of his silenced pistol, all was smothered in darkness. The guard, who had been watching a movie on a small television set, came out to inspect the lamppost. He threw a cigarette stub into the brush ahead and turned back to the relative comfort of his old chair and movie, apparently unbothered by the broken light.

Ridge's pistol coughed softly twice more, drilling into the guard's head.

•

Gibbs zoomed in on the guard box, using the night-vision mode as it allowed her to get a much tighter focus than the infrared. The box was a squat building made of brick with a flat roof. Long skinny windows gave it a bunker-like appearance. She targeted the head of one of the assailants, focusing on his left eye; she knew that even with all her experience she still squeezed the trigger a few millimetres per hundred metres to the left.

'Fox, I have a fix on the target closest to the door. The other seems to be lying on something to the far side. You have an easy entry,' she said over the radio. She didn't bother identifying herself as she had long got used to being the only female member of the GSR team. There was no mistaking her voice.

•

'Roger that, Gibbs. When the door goes down, take him out,' Fox replied.

He and Geiger ran towards the guard box and stood either side of the door. Fox gave Geiger a nod and the ex-marine hefted his boot against the latched side, splintering the doorjamb inwards.

The first guard was playing cards at a table and looked up at the intrusion. His surprise was short-lived as his head quietly exploded in a cloud of red. Gibbs was right on the money.

The second guard was startled awake. He grabbed the assault rifle resting by his side—half a second too late as Fox squeezed a three-round burst from his silenced MP5.

'Gatehouse secure,' Sefreid called over the radio.

'Guard box secure,' Fox followed. Geiger was peering out the open windows for any potential threats.

'Grounds clear to the south,' Gibbs called through.

'Grounds clear north,' said Goldsmith.

'Beasley, how's the transmission hut?' Fox asked of the last member unaccounted for.

'Job done, boss. Want me to head over now?' Beasley asked in his laid-back way.

'Thanks, Beasley, we move when you get here.'

Fox looked out the door, hoping the next assault would reunite him with his best friend.

25

ITALY

Popov awoke before the sun rose. Since he was a small boy he had suffered mild insomnia that left him with a pale, sickly appearance. Whenever he did manage to get some sleep—normally a few disjointed sessions through the night—he experienced a few moments of alarmed disorientation upon waking.

He lay motionless in the draughty room until he remembered where he was. He got up, pulled on his trousers and suit jacket and urgently made his way to the toilet outside.

The house was dark, the only light a dull illumination from outside coming in through the curtainless windows. Popov half ran for the back door, collecting his shin against a low-lying table on the way. He gritted his teeth, hobbled out of the back door and looked around in the dark morning haze.

Finding the small outhouse toilet, he fumbled hastily with the latch, dashed in and sat down—and none too soon. He reached forward and locked the battered old timber door, a contented smile settling on his face.

•

Beasley arrived at the guard box as Fox and Geiger were exiting. The headless guard had been heaped onto the other who lay on a small cot bed; a pool of blood trickled to the centre of the dirty concrete floor. Fox had thrown the dead men's assault rifles on the roof of the structure, so they wouldn't be found in a hurry in the event the position was lost.

'Wow,' was all Beasley said at the sight before him.

'This is Fox. We're ready,' Fox said over the radio to the other members of the GSR team positioned around the compound.

'Copy that, Fox,' Sefreid responded. 'Let's move!'

•

Goldsmith and Pepper had entered the compound the long way, through the pine plantation and over the tall wire fence. Now they were moving in a crouched run through the spindly trees to the northeast, making as little noise as possible. Halfway there, the deep growls and barks of large dogs broke the silence of the night and their stealthy approach.

'Damn!' Goldsmith said as he and Pepper sprinted to neutralise the sound.

•

Sefreid and Ridge heard the dogs as they were quietly making their way to the main house. They picked up their pace.

'Gibbs, do you have a line on the kennel?' Sefreid asked.

Gibbs could barely hear the dogs from where she lay, but swept her rifle in the direction she knew the kennel to be.

'Negative, no sight line on the kennel,' she replied.

•

Fox and Geiger were making their way around the back of the motorbike garage when they heard the dogs and subsequent transmissions between the other team members. Fox nodded at Geiger and the pair split up—Fox set to enter the rear door of the main house, Geiger moving to flank the barracks.

'I'm in position,' Fox announced and waited for the others to do the same.

•

In the barracks, the dog handler rolled out of bed and donned a coat. He did not bother picking up a weapon as he knew the dogs would be barking at a fox, as quite often happened in the early morning. He went out into the darkness to give them a scolding.

•

Popov, too, heard the barking. He had a mutual understanding with these particular dogs—he didn't like them and they didn't like him. Earlier in life he had been the one bullied and picked on; now he looked forward to poking a stick through the cage at them when he had finished his business.

•

Pepper—now at the edge of the tree line with Goldsmith— saw the guard approach the kennel, a large caged area with some timber sleeping boxes to one side. From his position downwind he could smell the stench of the dogs' faeces in the seldom-cleaned pen. He and Goldsmith shouldered their weapons.

'We have a target moving towards the kennel,' Goldsmith whispered.

'Take him down,' Sefreid ordered.

•

'Shut up!' the dog handler yelled in Russian to his animals, but they only barked more, in the direction of the trees. The handler glanced over, but could see nothing but darkness. He unlocked the latch, commanding the dogs to be quiet.

•

Goldsmith had fallen in love with his weapon during his five years spent with the US Navy SEALS. He got down on one knee and held the pistol grip with both hands as he aimed the cross-haired sight on the target's torso. An eight-centimetre bolt flew from the compact crossbow with incredible power and silence and pierced the man's chest, dropping him to the ground.

'Target down,' Goldsmith called as he holstered the crossbow to his thigh and picked his M16 up off the ground. He and Pepper ran for the kennels.

•

Sefreid and Ridge reached the corner of the main house and peered in a window—an empty bedroom. They continued towards the front door, crouching along the side of the building.

Once they were in position at the front door, Sefreid called into his mike: 'Fox, we're ready to go.'

'Let's do it!'

At both ends of the house the doors were kicked in.

•

Goldsmith and Pepper were halfway to the kennel when the dogs got out. There were three of them and Goldsmith could see with his night-vision goggles that one had some crude gauze bandaging around its snout.

The three Alsatians bounded towards them, vicious teeth bared for attack.

Goldsmith took his crossbow from its Velcro strap and fired another stainless steel bolt. It missed the bounding dogs now speeding closer towards them. The next shot hit the lead Alsatian, now only fifteen metres away, tunnelling its way through the dog's hindquarter. It fell, spasming and yelping, but the other two dogs bounded by without even noticing, intent on the kill.

•

Popov heard the injured dog's whimpering and smiled, thinking the dog handler must have given it a hiding. Satisfied, he began feeling around in the dark for some toilet paper.

•

Inside the house, Fox scanned everywhere. He was momentarily startled to see two figures in front of him across the main room, then relieved a millisecond later as he noticed the fluorescent neck straps.

Sefreid motioned to Fox to check the two rooms closest, whilst he would do the same in the rooms near him. Ridge was to check just one room and then cover the others.

•

Geiger used a small mirror—not unlike that used by a dentist, only on a long extendable stem—to see into the barracks room via the rear windows. Everybody inside appeared asleep. He pushed the mirror into a pouch in his Kevlar vest and ran, crouching, under the window line to the other side of the building and the only door.

•

Goldsmith loaded another three-bolt clip into the top of his crossbow. The dogs were nearly on top of them.

Pepper hefted his big M60 machine gun above his head and, using it like a club, swung at the Alsatian as it leaped at him. It moved with the blow and lunged again, this time getting past the machine gun and sinking its teeth into Pepper's forearm. The large man grunted in pain and punched the dog off him. It snarled even more ferociously, blood dripping from its fangs.

Goldsmith pulled back on the lever that moved the heavy duty firing cord of the crossbow into its primed position. He looked up in time to see the other Alsatian begin its leap through the air, its gaping gauzed mouth aimed at his jugular. He raised the crossbow to fire, but the force of the dog's weight knocked it from his hand and it discharged into the air as the dog brought him down.

Rolling around, he saw his M16 to the left and lunged for it. The dog bit fiercely into his face.

Nearby, Pepper took another swipe at the dog attacking him, but it was too fast, skirting his blow and moving in for the kill.

•

In the main house, the GSR team could just hear the attacking dogs above the kicking-down of doors.

The first room Fox entered was occupied by a sleeping hulk of a man snoring under a blanket, the old steel frame bed buckling under his weight. He stirred at the noise and looked up at Fox, who must have appeared like death itself in his black fatigues and face paint, night-vision goggles protruding from his face and MP5 levelled out.

Fox noticed the man glancing from him to a pistol on the bedside table. He quickly squeezed the MP5's trigger. Three rounds spat from the silenced submachine gun into the man's forehead.

•

Geiger had the door to the barracks covered and was waiting for Goldsmith and Pepper to arrive. He could hear the dogs' snarling over in the direction he expected his two teammates to come from.

'Geiger to Goldsmith, I'm in position. What's the hold-up?' he asked.

•

Goldsmith couldn't see or hear anything. The Alsatian had torn off his night-vision goggles and his earpiece when it attacked his face. Now all he could see was darkness as his eyes took their time to adjust. Two lines of blood ran down his cheeks where the dog's bottom canines had pierced the flesh.

'Doug, I can't see!' he called out to Pepper, who had answered Geiger's radio call, saying they would be there soon.

Turning around, Pepper saw his fallen comrade. The dog spat out Goldsmith's goggles, freeing its jaws for another attack.

'The hell with this!' Pepper said, and pointing his machine gun at the dog, he squeezed the trigger.

•

Popov opened the toilet door a little to let in some fresh air. Finding only an empty roll of toilet paper on the floor, he was deciding what to do next when the sound of heavy machine-gun fire ripped through the still morning. Stunned, he looked out the door, wondering who was shooting at what.

•

The dog was snapping at Goldsmith's jugular as he reached for the pistol in his hip holster. He was still pulling it out when Pepper's M60 roared to life and the dog was cut down. Again the gun roared, then Pepper came over to Goldsmith and easily hefted the smaller man up by the arm.

•

Sefreid was kicking in his second door when he heard the distinctive sound of Pepper's M60—and thought he and Goldsmith must be rounding up the men in the barracks.

The first room Sefreid had checked was empty, but the bed had been slept in and was still warm to touch. He warned the others over their headsets that there may be someone loose in the house, but thought it was probably the man who had gone to the kennels earlier.

In the second room, the occupant awoke at the sound of the gunfire, only to be knocked unconscious by a blow to the head from Sefreid's rifle.

•

Geiger was running back from his vulnerable position to the cover of the main house when he heard the M60 fire. It would surely rouse the occupants of the barracks.

'We're on our way!' Pepper's booming voice came over his radio earpiece.

The door to the barracks flew open and two figures came out into the dark morning. They were wearing hastily donned fatigues and each had an AK-47 assault rifle raised to his shoulder, scanning for a target.

They were both looking in the direction of the gunfire, away from the corner of the house where Geiger was located. He sighted them up and squeezed the trigger of his M16 twice in quick succession. The sharp *crack-crack* felled the two guards in front of him.

'Two targets down,' Geiger called over the radio. 'I could use some help, guys!'

The windows of the barracks smashed out and the flaming tongues of fully automatic fire pointed everywhere. Geiger loosed another well-aimed shot through a timber window frame and wounded a guard in the neck.

•

Sefreid had just called 'All clear!' to the others in the house when they heard the firefight outside.

Ridge tied the semi-conscious guard up in one of the bedrooms and stood by him, intimidating the man with his combat knife. Fox had made a second search of the house in vain. Gammaldi was nowhere to be seen.

'Geiger, this is Sefreid. Fox and I are on our way,' Sefreid said as he ran out the front door.

Fox looked at the man tied up and turned to Ridge. 'Find out what they've done with him,' he said coolly as he made for the back door.

Ridge stood over the man, holding his knife out so that it glinted in the minimal moonlight.

•

Popov was glad he had gone to the toilet when he had. Peeking through the partially opened outhouse door, he listened to the assortment of gunshots and watched as a large black-clad figure ran out the back door of the house and took cover at the side.

He pulled up his trousers and readied himself to run.

•

Fox crouched next to Geiger behind the cover of the main house. Wild shots flew from the barracks in every direction, the guards not game enough to go out the door or get too close to the windows. Geiger took a quick look at Fox's face and knew he had not found his friend in the house.

'There are five left in the barracks by my reckoning,' Geiger said. 'Think Gammaldi may be in there?'

'We can't take a chance in case he is,' Fox replied. 'Gibbs?' he called over the radio.

•

'I'm on my way, Fox,' Gibbs said as she ran along the runway and climbed some stacked crates that allowed her access to the roof of the hangar. Whilst her position on the roof of the transmission building had been the highest point in the compound, the hangar had blocked her view of a couple of the buildings. On hearing the firefight and Geiger's call for assistance, she had taken the initiative to move.

•

On one side of the main house, Sefreid fired short bursts from his silenced MP5 into the barracks, ensuring that the guards inside kept their heads down.

'Goldsmith, Pepper, what's your position?' he barked as a few bullets shredded the timber near his head.

'We're covering the rear of the barracks,' Goldsmith said over the headsets.

'Gibbs, talk to me,' Sefreid said as a burst of bullets tore into the ground near him.

•

'Just a sec,' Gibbs responded as she dived and slid along the roof to its edge, sighting her rifle as she went. She was just in range to use her thermal scope setting.

'Okay, I have five figures in the barracks; repeat, five in the barracks.' As she spoke she steadied her long rifle.

'Gibbs, are they all aggressive?' Fox's voice came over the radio.

She looked through her scope, silent a moment.

'I'm just out of range to be absolutely sure,' she said. 'You think Gammaldi's in there?'

'Could be,' Fox admitted.

'Okay, everybody, listen up,' Sefreid ordered. 'Call out the known targets for Gibbs to fire on!'

'Okay. We have one southeast window,' Geiger called over the radio.

Gibbs sighted up the red shaded blob in the designated area. With gentle pressure on the trigger, her rifle fired silently. Only the split-second mechanical sound of the bolt recoiling and driving another bullet into the chamber was audible. The empty cartridges were collected in a specially made canvas pouch.

The large bullet went through the timber wall of the barracks as if it were cardboard, and the vertical shape in her scope changed to a motionless horizontal one.

'Target down!' she confirmed for everyone's benefit.

'Northeast window and—' A short burst of gunfire came from Sefreid's position. 'North window, a target in each!'

Gibbs sighted up the first target. With a loud *whack!* the bullet passed through the tin roof and the target fell.

'One down,' she said calmly and sighted again.

Whack!—this time the bullet did not hit its target. *Whack!*—still the figure remained standing. Something was absorbing her bullets.

'I'm still getting fire from the northeast corner!' Sefreid yelled over the radio.

Gibbs got up on one knee to increase the angle of attack and fired again—*whack! whack! whack!*—then the eight-round magazine of her sniper rifle was empty.

'Damn!' she said as she opened one of the pockets on her pants.

•

All firing stopped for a moment and Sefreid looked around the corner. The gunman from the northeast corner was no longer there.

'Goldsmith, you lay down cover fire to the rear of the barracks,' he said. 'Pepper, cover my approach to the door!'

He ran under the heavy suppressing fire from the M60, which splintered high around the roof line of the barracks.

'Geiger, meet me with a flash-bang!' Sefreid called as he approached the door.

'On my way!' Geiger responded.

He ran towards the door of the barracks, assault rifle leading the way. From behind, Fox closed in slowly, scanning the windows as he went.

•

Inside the barracks, the two remaining unscathed Chechens looked at the carnage around them. Two of their number had been slain as they went outside, two lay dead in corners, and another was writhing in pain, having been shot in the hip moments before.

They opened the windows on the western side of the barracks, at the back, and began climbing out.

•

Geiger was opposite Sefreid at the door to the barracks. He pulled the cap and pressed the button on the flash-bang grenade and tossed it through a smashed-out window.

'Fire in the hole!' he called over the radio.

A loud boom came out of the barracks, accompanied by the blinding light of burning magnesium. The SAS-developed flash-bang grenades would disorient and possibly incapacitate anyone left inside the house for several minutes.

•

Goldsmith looked back towards the barracks in time to see two figures climbing out the windows and running away.

'Stop or I'll shoot!' he yelled after the fleeing men. He fired his M16 at them—catching one in the arm—as they disappeared around a corner.

'Gibbs, you have two targets heading your way!' he called over the radio.

•

'Got 'em!' Gibbs responded and sighted the two men in the night-vision scope. One appeared to have dropped his weapon and was holding his arm; the other was charging away. She shot him in the head.

Seeing his fallen comrade and realising he must have been killed by a sniper, the second man stopped dead in his tracks, surrendering.

•

'Compound secure,' Sefreid called over the radio.

The Gulfstream had also been listening in, the pilots flying in slow circles above and tailoring their flight pattern as the situation on the ground neared completion. Now the flaps came up and the bright landing lights illuminated the runway as the aircraft came in to land.

26

ITALY

The conflict appeared to have died down, so Popov took his chance. He left the toilet and ran as fast as his bare feet would take him. His first thought was to escape on one of the motorbikes he had seen before, but he decided against it for two reasons: he did not know where they were kept, and he assumed that the attackers had to have come from the road as it was the only entry.

Then he remembered the lagoon and the small boat he had planned to take in the morning. Although it was still dark in the pre-sunrise, he ran in the direction he remembered the jetty to be.

'Please be there,' he whispered over and over as he ran.

•

Fox had a quick look in the barracks then headed back to the main house, where Ridge still stood guard over the tied-up prisoner.

'He tell you anything?' Fox asked as he neared them. He noticed Ridge still had his mean-looking knife out and that there was a long gash under the prisoner's eye.

'He doesn't speak much English,' Ridge pointed at the man menacingly with the knife 'but he seems to be saying Gammaldi was taken to another place.'

'Where?' Fox asked. 'When?'

'Yesterday. And he has no idea where. Apparently a secret hideout that only the base commander knew about.'

'Knew, past tense?' Fox asked, hoping it wasn't the answer he was expecting.

'You nailed him in his room—'

Fox went outside before Ridge finished, his fists clenched into balls. When the Chechens heard of the attack on the compound and the deaths of so many of their men, they would surely execute Al.

The voices of the GSR team were chattering away in his earpiece but he ignored them, staring at the ground, his night-vision goggles atop his head now. In his peripheral vision he thought he saw something—like a figure running away. He looked up but couldn't see anything, so looked back down at the ground—and there it was again, only more distant this time.

He slid the night-vision goggles over his eyes and saw the outline of a man running into the cover of the spindly trees near the guard box.

'Beasley! Someone just ran by your position!' he yelled as he bounded into pursuit.

'I haven't seen anyone!' Beasley yelled, leaping from his position in the guard box and scanning the area around him.

'I'm backing you,' Geiger added as he joined the chase.

Fox ran past Beasley, who immediately followed, in the direction of the trees. At the thicket, they split up, Fox ploughing on dead ahead, Beasley running along the length of the tree line as it moved away from the compound.

Pushing his way through the scratchy branches, Fox stopped momentarily as he heard a noise—the sound of an outboard motor. Suddenly, it dawned on him: the man was trying to escape via the lagoon.

'He's going to get away in a boat!' Fox yelled over the radio as he ran faster towards the water, branches scratching at his face.

•

Geiger, halfway to the thicket, heard Fox and did a quick about-turn. After a few seconds' sprinting, he met up with the Gulfstream as it completed its landing at the edge of the runway. Over the radio, he instructed the pilots on what he needed to do.

Gibbs came across from the hangar and met up with Geiger at the aircraft's still moving fuselage. 'What are you doing?' she asked over the whining of the jet turbines.

'Just give me a hand!' Geiger said as he unclasped the latches on the first starboard storage compartment. He reached in and dragged out a long, wide black cylinder.

'Help me carry it!' he said.

Together, they ran in the direction of Fox and the escapee, the cylinder straddled across their right shoulders.

•

Fox had cleared the tree thicket and could see the jetty less than five hundred metres ahead. He couldn't see the boat but the outboard motor could be heard as it picked up revs.

Beasley came abreast of him at the water's edge and they went onto the creaky old timber jetty in stride. It was short in length and at its end Fox sighted his weapon. The scope on the MP5 magnified only three times—relative to its effective range—and the small boat bumping over the waves of the lagoon made a near impossible target. He fired anyway, on fully automatic, and the silenced submachine gun soon emptied its magazine.

'Damn it!' Fox roared, and threw his gun onto the jetty with a metallic thwack. Beasley just looked on, the automatic shotgun in his hands useless at a target over a hundred metres away, let alone almost a kilometre. As Fox turned and began walking back along the jetty, Geiger and Gibbs rounded the bend of trees at a jog, the black cylinder over their shoulders.

'We get here in time?' Geiger asked as they set down the cylinder. He lifted the cover, pulling on a rope at one end. The sound was like a party popper that shoots small streamers into the air. The corner of Fox's mouth twitched into a grin as the canister split in half lengthways and the black mass inside quickly inflated into a rubber zodiac, the two long halves of the container reinforcing the pontoon bottoms.

After putting the craft into the water, the four of them jumped in and Geiger assembled the electric motor. Stored in three parts for compactness, it came together with the ease of Lego blocks. The engine itself had very little horsepower or torque, but its top speed was reasonable at fifteen knots. The zodiac's main use was for short, stealthy incursions to which the quiet hum of the electric motor was well suited.

Fox and his GSR team soon caught sight of their quarry, but kept as far from him as they could to see where he would lead them.

27

NATIONAL RECONNAISSANCE OFFICE

Kopec had just come back from the bathroom where he'd washed his face in an attempt to keep under control the cold sweat dripping off his forehead. He looked at his watch—he still had around an hour to find the target before the deadline.

'Yee-hah!' a young analyst hooted suddenly.

'What is it?' Kopec rushed over to group two as they filled the largest screen in the room with an enlarged section of their search area.

'Huge signature—faint but huge!' said the analyst. Every head in the room had turned and was looking at the screen, which showed a glowing area near the bank of a body of water.

'Can you get closer?' Kopec asked, moving nearer to study the projection. The heat signature was big—the biggest they had come across—but very faint.

'It should be coming through any second from a better angle,' said the analyst, conviction in his voice and on the faces of his search team.

Two hours earlier, another team had come across a large and bright signature that had brought the whole room to their feet in triumph. At closer magnification they'd found their discovery was in fact an old US nuclear waste dumping ground, with the toxic waste seeping through the stacks of unmarked drums; information that the press and the UN would have a field day with.

The room was tense, waiting for the next feed of shots to come through. Kopec was the only one standing—in fact, he hadn't sat down once this shift—and he used the opportunity to stretch the tension out of his back.

'Bingo!' yelled the analyst, sharing a high five with a colleague. He bashed away at the keyboard in front of him and the image zoomed in further until the heat signature filled the entire screen.

Kopec smiled, taking a few paces back to get the full effect, as though appreciating a painting by an old Master. There was no mistaking it. The heat resonance was nowhere near as strong as that from the nuclear material found before, but it stood out against the barren sands of Iran. A long stretched teardrop, at least fifty metres long and around ten metres across at its widest. Like a comet burning through the sky.

28

GROZNY

Ivanovich walked from his car to the waiting plane. He returned the salute of an elite soldier waiting beside the bottom stair of the aircraft and briskly climbed his way inside and out of the early morning cold.

Most would have found the opulence of the interior quite obscene, especially the hungry Chechens who survived on the meagre social security benefits their government handed out monthly. It was more reminiscent of a Renaissance king's bedroom: rich burgundy felts lined the walls and ceiling with gold embroidery at measured intervals; the carpets were made from the fur of three Siberian black bears; and the windows sported mink curtains. There were only four seats in the cabin, covered in soft brown leather, which could recline into comfortable sleeping positions. A thin floor-to-ceiling curtain fashioned from a tapestry from the Tsar's collection separated the rear section of the cabin, which was fitted out with a round double bed and ensuite. Apart from the flight crew, the jet was staffed by two scantily clad stewardesses, women who followed Ivanovich most places and fulfilled all his whims.

The jet took off and flew low until they were well out of Grozny, then climbed to cruising altitude. Ivanovich was reclining in one of the chairs, drinking a tumbler of vodka, one of his girls perched daintily on his lap, the other laid out on the bed.

'Sir, I cannot tell you how glad I am that you have finally heeded my advice on leaving the capital. Things are getting much too dangerous,' Ivanovich's Chief of Intelligence said to his commander, mesmerised by the raven-haired woman on the bed.

'It was not your words that made me leave, Mishka,' Ivanovich replied, noticing the way his advisor was ogling the woman.

'But the Russians are sending an assassination team after you,' Mishka said, averting his gaze.

'Then let them try and find me!' Sergei Ivanovich said with a laugh. He motioned for the woman on his knee to join the other on the bed. Then he got up and slapped a large hand on Mishka's shoulder and handed him his half-drunk glass of vodka.

'You need to learn how to relax a little, my friend,' he said and disappeared into the bedroom area. The second woman closed the tapestry behind them.

Mishka could no longer see the women but heard their expensive giggles and moans during the remainder of the flight.

29

WASHINGTON

McCorkell awoke to the chiming of the telephone on his bedside table. The phone was linked to the bedside lamp, which lit his modest-sized bedroom with a golden glow.

'Hello?' he said groggily into the receiver, looking over to the clock and seeing the ungodly hour.

'Sir, I have Paul Kopec from the National Reconnaissance Office on the line for you.' The efficient and pleasant voice of one of the White House telephonists came over the line.

'Thanks, put him through.' McCorkell sat up and took a sip of water from the glass he always had by his bed.

'Mr McCorkell, sorry for calling at this hour,' Kopec apologised.

'Quite all right, Kopec, I assume you have good news,' McCorkell said, thinking of only one reason why the NRO would wake him today.

'Yes, sir,' Kopec said. His smile of pride was audible over the phone line. 'We have found the location of the theterium, sir, not far from the Iraqi border with Iran, and around six hundred kilometres from the Azerbaijan–Iran border.'

'Thank you, Kopec. Pass on my congratulations to all involved and have the information and an analyst sent straight to the White House. And send the information on to Larter and the Joint Chiefs at the Pentagon,' McCorkell said as he swung himself to sit on the edge of the bed and put his feet into a pair of neatly laid out slippers.

'On its way, sir.'

McCorkell hung up the phone and walked to the front door of his one-bedroom penthouse apartment, donning his robe as he did so. The Secret Service agent sitting on a chair outside the door was startled from reading his magazine, and stood up on seeing his principal.

'Have the car ready to go to the White House in fifteen minutes,' was all McCorkell said and closed the door.

McCorkell took the time to shave and shower and don a fresh suit, then grabbed a couple of pieces of fruit as he went out of the apartment. He carried his attaché case and passed a sports bag to the agent as they waited for the lift.

'Taking your run at work today?' the agent asked as the lift opened.

'I have a shit of a day if I miss my five kilometres,' replied McCorkell as they rode the lift down. He reminded himself to give his running partner a call when the sun rose, to make other arrangements.

30

GROZNY

Captain William Farrell of the British 22nd Special Air Service Regiment walked through Grozny's recently coined State Square like a local.

He had arrived in the capital only two hours before, driving in an inconspicuous van he'd commandeered in Georgia, together with Sergeant Jenkins and four other SAS members, who'd now left for another mission to the north of the city.

Farrell and Jenkins did not look like soldiers—especially not members of the world's elite Special Forces fraternity. Farrell was dressed in the kind of old clothes one saw everywhere on the streets of the former Soviet Union. His hair was dark and shaggy, and his beard was in need of tidying. Jenkins was dressed in a pair of old overalls, polyester jacket and work boots and carried a toolbox. His wide chiselled jaw, highlighting his Viking ancestry, sported a few days of stubble and the thick

blond hair that touched his shoulders was held out of his face
by a black hat of knitted wool.

The pair soon found their destination—a narrow café in an
old building, recently redecorated in a Western European style.
The interior was perfumed by the myriad of cheeses that were
displayed in the window and the sausages and onions being
cooked on a hotplate for early morning breakfasts.

Sergeant Jenkins ordered two of the morning's specials whilst
Farrell headed out the back to the toilet. He used the journey
to take in the people sitting in the café. There were only a
dozen, mostly people in cheap business attire. In one of the
small booths along the side wall, two men sat with full plates
of breakfast in front of them, untouched except for the steaming
coffees. Both big burly men, one was dressed in casual Eastern
European wear, the other in overalls and woollen hat. The latter
had a beaten old toolbox by his feet. One of them Farrell
recognised.

When Farrell returned from the toilets, Jenkins was paying
for the meals.

'Why is it always my shout?' asked Jenkins as he handed a
heavily laden plate to his senior officer.

'Because you rob more people,' Farrell replied with a grin,
and led the way to a table.

For the past fourteen months, Farrell and his SAS squad
had been living between Russia and Georgia. It was a three-
year tour of duty that had been an entrenched part of SAS
tradition since the late sixties. Squads were sent the world over,
taking with them only the clothes on their backs and a few
hundred US dollars—it was then up to them to live and mingle
with the locals in whatever community they chose. Unknown

to each host country, the SAS teams would get first-hand experience of the culture, learn self-sufficiency in field operations, gather bits of information here and there, and occasionally be called on for a specific task, such as this mission.

Two of Farrell's team had been recruited into the Russian Mafia; the others did some occasional legitimate work, usually on projects of interest back home, but they soon found that crime was the most satisfying way to live.

Farrell put his plate on the table and sat down in the booth, next to the man he knew. Jenkins took the seat opposite.

'Good morning, comrade,' Farrell said in Russian. To the tuned ear his accent was unmistakably Muscovite.

'Good morning, Comrade Farrell,' said the burly Russian as he laid his paper down. 'You've been well?'

'I cannot complain,' Farrell replied to his old friend. Antinov was a major in Russia's KRV, the country's elite fighting and saboteur unit. The two had trained together a few times and liaised socially whenever Farrell was in Moscow.

'How's the family?' Farrell asked as Jenkins and his counterpart got to know each other.

'They are well, thank you. Although my daughter is starting to worry me,' Antinov replied as he ate his breakfast sausages. Farrell ate, too, and noted in his mind the courtesy the Russians had displayed at waiting until they arrived.

'How old are they now?' he asked as he demolished his sausages ravenously. He hadn't eaten properly since lunch the day before.

'Natalia just turned sixteen and Joshua is nine. It wouldn't be so bad but she has a crush on one of the stars of our local hockey team, a boy of twenty who seems to display similar affections,' Antinov said as he sipped his coffee. Farrell noticed the white knuckles on his friend's hands as he unconsciously squeezed the mug in frustration.

'I'd be glad to have my boys pay him a visit when we return to Moscow,' Farrell said. This made Antinov chuckle.

'Thank you, Comrade Farrell, but that will not be necessary.' He paused to shovel a forkful of browned onions into his mouth. 'I have arranged similar plans myself. I have been waiting for the opportunity to be out of town. How you say, an alibi?' Antinov said the word in English.

It was Farrell's turn to laugh, nodding his head at how the world worked.

31

THE WHITE HOUSE

McCorkell sat at the head of the table in the Situation Room. The high-backed leather chair was reserved for the President, who was sound asleep in his bedroom upstairs. McCorkell had no need to wake him yet as exact plans had to be made first with the new data; then he would present these to the President for an absolute decision.

McCorkell watched as Paul Kopec from the National Reconnaissance Office inserted a CD into a computer on a side table. The young man was clearly overawed by the occasion and an army staff aide came to his assistance. With a few clicks of the computer's mouse, Kopec had the close-up shot of the theterium area beamed in great clarity by a digital projector.

McCorkell was amazed at how expansive the area of theterium was and wondered how deep it would be. It was a much larger amount than they had all been expecting, which certainly upped the ante on the decision-making process.

'Sir, the area you see highlighted is the theterium,' Kopec said, indicating with a red laser pointer. 'However, it does not all lie exposed on the surface. In fact, very little of it does. Because this image is picking up the heat signature, think of it as being like an X-ray of the site.

'Now, when I overlay a standard photographic image on top of this one . . .' Kopec made some adjustments on the computer, 'we can see exactly where it is exposed.'

McCorkell looked closely at the projected image, which showed the superimposed shape of the theterium in its surroundings. It was highlighted on the black and white photograph as a soft orange colour, brighter in the areas where it lay exposed on the desert surrounds.

'What's that dark patch in the centre?' McCorkell asked, just as the doors to the Situation Room opened.

First to enter was Admiral Donald Vanzet, Chairman of the Joint Chiefs, followed by his personal aide. McCorkell allowed himself a smile as Kopec gaped at the sight of the admiral, before quickly recovering his composure.

'That, sir, is the mouth of a large cave, with a smaller one here,' Kopec said, tracing over the two openings with his laser pointer.

'Morning, Bill,' Admiral Vanzet said as he took his seat and helped himself to the pot of coffee on the table. McCorkell was always amazed by how fresh the man appeared at any time of day or night, no matter what stress load.

'Admiral, this is Paul Kopec from the NRO, running through the findings,' McCorkell told Vanzet. The JCS Chairman was one of the few military minds whose views McCorkell respected as God's honest truth.

'I hope I haven't missed too much. Please continue,' said Vanzet as he took in the image projected before him.

'Thank you, sir. I was saying, these dark sections in the centre of the image are the openings of two caves. How deep they run we cannot tell, but we would assume that the bigger of the two allows access to the theterium.'

Kopec paused to look at some notes he had scribbled on his hand.

'To the west of the caves we have a campsite with a few tent-like structures that, as of two hours ago, hold only three people. You can just make out two here . . .' Kopec again used his laser pointer. 'Both armed men walking a perimeter line, as evident from the footprints here. The other figure is in the larger of the tents. There are three vehicles at the site: a tanker truck and two standard four-by-fours.' Kopec pointed out the vehicles and concluded his report.

'I imagine you have checked the surrounding area for a larger force?' Vanzet asked of Kopec.

'Yes, sir, the closest other people to the site are civilians in the town of Maragheh over a hundred kilometres to the northeast, along the bank of Lake Urmia. This is an extremely remote area of Iran.'

'Thank you, Paul, we are grateful for your team's efforts on this,' said McCorkell by way of ending the presentation.

'Get me a visual link to Major Scot on the *Carl Vinson*,' Vanzet said to his personal aide once Kopec had left.

'It's a much greater deposit than we thought possible,' McCorkell said to the Chairman of the Joint Chiefs, who was in the process of lighting a cigar—something which was against White House protocol in staff areas, yet rarely ever observed by such people.

'It is much larger than our estimates,' Vanzet admitted, 'and could potentially create hundreds or possibly thousands of projectiles. And that use aside, who knows what other weapon systems could be developed if we researched the possibilities held within this theterium.'

'It's settled then. We must get our hands on it before the Chechens,' McCorkell stated matter-of-factly as the double doors of the Situation Room were pushed open.

'Like hell the President's sending American forces into Iran to fight the Russians!' said Tom Fullop, the White House Chief of Staff, his face red with anger. His thinning black curly hair was messier and greasier than usual and it was apparent he had rushed to get to the White House.

'Why don't you go upstairs and lick some envelopes where you'll be useful?' Admiral Vanzet said to Fullop, the pair having a long history of arguments.

McCorkell had never become involved in the political dogfights that were commonplace in the city he now lived in. Whilst he had an inherent dislike for Fullop, the Chief of Staff was without a doubt very good at his job, and thus the overall administration benefited. At the end of the day, McCorkell was never one to stand in the way of someone voicing his opinion— especially when that someone had more professional access to the President's ear than he did—and he took the situation in his stride as an invaluable part of the democratic republic he lived in.

'Tom, the situation is this: if the Chechens get their hands on this deposit of theterium—' McCorkell motioned over Fullop's shoulder at the projection '—it will make them a military superpower, able to strike at cities at will and with no warning.'

'I know the consequences,' Fullop interjected, 'but putting an incursion force into Iran is unacceptable.'

'Baker's getting nowhere with the Iranians, so where does that leave us?' McCorkell asked.

The fact that the Secretary of State had been received by Iran at all had given the administration some hope; a chance of the two countries working together to try to broker a peaceful outcome to the escalating situation. However, Baker's presence had not only added fuel to the fire in Chechnya—President Ivanovich had been openly dismissive of US intervention in the area—but also in Iran, as people screamed for bloody revenge after the destruction of Bandar-e Anzali. The decision had been made not to reveal to Iran the true reason behind Chechnya's invasion, for fear the Iranians might use whatever theterium there was for themselves. The amount of theterium found by the Warfighter satellite confirmed the wisdom of this move.

'What about the anti-sat missile launch today? Won't that end the situation?' Fullop asked the two men before him.

'Provided we find the Dragon in time, it's within range of the Pegasus and we destroy it, then yes, it may change the time frame of the attack on Iran—but not for long.' Vanzet spoke to Fullop in a condescendingly clear manner, as if explaining the situation to a child. 'The Chechens have gone too far already to back down now. They won't withdraw their troops unless their objective is totally lost.'

'Well, then, that is our only choice,' Fullop said and headed for the door.

'And how do you suppose that?' Vanzet called, puffing a ring of smoke at the disappearing Chief of Staff. 'I really can't stand that man,' he muttered.

McCorkell did not comment; he was turning facts over in his mind, trying to work out the situation as he saw it. His thoughts were interrupted when one of the military aides in the room announced a visual connection had been made to the *Carl Vinson*.

The USS *Carl Vinson* was a Nimitz class of nuclear aircraft carrier and had more combat aircraft and naval assets attached to its group than most countries boasted in their entire military forces. She was currently on station in the Persian Gulf to augment the US military force there, and included several marine vessels.

A large flat-screen television on the wall came to life with a live video image of a man in desert combat fatigues. His hair was shaved short back and sides, common to all marines, and he had a long scar running from his eye to his chin. His eyes were the lightest and most piercing grey McCorkell had ever seen and he had the sense that he was looking at a remorseless killer.

32

VENICE

Gammaldi checked his injuries in the darkness of his cell, massaging the stiffness and bruising out of his joints. Once he was sure there was no one within hearing range outside, he went to the small crevasse between two of the floor's stone blocks where he had hidden his tool. It was the small metal handle he had prised from the interior of the jet he'd arrived in, and he thanked his foresight at taking it.

He went back to work on the door, chipping away furiously at the brittle old sandstone, stopping every now and then to listen. It was painfully slow going, but Gammaldi had thoughts of the Doctor and Orakov's hints of his interrogation techniques to urge him on.

The latch of the solid steel door had cut a groove into the stone doorjamb it swung upon. It was this groove that Gammaldi was exploiting. Soon his hands became red and bloody from the improvised tool but he kept on, the urge to escape over-powering any pain. Freedom from his cell was within sight.

•

Popov was unaware he was being followed—not that he had really checked. It was still dark and he only had a vague idea where he was heading. He saw a channel marker in the distance ahead and recalled from the other time he had taken a boat ride here that there was a similar marker right by the island hideout.

The boat he was in was a restored water taxi, the kind that litter the canals of Venice. Its classic timber hull was beauti-fully polished and the red leather seats were well loved. The inboard engine was larger than the more modern outboards adorning the stern of speedboats, and produced a deep, satis-fying note and a smooth ride.

Initially, Popov had pushed the craft full-throttle to put distance between himself and the attackers at the farmhouse. Now he was advancing slowly, attempting to find his way in the dark. He came to the first set of channel markers, two anchored buoys three hundred metres apart with tall fluores-cent tubes. Popov brought his craft up to top speed to enter the shipping lane. He knew the island he was heading for butted up against one side of this lane, but how far he could not quite recall. He was also hesitant as to which way to go, but seeing the dim lights of the city of Venice in the distance jogged his memory.

He looked over his shoulder as he entered the waterway and squinted in the darkness. There was nothing but blackness behind him, with the far off lights of the occasional boats and the houses on shore. He looked ahead and powered the antique boat along, hoping as he neared each buoy that he would find the one he was looking for.

•

Geiger was manning the electric motor on the rubber zodiac. The engine was nowhere near as powerful as the petrol one at Popov's disposal, but the large battery pack that slotted into place, forming the top half of the engine's bulk, was capable of lasting just over two hours at medium speed. They were currently running at around two-thirds speed, and an electronic display showed the exact measurements of distances, speed and battery power left. It also counted down the time to the halfway mark of the battery power, so that a point of no return could be monitored. They were a few minutes away from that mark.

'It would be so easy to take him. He has no idea that he's being followed.' Gibbs was sitting at the bow of the zodiac. She'd taken the scope off her sniper rifle and was using it like a telescope.

'I'll bet a round of celebratory drinks this guy will lead us to the "secret hideout",' Fox said. He grinned, but he was anxious underneath.

'I'm not one to bet, but I wouldn't say no to a beer tonight,' Geiger said over the quiet whirr of the electric engine.

'Make mine a Pepsi,' Beasley added, as he had long learned alcohol and he did not mix.

'Excellent, sounds like a cheap shout then,' Fox said with a laugh.

'Not so fast, tough guy.' Gibbs turned around from her perch. 'I only drink Bollinger. A pre-nineties vintage will be fine.'

They were interrupted by Sefreid's voice over their headsets, wanting a status report.

33

GROZNY

In the café the four men looked over the several sets of blueprints that were folded into the centre of the Russian's newspaper. The blueprints detailed the basement of the capital's main hospital, including a sub-basement that held large boilers. One third of this level was walled off, labelled as a coal storeroom.

'This room has been redundant for the past twenty years, since the hospital's heating was linked to the city's main oil supply, and backed up on site by a gas-fired unit,' Antinov said.

He had already described the workings of the Dragon in great detail, and the two British SAS men had read a sketchy report passed on to them the day before by MI6. The weapon was truly amazing—an engineering masterpiece from the old Soviet superpower. The thought of a nation like Chechnya wielding such power—at the whim of an unpredictable mega-lomaniac like President Ivanovich—was a nightmare.

'And this is where the controls for the Dragon are . . .' finished Farrell.

'Yes, locked away for the past twenty years, unknown to all since the collapse of the Union,' Antinov said.

'How could something like this go missing?' Jenkins asked in a frustrated tone.

'The Dragon project was shelved in 1986; the secrecy surrounding it was so tight that only the Politburo members and a few engineers knew of its existence. All of the techni-cians on the project, including those who installed the controls in the original military facility in the outskirts of this city, knew nothing about what they were working on. It was passed off as a ballistic missile tracking device. Any with greater knowledge were killed. Only yesterday, through the confessions of two of the surviving Politburo members of the time, did the truth come out. Oh, and the head of the department responsible for such weapons systems at the time was one Sergei Ivanovich.'

Antinov's own frustration was evident as he spoke—it was a feeling so many ex-Soviets had experienced after their Union's collapse. The task of socio-economic reform was hard enough without the immense logistical task of accounting for every piece of the country's military hardware. And then all those ex-political types taking anything not bolted down . . .

'You're sure they haven't been moved since?' asked Jenkins, the SAS squad's electronics expert.

'We have confirmation as of thirty-six hours ago. The weapon was fired from this location.' Antinov tapped his finger on the particular section of the blueprints.

Farrell checked his watch, an expensive Rolex he had acquired from the still warm corpse of a Muscovite drug lord. 'Let's make a move,' he said and led the men out of the café.

34

VENICE

The island was small, no more than six hundred metres in diameter, its shores high and rocky. The only foliage, bar the tall grasses that grew between the rocks, was the same type of spindly trees Fox's GSR team had encountered at the farmhouse.

From their positions in the zodiac, the team scanned the rocky shore, concentrating on the stone pier that the wooden speedboat was now moored to. They watched as the figure they had pursued ran from his boat up some ancient stone stairs that eventually led to a low squat stone building.

'Okay. Gibbs, we'll drop you first—make your way up that rocky side there and find a good vantage point,' Fox ordered. 'Geiger and I will take the stairs and enter that structure. Beasley, you keep the boat away from the island, out of sight.'

The team confirmed their tasks and Gibbs was dropped off, soon climbing up over the huge boulders with the agility and speed of a mountain goat. Beasley dropped Fox and Geiger at the pier, then took the little zodiac a few hundred metres offshore, vanishing into the darkness.

Fox crept up the stone stairs, his silenced MP5 leading the way as he hugged the submachine gun into his shoulder and looked down its sights. Geiger was close behind, carrying his larger M16 in much the same fashion.

The stairs were made from single blocks of granite, the run of each worn down by centuries of use. The squat square building revealed itself to be of the same material, just a blank wall at the top of the stairs, not much higher than Fox's head. Where the stairs ended the same dark stone was used to pave two paths, each leading around opposite corners of the structure.

Motioning for Geiger to take the right, Fox took the left path and made his way to the corner to peer around the side.

'Fox, I have a bead on the structure. Can see you both clearly.' Gibbs's voice came over the radio, crackling with static.

'No hostiles?' Fox whispered as he poked his head around the corner, seeing nothing but another ten metres of blank wall.

'Negative, not from this angle, but I have a good cover on the stairs.'

'Okay, sit tight,' Fox said, making his way to the next corner.

'I have two contacts.' Geiger's voice crackled over the radio.

Fox had trouble making out the words—something was interfering with their equipment. But Geiger's report became clear as Fox glanced around the next bend. Two burly men— dressed in the same jungle green fatigues their countrymen at the farmhouse had worn—stood barring the path, their rifles slung over their shoulders.

'Geiger, can you hear me?' Fox whispered as he leaned up against the wall, out of sight of the guards. The only response was the static crackling in his earpiece.

'Gibbs, do you copy?' Fox tried; he received the same noise over the radio in reply.

Damn! he thought. He cursed again when he heard the guards' footsteps coming closer and their conversational tones growing louder. He looked ahead of him, but a steep rock wall formed a dead end. He glanced back in the direction from which he had come, but it seemed too much ground to cover, and if he ran they would probably hear his footsteps. He noticed that the stone path was littered with hundreds of tiny objects, and with a closer look he realised they were the butts of cigarettes.

The guards were constantly patrolling the perimeter.

•

Clink! The latch freed itself from the groove Gammaldi had created in the stone. He did not dare venture outside yet; instead he stood still and listened. Not a sound was to be heard. With great trepidation he opened the ancient steel door, knowing the hinges were creaky from when the guards had opened it to throw him into the cell. He cringed as the metal on metal squeal pierced the echoing silence of the corridor, but quickly discovered that if he lifted the door while moving it aside, the noise diminished.

Once in the corridor, he examined his options through swollen eyes. He could not recall the way he had been led down here, except that he had come down a great number of steep stairs. To the left he saw doors like the one he had just emerged from. To the right the passage was illuminated by light spilling from a room. He took off in the direction of the light and stopped at the source's ajar door, peering inside. Some guards were playing poker. There was no mistaking the bulk, big shaved head and round shoulders of the pirate amongst them.

Gammaldi gripped the small metal lever in his hand, its end sharpened from the use against the stone wall. For a fleeting moment he considered exacting some revenge.

Then the men broke their silence as they showed their cards and he used the lively distraction as cover, running past the open doorway towards the dark end of the corridor.

A faint draught blew on his face as he rounded the bend and he smiled in triumph as he bounded up the stairs.

•

Popov knocked frantically on the door, as he had been doing for the past few minutes. Finally, he heard a heavy latch lift and the door parted enough for a man's head to poke out. It was the tanned, craggy face of Dimitry Orakov.

'What the hell is it?' Orakov demanded, his eyes groggily focusing on the dishevelled man in a suit and no shirt before him.

'Comrade Orakov, it is Popov,' he said. Orakov opened the door a little more, although he looked annoyed.

'There has been an attack at the airfield. I managed to escape and make it here,' Popov said quickly.

'What?' Orakov's expression changed from annoyance to disbelief.

Popov frantically relayed everything he had witnessed.

•

The two guards rounded the corner and kept on walking, chatting in Russian. Having learnt rudimentary elements of the language at the Academy, Fox got the gist of what they were saying—the unexpected arrival of Popov earlier had animated them and they were looking forward to some action. Their discussion was cut short as Fox squeezed off three rounds into the closest man, then pointed his silenced MP5 at the next, only to see him drop to the ground like a sack of potatoes, the contents of his head painting the wall behind.

Fox stood up from the shadows he had been hiding in and looked around. He heard a crackling voice over his headset, which he just made out to be Gibbs. Knowing she had felled the other guard, he gave an acknowledging wave in her direction and bounded over the corpses, running around the corner of the structure to the door, where he found Geiger waiting.

'The terrace is clear,' Geiger said. 'Take a look over there,' he added, nodding to the edge of the path.

Fox looked around. At the eastern edge of the island, bright halogen lights lit up a long modern pier. Two boats were moored there: a sleek sixteen-metre cabin cruiser, and an older, nondescript craft of similar dimensions. Fox noted that he was standing on the third and top storey of a large building. He counted six figures walking the area below him, assault rifles slung over their shoulders, unaware of any pending danger.

'Shall we see what's behind door number one?' Geiger asked, his M16 level with the wooden door.

Fox nodded, then motioned with military hand signs their intention for the sake of Gibbs, watching from afar.

'Let's go.'

•

Gammaldi continued up the stairs, stopping only once when he heard footsteps along one of the corridors. He had climbed two levels so far, and thought that was about the same distance that he had descended when blindfolded.

At the next level he came to he looked down the length of dimly lit corridors, only to find the space full of talkative Russian voices. He assumed this level to be where the guards' sleeping quarters were located.

Gammaldi scuttled back down some steps as two men carrying large steaming pots walked along the corridor. He exhaled upon realising he had not been seen, then raced back up the stairs, turning the corner to climb the next set. The smell of fried eggs and honeyed porridge made his stomach groan like a birthing buffalo.

A wooden door loomed ahead at the next level and the corridors were deserted. Gammaldi approached and saw the door had no lock. With a smile, he grasped the handle; a cold draught blew on his feet, hinting at the outside world that beckoned him to freedom.

•

The alarm screamed as Geiger and Fox leaped through the doorway. Geiger went first and smashed the butt of his M16 into the face of a man behind the door, sending him unconscious to the ground.

'Shit!' Geiger paused at the sound of the sirens, uncertain whether to continue.

Fox ducked through the low doorway and past Geiger, not seeming to notice the siren. He bounded down the stairs with little heed for personal safety. Geiger followed.

•

Gammaldi opened the door and ran for his life. The sound of sirens filled the early morning and drowned out the birds that were chirping at the first hues of sunlight.

Two guards were running about to his right so Gammaldi turned left, to find a steep rocky wall in his path. The sound of a small army hurrying to alertness sent the stocky Australian climbing up the wall, his hands and feet bleeding as he scraped his way up.

•

Fox had already passed one eerily empty level. The next floor he came to was also deserted, but with an open door leading outside. Looking through it, Fox saw at least four guards running about, looking for any potential danger. The corridor was empty and dark so he proceeded down another level.

•

Gibbs was lying on the highest boulder at the top of the hill that made up the island. From this vantage she was level with the roof of the structure—covered with satellite dishes and antennae—and had a good cover of the northern section of the island. She'd heard the sirens and knew their mission was coming to an end. She tried again to raise her teammates over her throat mike, but the same electronic interference just crackled over. She considered making her way back down to the stone pier, but the idea was short-lived. There was no way she would leave without knowing the fate of her companions.

Then another reason for staying in position came into Gibbs's scope—a target. It was a stocky shape emerging from the scrub at the edge of the area she was covering. The figure was hard to make out through the thatch of short trees, so she gave her sight a twist to reveal the target in infrared.

'Come to momma,' she whispered as she adjusted her scope again to line up the target's head. Then she noticed the figure was unarmed and limping slightly, and her finger eased its pressure on the trigger.

•

Fox was at the landing of the stairs a level below ground. He watched as guards ran out of rooms and down the corridor, and tried to make sense of the orders being barked all around. His eavesdropping did not go unnoticed. A guard turned the corner in front of Fox and stood there, stunned, his assault rifle hanging loosely in his hands. He was a young man, no older than twenty, and shook his head with wide eyes at the MP5 Fox was pointing at his face.

'Sorry,' Fox said quietly as he swung the butt of his sub-machine gun up. It connected heavily with the man's jaw, knocking him cold.

Another man came around the corner, this one more alert. He raised his weapon to fire just as Fox felled him with a quick *thump-thump-thump* from his silenced MP5.

'They're coming!' Geiger said as he looked around another corner. 'About a dozen or so.'

Fox weighed up the odds: they weren't good. The boom of automatic gunfire was deafening in the confines of the stone corridor. He turned to Geiger, who was just beginning to return fire around the corner at the mob approaching them.

'I think I can hold them down if you want to— Ahhh!' Geiger fell to the floor and slid to Fox's feet, clutching his arm.

Fox thumbed the selector of his MP5 to fully automatic, and emptied his magazine at the approaching guards. The first three fell to the ground in a heap; the others ran for cover into the rooms off the corridor.

'I'm okay,' Geiger said as Fox helped him to his feet. In an instant, Fox realised how selfish he was being, risking the lives of the GSR team for a slim chance of rescuing his friend. That task should be his alone.

'Come on, we're getting out of here,' he said. He slung his empty MP5 over his shoulder and picked up Geiger's much heavier M16 with its underslung M203 grenade launcher.

Unleashing a heavy torrent of fire down the corridor, Fox followed Geiger back up the stairs.

•

Gammaldi ran along a path overlooking the eastern side of the island. He considered making for the pier, but changed his mind when at least a dozen armed guards came into view. They took positions by a big sleek yacht that sported a massive antenna that wouldn't be out of place on a battleship. Instead, he ran towards the squat building at the top of the complex he had just escaped from.

When he saw the crumpled bodies of two guards he looked around anxiously, but the sound of the alarm siren dismissed his thoughts of caution and he hobbled along the path towards the guards.

Staring at an AK-47 lying beside one of the dead guards, Gammaldi detected movement to his left. A huge bulk squeezed out of the open doorway and stood to full height. It was the pirate, moving to block the way between Gammaldi and the weapons.

'Bluebeard!' Gammaldi said, a little too startled for it to be a wisecrack. The hulk of a man laughed deeply in response and lunged out at Gammaldi with a flying fist.

The smaller man managed to parry the blow and moved in to sink his own fist into the pirate's chest. Gammaldi wondered who came off worse from the impact: his whole arm jolted and his shoulder threatened to dislocate, while the pirate merely took a step back and grunted.

•

Gibbs was watching the David and Goliath struggle unfold in her scope. She knew she had to intervene for the sake of the proportionally outmatched figure. The attacker's head was the size of a watermelon and she had no trouble putting the crosshairs of her scope in the centre of it.

'Pick on someone your own size,' she whispered down her barrel.

•

The pirate smiled at his quarry, revealing gums in severe need of specialist attention. Gammaldi saw only one front tooth in the cavernous mouth and took aim with his fist, launching himself with all his might.

'My dentist and I owe you something,' he said.

Gammaldi was dumbfounded by what occurred next. Just as his knuckles touched the dinner-plate-sized face and he was expecting the shock of impact, his fist flew on through the empty space where two hundred kilograms of man should have been. In the same instant he was covered in blood as the pirate's colossal skull blew apart.

Gammaldi stood frozen for a full minute, looking between his still clenched fist and the headless corpse of the pirate spread on the ground. He looked about him and saw nothing. He then looked up and said a quick prayer to God, reverting to a faith he had not practised for years.

Then he ran for freedom.

•

Gibbs's rifle was still smoking as she made her way down from the boulder and towards the structure. She had the sneaking suspicion that she had just helped Gammaldi escape, but couldn't be sure until she saw him for herself.

She half ran and half slid down the rocky slope, then pushed her way through the spindly trees that screened her from the stone structure, trying to catch up with the fleeing figure.

•

Geiger fired his pistol again around the corner and the shooting stopped. He and Fox had been held up at the next landing by a sole gunman, whom they now heard crying out in agony.

'I'll cover you,' Fox said as he ran around the landing and fired the M16. Geiger used the time to run behind Fox and bound up the stairs two at a time. Fox soon followed, his longer legs managing three steps per stride.

'This is it,' Geiger said, surprised to discover Fox was right behind him. They burst out of the doorway into the brightening morning.

'Jesus!' Fox exclaimed at the sight of the huge headless corpse before them, looking like a beached whale. He turned back and used his MP5 to jerry-rig shut the heavy wooden door to the structure.

'Let's go,' he prompted Geiger, who was still stunned at the sight of the enormous man bleeding litres of blood across the path.

'Hey, guys!' Gibbs came crashing through a wall of spindly trees. The pair looked up, alarmed at first, then glad to see who it was.

'Hey, Gibbs,' Geiger replied, poking the toe of his boot into the hulk lying before them. 'You get all the easy targets.'

'Yeah. He was just about to—'

Gibbs was cut off by a smashing on the wooden door as the guards within tried to kick it down. Fox knew the MP5 would buy them a little time but not much.

'Let's get out of here!' he ordered reluctantly. They ran down the path and stairs, Gibbs assessing Geiger's injury as they went.

•

Gammaldi was in the timber boat at the short stone pier. He had tried in vain to start the engine; it was impossible without a key. He heard noise coming from atop the high stairs he had just descended and leapt from the boat into the frigid water.

He swam as fast as he could towards the sparse lights of the mainland shore.

•

'Beasley, come in! Beasley!' Fox called over the encrypted radio throat mike, which had less static interference as they came down the stairs.

'I read you, Fox.' Beasley's voice came clearly over the radio.

'Meet us at the pier!' Fox yelled, running down the last, long flight of stairs.

Whilst waiting for his other two team members at the pier, Fox shot holes into the bottom of the timber speedboat with his pistol, remembering one of his many lessons from the Defence Academy: never leave an enemy's equipment intact.

Beasley hummed the electric zodiac alongside the pier and Fox got in.

'What the hell is up with the radios?' Beasley asked Fox, who was helping Geiger down into the craft.

'Something up there's jamming the signal,' Fox replied as Gibbs jumped aboard.

'I noticed some pretty heavy-duty antennae atop the structure up there,' Gibbs said as she wrapped a tight bandage around Geiger's left bicep.

Beasley motored the electric-powered craft away from the island. 'No sign of Gammaldi?' he asked the team.

'No, ' Fox said. He was contemplating telling the team to leave him behind to continue the search alone, when Gibbs interrupted.

'That's what I was trying to tell you!' she said urgently, leaving Geiger to tie off his own bandage. 'When I drilled that ogre up there, he was in the process of pummelling a guy. He ran off towards the pier.' Gibbs pointed over her shoulder at the disappearing island.

'That means he may still be there!' Fox said. He scanned the side of the island they had just left, but his night-vision goggles were useless in the sunrise, and the shore was too craggy and distant to spot a person with the naked eye.

'Or more likely out here,' Gibbs said as she shouldered her sniper rifle and looked around them with its infrared scope.

It took only seconds to locate the splashing swimmer in the water.

•

Not the greatest swimmer at the best of times, Gammaldi went as fast as his short, stocky arms would carry him, but his lungs were burning from exertion. It was the fatigue brought on by lack of food and sleep, and the cold salty water bit at his swollen eyes and body cuts.

He thought he heard a slight hum in the water, but assumed it was his ears giving in like his closed-over eyes had. Then he thought he heard a voice—Fox's voice no less—and deduced his mind was going as well. He must be nearing the end.

He was about to resign himself to his fate, stop swimming, and let the sea consume his tired and battered body, when a hand came down on his shoulder. It was a big hand, strong and warm.

Gammaldi turned on his side and faced up, but he couldn't see a thing through his eyes any more. As strong arms hefted him out of the water his body went limp.

•

Fox barely recognised the man before him, even though they'd been friends since high school.

'Need a lift, mate?' he asked.

Gammaldi collapsed into the embrace of his old friend, laughing with relief through chattering teeth.

35

WASHINGTON

McCorkell ran through The Ellipse to the Constitution Gardens, where he met his jogging partner at the Washington Monument. The pair were of similar fitness levels and managed to easily keep in step along the five-kilometre run. A Secret Service man ran thirty metres behind his principal, talking with the other man's bodyguard.

'They found the theterium this morning,' McCorkell said quietly, his breath fogging in the early morning cold. 'A huge deposit—45.5 East, 37 North—found mostly in a cave and close to the surface,' he added, then paused as they passed a group of corporate joggers being egged on by a personal trainer.

'So where does that leave you?' his companion asked.

'I've yet to speak to the President, but we have two likely options: a quick extraction followed by the destruction of the site; or just the latter, if Fullop has his way—which I'm quietly counting on.' McCorkell picked up the pace as they always did on passing the halfway mark.

'How will they extract the theterium?' the other man asked with interest.

'A specialist army engineering outfit, backed by a black-ops marines unit—how exactly I don't know, nor the method of incursion, but the deadline's ticking closer.'

'How soon could they be on the ground?' the man asked in a worried tone.

'Within the next twenty-four hours—logistically no sooner, and certainly strategically not much later,' McCorkell said, passing on information that he knew would result in the deaths of some of his countrymen.

'Any movements towards the objective by the Chechens?'

'No. We assume they are waiting for the deadline in around forty hours' time—but they have a force ready to deploy directly to the site from the Iraqi border.' McCorkell was labouring for breath now.

'They were the hundred or so troops spotted yesterday?' The other man breathed easier, as he was mostly listening.

'Yeah. Hopefully everyone can be in and out in time to miss them. Do you still think you can succeed?'

The pair slowed down for the last part of the jog towards the mall, where they had agreed to stop for a drink and general chat about life for the benefit of anyone listening in. McCorkell was sure his Secret Service agent had been ordered to do so: his running partner was a person of interest to the United States Government.

The other man took his time before replying. 'Yes, I think we can get there first.'

He was confident, a trait McCorkell had always known in him, and it instilled a degree of hope. Even though the National Security Advisor was committing treason, he felt comfortable in the knowledge of how the information would be used.

The pair slowed to a stop and stretched, before walking into a small, well-heated coffee shop open for the early morning trade. The owner smiled on recognising the men and served them their usual.

36

GROZNY

Farrell and Antinov walked in the main doors of the hospital and introduced themselves at reception. The clerk checked in the appointment books and confirmed that the men had a booking to assess the boilers in the basement. It had been made the day before by Russian Intelligence.

'We have some service men waiting with a van outside. Is there a service entry to this section of the basement?' Antinov asked, knowing the answer.

'Yes, sir,' replied the clerk, handing back the City Works identity cards the men had produced. 'At the east side of the hospital, door . . .' The clerk had to check a laminated map on the desk.

Three, Farrell recalled in his head.

'Door three,' finished the clerk with an efficient smile.

'Thank you. We will leave a service report here when we are done,' Farrell said as they walked away.

'Oh, sir?' the clerk called after them as they neared the door. 'Don't mind the soldiers guarding the service areas.'

'Yes, thank you, comrade,' Antinov said. They knew exactly how many soldiers were guarding the hospital.

•

Door three was the only service door on the east side of the hospital in good repair. It was also the only door guarded by a pair of soldiers. The van pulled up and Antinov jumped out to greet them.

'Comrade Milovich, City Works,' he said, presenting his identity card.

'Yes, we have been notified of your arrival,' one of the guards said, motioning to a wooden box on the brick wall that contained an old telephone.

'We're here to inspect and service the boilers,' Antinov said as Farrell, Jenkins and his Russian counterpart, with their overalls and toolkits, joined him.

'No problem,' the second guard said, and opened the door for the City Works men. Antinov led the way through the door and down the stairs, the pair in overalls close behind him, once their toolboxes had been inspected.

That was easy, thought Farrell as he went to pass through the doors. He was stopped by the outstretched arm of one of the guards.

'Why do you need a camera?' asked the guard.

Farrell glanced down at the Polaroid hanging around his neck and shifted the large roll of boiler plans under his arm. 'Oh, to take photos of the state of the boilers,' Farrell said innocently. 'A necessity since we are personally liable these days if our work is faulty.'

The guard thought for a moment, then gave a shrug and let Farrell pass.

37

THE WHITE HOUSE

The President entered the Situation Room at 0800 hours to find McCorkell and Secretary of Defence Larter in conversation.

'Morning, boys,' he said jovially and sat at the head of the table. He shifted a little upon noticing his leather seat was already warm.

'Mr President,' they replied in unison.

'I hear we found the theterium. Well done all round,' the President said as he sipped a fresh coffee set in front of him.

McCorkell frowned at Larter, who returned a slight shrug. *Fullop*, McCorkell thought; the President's predictable political lap dog had already gotten to his ear and stolen the National Security Advisor's thunder. He wondered what sort of spin the Chief of Staff had put on the situation.

'Yes, sir, the deposit was much more extensive than we had estimated,' McCorkell said.

'Obviously we have the option to . . . how can I say this . . .'
The President searched for non-incriminating words. 'To remove
the site, perhaps in the process averting the pending conflict
between Chechnya and Iran.'

'That is correct, Mr President,' Larter allowed, 'but the
advice from the Joint Chiefs is unanimous. We have over a day
and a half, with the resourcers in transit, to obtain some
theterium for ourselves before we have to commit to a destructive course.'

'So it's the view of your people that we should obtain the
theterium for our own purposes?' the President asked.

'That is our position, yes, sir.' Larter looked over to McCorkell
for support.

'And what say you, Bill?' the President asked.

'Sir, we don't know what sort of potential uses this theterium
may hold, but we have to ask ourselves: is it worth the risk?
I mean, sending American troops into Iran poses all sorts of
problems, as I'm sure has been pointed out to you already.'
McCorkell added the last at the expense of Fullop. 'And for
the purpose of obtaining material for a new weapon of mass
destruction.'

'Hmph.' The President sat in thought a moment. 'Peter, can
you guarantee the incursion force could excavate and leave the
area in time?'

'Mr President,' Larter said, with what McCorkell pegged as
a nervous smile, 'you know the capabilities of the resourcers
as well as I, and the marines unit is made up of some of the
toughest fighting personnel we have—but nothing is guaranteed in warfare—'

The President cut him off by pounding his fist on the table. 'Damn it! What's the success rate on this one? Because if it's a shade less than one hundred per cent, we're not doing it.' His cheeks flushed. 'We've lost enough boys in uniform in the Middle East already. Failure this time is not an option.'

Silence.

'Is there enough time to have these marines get in and out and still leave time to wipe the site?' McCorkell asked, knowing the answer.

'Yes, sir, there is.' Larter's reply was directed to the President. 'How much they extract depends on time and methods of transport used, but they should be able to obtain a worthwhile amount.' He looked down at a printed estimate of the extraction process on the desk as he spoke. 'Under the circumstances, I think we'd be missing a huge opportunity by not attempting a mining op.'

'All right. Go in for the damned element, leaving enough time to eliminate the site, and make that destruction damn well known to the Chechens afterwards.' The President got up and moved towards the doors. He paused there, casting a look of trust at his advisors. 'With any luck, a conflict in Iran can be avoided, with us scientifically profiting from the whole ordeal. I have to give a press conference now. I'll leave the floor to you, gentlemen.'

'Just to be clear, Mr President, you are green-lighting a United States military incursion into Iran?' McCorkell said, not wanting to be party to any blame should things go wrong.

The President knew the game all too well.

'I think we're all clear on what needs to be done, Bill, Peter,' and he exited the Situation Room, leaving the responsibility and accountability of the mission to his Defence men.

'Bastard,' Larter muttered.

38

GROZNY

In the basement of the hospital, the four Special Forces men went about their subterfuge task.

Farrell crouched down, ostensibly to take photos of the boilers, but focusing instead on the pair of uniformed Chechen soldiers guarding the coal storeroom's doors. Beyond those doors lay their objective: the Dragon controls. Jenkins and the Russian set their toolboxes on the ground, while Antinov scanned the room for cameras and alarms.

Satisfied there were neither, Antinov and Farrell made their move.

'Excuse me, can we inspect through there?' Antinov asked one of the guards while Farrell moved close to the other.

'It's strictly off limits beyond these doors,' the guard told Antinov.

'Do you know the penalty for interfering with high-ranking city engineers, soldier?' Antinov prodded as he moved within reach of the guard.

'Strictly off limits!' the guard enforced, raising his assault rifle loosely in his hands and pointing it at Antinov.

In the blink of an eye, the Russian Special Forces leader twisted the rifle from the guard's hands and knocked him across the head with it. In the same instant, Farrell disarmed his quarry and head-butted him in the face, smashing the guard's nose, and following up with a chop to the man's neck.

Jenkins and his Russian counterpart dragged the unconscious guards to the back of the boilers where they tied them up together and gagged them with thick cloth tape. Antinov and Farrell screwed silencers into the pistols each had concealed in the small of his back and pushed through the doors.

Inside the control room, two soldiers stood up quickly from a game of backgammon. Antinov put a nine-millimetre slug between each man's eyes with his huge Soviet automatic.

Farrell rounded up a technician in civilian clothes who was pulling apart a large piece of equipment with a screwdriver. He was of medium height, with short sandy hair and glasses sitting crooked on his face.

'Please don't hurt me!' the technician begged as Antinov took him by the scruff of the neck.

'If you remain quiet, no harm will come to you,' the Russian said.

Farrell began photographing the equipment, making sure the shots met side by side so nothing was left out, while Jenkins and his partner prepared to set charges around the room.

The explosives were ingenious. Jenkins opened the battered old toolbox and looked in the separate compartments. There was a hammer, several spanners and ratchets, some assorted nuts and bolts, a screwdriver set and a tape measure. Tucked next to the tape measure was a small reel of wire and some snips. The Russian's toolbox was identical, right down to the wear marks on the hammer's handle and mismatched spanners. The toolboxes were the latest in plastic explosives disguised as everyday objects. They'd been moulded by expert model makers and tinted to the correct colours.

With care, Jenkins took out the hammer and pushed it into the seam between two huge computer cases. Next the screwdrivers were worked together into one mass and stuck under another control box.

'Why are you the only technician here?' Antinov asked the trembling man, who'd wet his pants and made a puddle around both their feet.

'What do you mean?' the Chechen said, unable to take his eyes from the dead guards on the floor.

'All this equipment—it needs at least several people to work it, no?' Antinov said, noticing Farrell was finishing up his photographs.

'I have been the only one here for three days, since they removed the firing controls,' the man said nervously.

'What?' Antinov gave the trembling technician his full attention.

'Shit!' Farrell suddenly said in English from the other end of the room. 'Something is missing here!' he hissed.

Antinov dragged the technician over to where Farrell stood staring into a gaping hole in the top of a large metal box, with loose wires spilling out.

'That was the firing board,' the technician said simply.

'Talk!' Farrell said as Antinov shook the man.

'The controls here were duplicated some time ago. Three days ago, Comrade Popov came and removed the coded firing panel,' the man said, reeking of urine.

'Where are the second controls?' Antinov growled. He shook the man by the lapels, lifting him off his toes.

'I swear I have no idea!' The technician was quivering in terror.

'Then who does?' Farrell could see the technician was holding nothing back. The hot end of Antinov's silencer against his temple heightened his frantic state.

'I swear I have no idea. I am here merely to dismantle what remains of the controls.'

'Don't worry. We'll do that for you,' Jenkins said as he and the other Russian finished their work.

'The controls could be at the farmhouse perhaps!' the technician said, apparently clutching at straws.

'What farmhouse?' Antinov said, pushing his pistol harder against the man's head.

'About half an hour's drive north of the city. Popov told us he went there and met with President Ivanovich himself.'

'We're done,' Jenkins said, looking around at their handiwork.

'That is all you know?' Antinov asked the technician.

'That is all,' he answered, then shouted in a panicked, desperate voice: 'Guards!'

Without hesitation, Antinov pulled the trigger and the technician was blown across the room.

'You can't say I didn't warn you,' Antinov said to the dead man.

They moved to the door, pausing a moment to see if the technician had been heard. After a minute no one had showed, so they hid their weapons and walked up the stairs to exit via door three.

'Let's hope the chaps at the farm have better luck,' Farrell said.

39

SPACE

The Dragon was loaded and nearing readiness to fire. With incredible slowness, the pod had docked with the weapon, expelling its canister and leaving behind the theterium sphere and the larger depleted uranium counterweight.

The solar power of the Dragon had been fully drained during the reloading and the compact nuclear reactor was still working to recharge the immense current in the coil.

But now the seven-day fire-and-recharge cycle was nearly complete. Soon the Dragon would be ready to breathe fire again.

40

ITALY

The zodiac's small electric motor ran out of life just two hundred metres from the timber jetty at the farmhouse. The little craft had performed well, but now, to their dismay, the occupants found themselves slowly floating away from the jetty as the tide ebbed from the lagoon.

'What's happening?' Sefreid asked over the headsets. He and Ridge waited on shore with a pair of four-wheeled motorbikes.

'The engine's cut out,' Fox replied, paddling furiously on one side of the zodiac; Beasley followed suit on the other. The small black plastic oars were agonisingly slow going in the water.

'You'd better hurry. You've got company,' Sefreid added.

Fox looked over his shoulder and saw the backlit shadow of a large boat on the horizon. He powered his strokes into the water with added haste.

'Can you swim for it?' Sefreid suggested.

'Not with the injured,' Fox replied through a grunt of exertion.

•

Ridge pulled off his boots and tossed a greasy loop of rope to his commander. 'Hang on to this!' he yelled as he ran and leapt off the jetty, his end of the rope tied to his belt.

Sefreid held onto his end of the rope in wonder, watching as the whippet-framed Ridge swam through the water at speed. It only took a few seconds for him to realise what was happening and he promptly tied the rope onto the back metal grate of his bike.

'Ridge is heading your way,' he told Fox and his team.

•

'I see him,' Fox replied as he watched Ridge coming through the water with torpedo speed, already two-thirds of the way across the distance. In the time they had been paddling, Fox guessed they had only covered around forty metres.

Gibbs pulled Ridge out of the water and the sopping man quickly transferred his end of the rope from his belt to the eyelet at the tip of the zodiac's prow.

'Ready!' he called in exhaustion.

•

Sefreid turned his four-wheeled motorbike in a tight circle, away from the shore and in the direction of the airfield. He noticed that the spool of rope coiled on the ground had only two loops left to unreel—it had been that close.

With a rev of the two-stroke engine, he let the clutch out and the wheels of the bike bit into the soft muddy bank. For a moment nothing happened, then the wide, knobbly tyres bit and the bike leapt forward. When the rope went taut the motorbike slowed, but he kept the revs high, soon changing up gears.

•

The roar of heavy machine-gun fire ripped through the morning and drowned out the motorbike noise. Looking back, Fox saw the blaze of fire was coming from the muzzle of a heavy-calibre machine-gun on the deck of the pursuing boat. Jets of spray erupted in wild zigzags along the wake of the quickly escaping zodiac.

Fox sat back in the boat and took aim with Geiger's M16. With a squeeze of the secondary trigger, the big M203 under-slung grenade launcher belched fire, but the forty-millimetre explosive projectile splashed into the water, shooting a huge geyser into the air.

'Pump to reload and aim higher!' Geiger called out.

With a higher inclination of the weapon, Fox fired again. This time the round flew through the air as a hail of heavy machine-gun fire churned the water to the side of the zodiac and headed straight for them.

The grenade hit the water directly in front of the pursuing vessel, which veered off abruptly, sending several uniformed men into the water. The heavy machine-gun crew lost control of their weapon, firing off into the air.

'That'll give them something to think about,' Fox said with a grin. Just then, the zodiac hit the muddy embankment and slowed down. 'Sefreid, keep going!' Fox shouted, as he could see the pursuing craft turning again.

Sefreid gave the four-wheeler's engine more juice, and soon it and the zodiac were hidden behind the tree line, travelling at around thirty kilometres per hour. The zodiac rode with incredible smoothness across the grass, which was damp with morning dew.

Beasley gave out a hoot as they slid out of the thicket of trees and headed for the Gulfstream idling on the gravel runway.

●

Goldsmith was waiting at the bottom of the retractable stairs of the jet. He grinned at the sight in front of him—Sefreid hammering the bike across the home straight, the occupants of the zodiac hanging on for their lives, and Beasley upright in the prow, wind blowing in his face, hooting like a rodeo rider.

41

GROZNY

In the back of the van, Jenkins sat looking out of the rear window. In his hand was half of the tape measure, which was in fact a remote detonator. Just before they rounded a corner and the east side of the hospital was lost from view, he pressed the detonate button.

In the old coal storeroom of the basement, the other half of the tape measure received the signal via its radio antenna and in turn sent a current down the dozen wires that led to different parts of the room. The wires each ended at the toolkits' bolts: disguised detonators that triggered the main explosion.

The door-three guards were thrown through the air by the exploding fireball. With a satisfied nod Jenkins turned back to face his fellow soldiers.

'Control site number one is no more,' he said.

'I thought the controls were encrypted, not able to be duplicated,' Farrell said to Antinov.

'It seems that the panel is what cannot be duplicated,' Antinov replied, pulling into a nearby laneway and stopping the van by the parked Fiat he had placed there the day before.

The four men alighted from the van, Jenkins and his Russian number stripping off their overalls before closing the van doors behind them and booby-trapping the handle with a fragmentation grenade.

'And if our team doesn't find the controls at the country house?' Farrell asked Antinov.

'We call our NATO comrades.' Antinov prayed the controls would be found by the other team, but he had underestimated his Chechen cousins thus far and dreaded doing so again.

'Let's get to a phone,' he said.

He put the Fiat in gear and they raced off.

42

ITALY

No sooner had the GSR Gulfstream X taken to the air than a notebook computer linked to the aircraft's telephone systems flashed with an email message. Beasley tapped in the security codes and brought the message up on the screen. Sefreid read it over Beasley's shoulder and promptly left the cabin for the cockpit where he told the pilots of their next destination. Coming out a moment later, he asked Beasley, 'That's it?'

'Yes, sir, just a couple of lines,' Beasley responded.

'Okay, team, listen up.' Sefreid looked about the cabin. Goldsmith was applying antiseptic to the shallow grooves cut into his face by the attacking Alsatian. Pepper and Geiger had removed the tops of their black fatigues removed and Ridge and Gibbs were attending to their injuries. It was already a joke amongst the team that the bite on Pepper's arm was worse than the bullet graze sustained by Geiger.

'We have just received word from home that mission two is a go,' Sefreid said. 'We are to fly to Iran straightaway, where we will make our way to the theterium site.'

Sefreid smiled, happy at the thought of more clandestine operations. To date his time with GSR had been mainly as a security advisor and facilitator. Wallace's hints of more 'hands-on' tasks in the future were finally coming to fruition.

•

'What's in Iran?' Gammaldi asked, sitting up against a padded bulkhead. He was consuming some packaged ration bars and had drunk over a litre of sports drink.

'Iranians.' Fox said. He was patching up his mate, using saline eye drops and an icepack to take down the swelling of his eyes.

'Really? I think I'd rather see the sights of Italy,' Gammaldi said, regaining his humour with his strength.

'I hear the Iranian dungeons are far more hospitable,' Fox baited, and left to have a look at the message on the computer for himself.

He read it in silence; then read it over twice more, trying to think of scenarios that it could be referring to.

Proceed mission two—employee waiting with details of takeover bid. Proceedings should not be hostile, but clock ticking fast.

Fox turned back to his friend, now covered in blankets in a corner. He was beginning to snore, a half-eaten energy bar gripped loosely in his hand, threatening to join a pile of similar silver wrappers on the floor. Fox smiled at the sight, knowing that when his stocky little mate awoke he would be prepared for any adventure, no matter what the odds.

43

MINSK MILITARY AIRFIELD, GEORGIA

A white unmarked Airbus A400M squatted at the end of the runway like a giant bug, its stubby nose and four huge propellers painted matte black. Four curved hangars lined one side of the two parallel runways, housing a squadron of Mig 29 Fulcrum jet fighters. Outside in the elements stood a row of ageing Hind helicopters, in the process of being overhauled by the base mechanics.

The morning sun was not visible through the cloudy sky and it looked like being another dark February day in Georgia.

Captain Farrell alighted from the Fiat and walked the stiffness induced by the non-stop drive out of his legs. Antinov, Jenkins and the Russian did the same. Nearby, the second team of Special Forces soldiers alighted from a Volkswagen van in low spirits. Their attack on the farmhouse north of Grozny had come up with nothing—no Chechen leaders, no military guards, and certainly no Dragon firing controls. Farrell had been disappointed to receive the news en route, but he and Antinov had used the trip to plan and prepare for their next task.

Now, he and Antinov followed the base commander, a tall colonel with thinning white hair and a friendly bearded face, to a fortified concrete office where a large figure in combat fatigues stood with his back to the door examining a wall map.

'Major Antinov, Captain Farrell, this is Captain Zimmermann of GSG-9.' The colonel made the introductions.

Captain Zimmermann turned and smiled briefly at the two squad commanders. 'Nice to see you again, Captain Farrell,' he said, and shook the SAS commander's hand in a firm grip.

'Likewise,' Farrell said.

'Major Antinov,' Zimmermann said to the KRV commander, 'I don't believe we have met.'

'No.' Antinov sized up the man in front of him. 'No offence to your unit's abilities, Comrade Captain, but when told of the German assistance in this matter I hardly expected a team of Border Police. Surely this is a military operation.'

The base colonel excused himself and left his office in search of coffee for his guests.

'A surprise to me as well, I assure you, Major, but orders are orders,' Zimmermann said. 'My team is from Group 9/3 and has done many training exercises with Farrell and his fellow SAS soldiers over the years.' Zimmermann spoke with utmost confidence, his Aryan blue eyes probing the Russian before him.

'Captain Zimmermann is right, Antinov,' Farrell began. 'GSG-9 are one of the world's top anti-terror units. I have personally trained with Group 3 members at NATO's

International Long Range Reconnaissance Patrol School and they almost whipped our butts.'

'In that case, it will be a pleasure serving alongside you.' Antinov slapped the serious-looking German on the arm with a laugh.

'Who will handle the explosives?' Farrell asked Zimmermann, now that everybody seemed to be getting along.

'I have two experts from our army engineers, along with our latest explosives,' Zimmermann said, somewhat guardedly, Farrell thought.

The base colonel entered followed by a sergeant with a tray of coffee. He was pleased to see the three Special Forces commanders smiling.

'Thank you, Comrade Colonel,' Antinov said to his countryman. 'Considering the situation, I think a brief celebration is in order to cement our alliance in the field.'

'Yes, a celebration, of course,' replied the colonel with a gleam in his eye. He went to a drawer and produced a tall bottle of a reasonably priced Russian vodka.

'Ah, excellent,' Antinov said as the colonel poured four glasses.

'To a successful mission,' Farrell toasted, licking his lips in anticipation of the stomach-warming liquid.

The four men threw their heads back in unison and emptied their glasses.

44

THE WHITE HOUSE, THE LAST DAY . . .

McCorkell had been in the Situation Room since before dawn, having slept the night on the comfortable couch in his office. NASA had located the Dragon over Iran in the early hours of the morning. The coordinates had been relayed to the air force, who quickly had an FA-18G Super Hornet jet in the air loaded with a Pegasus missile. The rocket that propelled the missile was capable of travelling over three hundred kilometres at Mach four and the missile's eighty-kilo high-explosive payload would toast any satellite-sized targets.

McCorkell was keeping close tabs on the Super Hornet's flight, awaiting news of the Pegasus missile's imminent launch at the Dragon. He had a quick run on the White House gym's treadmill, followed by a shower and a fresh change of clothes, before he continued catching up on the latest reports.

The first report he read from the stack on the conference table was of concern: the combined Russian–British Special Forces had not found the controls for the Dragon in Grozny. Both the team at the city's hospital and the team at the northern farmhouse had come up empty-handed.

He picked up another report. It had been decided—for obvious reasons—not to inform their allies about the theterium deposit, but now, reading a report from an operative in Moscow, it seemed the Russians might know of the location. Given the little time left until the deadline, McCorkell wasn't too worried however. What would the EU military team do now? Whether Pugh and the resourcers mined the element or not, the site would be levelled before the pending Chechen invasion.

McCorkell was talking to an air force ensign, getting a real time update on the Pegasus flight, when Tom Fullop and Robert Boxcell entered the room.

'Morning, Bill,' Boxcell said as he took a seat.

'Good morning, Rob,' McCorkell said, ignoring the Chief of Staff as he had ignored him—petty, but as common in politics as cereal for breakfast.

'What's the latest?' Boxcell asked.

'The Pegasus flight is on target, but the EU team failed to find the controls. Apart from that, nothing has changed.'

'I read a report on the controls on the drive in,' Boxcell said. 'The Russians suspect they were relocated to where Ivanovich lived before taking power in Chechnya.'

'Which we've narrowed down to somewhere in Europe, South America or the multitude of terrorist-friendly states in the Middle East,' added McCorkell.

'It's frustrating, but that's what we've got. Tracking his plane has so far left us with no fewer than eleven possible landing sites in seven countries,' Boxcell admitted.

'Can't we make a strike at these sites ourselves?' Fullop asked.

'Well, Tom, if you want to advise the President to launch cruise missiles at a number of civilian airports, go for it,' said McCorkell coldly.

'It's probably more proactive than the advice you're giving him,' Fullop retorted.

An uneasy quiet filled the room.

45

MARAGHEH, IRAN

The pilots of the Gulfstream X let out an audible sigh as they touched down on the private concrete runway of the Amahn Research Centre. Their fuel tanks were running perilously close to dry.

Only two structures stood beside the runway: a two-storey control tower and a long squat concrete building with an aircraft hangar at one end.

The control tower directed the GSR jet to the hangar. A tall steel door slid smoothly along runners as they neared, revealing a deep cavernous space. As the pilots shut down the twin engines, a dark-skinned Arab in khaki uniform pulled alongside in a golf cart with passenger trailer in tow.

Sefreid was the first to alight from the Gulfstream. He shook hands with the Arab whilst the rest of the GSR team, along with Fox and Gammaldi, emptied out of the jet. In transit they had all changed into desert combat fatigues.

'Okay, in the cart, people,' Sefreid commanded as he took a seat next to the driver in the lead electric car.

'What the hell have you got us into?' Gammaldi asked Fox quietly. They were the last to step aboard the cart.

'Me? It was you that dragged us into this, remember?'

Fox took in the inside of the hangar. The roof was relatively low, only a few metres' clearance over the Gulfstream, but it was a long narrow space—four aircraft of Gulfstream size could fit nose to tail with room to spare. In the direction they were headed, towards the far end of the hangar, sat a Lear jet in mint condition with custom chrome panelling around the twin jet engines and nose cone.

'I seem to recall that it was your driving that got us into this,' Gammaldi said, as the cart came to a stop by an elevator.

'Oh, you want to start on driving?' Fox said.

'Hey, at least I can fly a plane,' Gammaldi retorted with a grin, as the team crowded into the elevator.

'Yeah? Well, at least I can swim,' Fox said, returning the grin. Gibbs failed to suppress her laughter at the exchange.

The elevator sank five levels below ground, opening up to a concrete platform that overlooked a cavernous space the size of a football field. Dozens of people in lab coats milled about below, their various skin and hair colours indicating the multinational collaboration at the research site. The centre of the open expanse held a mass of computing equipment, surrounded by work desks, chairs and various banks of control panels. Fox didn't quite know what to make of the scene, but the answer came in the form of a tall distinguished-looking man of Arabic descent, dressed in a light grey Armani suit that matched the colouring of the hair at his temples.

'Richard! Good to see you again,' said the man as he strode confidently towards the band of fatigue-clad figures touting weaponry.

'Likewise, Dr Gunther,' Sefreid replied, shaking the offered hand.

'Please, come with me. We have prepared refreshments.'

Gunther spun on the heel of his expensive Italian shoes and led the way to a long glass-walled room that overlooked the work space below. Here a conference table had been converted to a buffet, holding piles of fresh flat breads, bowls of salads and exotically coloured dips. Trays of antipasto, with layers of different meats, pickles and cheeses, were also on offer.

'Thank you for your hospitality—' Sefreid said, but was cut off quickly.

'No need to thank me. Tasman and I are good friends, you know that.'

Gunther sensed the reluctance of the GSR team to eat with a deadline ticking. 'Your transport to the site is still an hour from being ready, and it will take half that time to get you to the dock,' he said. 'So you see, we do have some time to kill.'

'In that case, I'm sure my team is as famished as I am. Thank you again,' Sefreid said.

'It seems a couple of your team see no need to stand on ceremony,' Gunther replied with a laugh, motioning towards Fox and Gammaldi. The pair had loaded a couple of the fine porcelain plates to the brim and a waitress was already in the process of pouring them a beer each.

'They are mission specialists on this op. I'll introduce you,' Sefreid said, taking Gunther over to the two men.

Fox was busy eating and watching the activity below through the floor-to-ceiling windows, whilst Gammaldi was chatting up the pretty Iranian waitress.

'Dr Eric Gunther, this is Lachlan Fox, and that man over there is his partner in crime, Alister Gammaldi,' Sefreid said, then excused himself to attend to the buffet.

'Mr Fox.' Gunther shook Fox's hand.

Gammaldi gave a wave in acknowledgement of the introduction, then turned his attention back to the waitress, who he already had in fits of suppressed laughter.

'Lachlan is fine, Dr Gunther,' Fox replied, sizing up the man.

'In that case, it's Eric.' Gunther took a tall glass of gin and tonic from a nearby waitress.

'What is this facility for?' Fox asked between mouthfuls of food.

'It is the world's latest research centre into nuclear fusion. No doubt you were told that GSR has played a large part in funding the project,' Gunther offered, sipping at his drink. 'The operation is financed and run by my own company and staff, but the good Dr Wallace helped organise the building of the facility by lobbying some powerful people. And what you see with the eye, Lachlan, is just the staff work areas. We have almost ten kilometres of accelerators running under the sands here, making it the largest complex of its kind in the world.'

'That's impressive. You seem to have a good backer in Tasman Wallace.'

'We became friends when we were doing our doctorates at Oxford together,' Gunther said candidly. 'We always agreed that whichever one of us made it first, we would help the other in his quest.'

'So Wallace wants to change the world by reporting the real facts from places no one else will go, and you want to change the world by providing clean, sustainable energy,' Fox surmised.

Eric Gunther laughed. 'That was about it when we were young, idealising what we wanted to achieve—and I might say Tasman almost has.'

'And are you far from achieving your goal?' Fox asked with genuine interest.

'In the two years this facility has been operational, we have come a long way.' Gunther pointed to a large opening in a far wall that resembled a subway tunnel. 'We have just started testing in a kilometre-long vacuum tunnel, firing a hydrogen pellet along electronic rails into the core of a reactor, which, at great enough speed, should turn out favourably.'

'Can you achieve the speeds required?' Fox asked as he finished off his plate.

'We are still finding that out, but our best estimates indicate that with existing propulsion and power technologies it will take several years to reach the speeds required—then there is the hurdle of harnessing the resultant power. That, or we find an alternative to the hydrogen pellet to trigger the fusion process,' he finished.

A waitress approached and whispered in his ear. He nodded in acknowledgement.

'If you will excuse me, ladies and gentlemen,' Gunther said to the room. 'I must depart to conduct an interview on the facility.'

Sefreid walked over and shook Gunther's hand again.

'Good luck on whatever clandestine operation that old dog Wallace has sent you on this time. I am counting on seeing you all back in one piece.' Gunther spoke to Sefreid like a fond parent.

'We will scrape through. Thank you again, Dr Gunther.'

With that, Gunther left the room. Gammaldi joined Fox at the window overlooking the work area, where his friend had returned his attention to the scientists milling around below.

'I really do believe my taste in organising dates is better than yours,' Gammaldi said.

'Excuse me?'

'I think Anita will be much more enjoyable company over dinner than your good doctor,' Gammaldi said through a mouthful.

'You made a date with her?' Fox looked disbelievingly into the bruised and battered face of his friend.

'Yep. The next time we are in Iran,' Gammaldi replied, holding up a paper napkin with Anita's name and phone number scribbled across it.

'You're incredible,' Fox said, shaking his head.

'I thought that's why we joined the navy in the first place. A girl in every port, remember?' Gammaldi said deadpan, stuffing a large pickled gherkin in his mouth.

•

The boat Dr Gunther had organised had seen better days. It chugged along Lake Urmia as fast as the old diesel engine would take it. Pepper, who rebuilt engine blocks for kicks, had given it a tweak and three extra knots of speed were added to the twelve it had struggled to do since leaving port. Fox was at the helm in the small pilothouse, with Gammaldi alongside, familiarising himself with an MP5. The GSR team were in the hold below, getting their respective equipment ready.

'Let me see you load it again,' Fox said, watching his friend's actions with the submachine gun.

'Yes, sir!' Gammaldi ejected the magazine, inserted another and pulled back on the cocking slide, chambering the first round.

'Excellent. I know you can use a pistol so I won't ask for a demo,' Fox said.

They watched a small wooden boat holding two fishermen float by, the pair drawing near-empty nets aboard. Their craft was left bobbing in the larger vessel's wake.

'Hell of a way to make a living,' Gammaldi commented. He waved at the local fishermen, who were shaking their fists in fury at nearly being capsized.

'Yeah, you're right. It's a hell of a lot easier saving the world with a ticking deadline of certain death and destruction,' Fox said theatrically. 'And against unknown odds to boot.'

'Looking forward to it,' Gammaldi said deadpan, slinging the MP5 across his shoulder by the strap. The desert pattern fatigues he wore were a spare pair of Geiger's, too tight across the chest.

'Let me guess—this is what holidays are for,' Fox said, scanning ahead for any other craft. There was nothing but choppy, cloudy water.

'Something like that,' Gammaldi answered with a smile.

•

Sefreid joined the pair in the pilothouse fifteen minutes later, as the southern coast was growing closer on the horizon. It was a barren coastline, with no sign of habitation in either direction; a mixture of crumbling sandstone and thickly crusted salt flats left from the receding water over the ages. A hand-held GPS monitor let Fox know he was almost dead on course, and soon the low sandy humps that held the theterium deposits popped up on the horizon.

'There she is,' Sefreid said, magnifying the scene with a pair of binoculars.

'See a good spot to tie ashore?' Fox asked, picking what seemed an okay spot with the naked eye.

Sefreid looked along the coastline: most of it was a two-metre rock face with a slight gradient. The water in the lake had been kept at a fairly constant level for the past thirty years, as it was a vital irrigation resource for the pistachio plantations to the northeast, as well as supporting coastal communities with a dwindling fish supply and a general purpose water source.

'To the left a little. Over there,' Sefreid pointed. 'There's no sign of movement from the site, but better to keep a distance and we'll cover the ground on foot.'

'Couldn't agree more,' Fox said. He killed the engine and let the battered old boat drift the eight hundred or so metres to shore under its own momentum. Sefreid handed the field glasses to Gammaldi and went down the steep timber stairs to the hold, which was thick with diesel fumes.

'Are you sure about these guys?' Gammaldi asked under his breath as he examined the coastline and sand dunes himself.

'They proved their worth when they helped me rescue you,' Fox said quietly. 'And their intentions in this theterium matter seem clear.'

Fox looked at his friend, glad to have him back. He allowed himself a chuckle.

'What? You just got the last joke I told you?' Gammaldi said.

'Nah,' Fox said, turning back to the task. 'Hey, if you think these characters are a bit iffy, wait until you meet their boss.'

'The Wallace guy? I thought you liked him?' Gammaldi put the binoculars down. Through the window he could see they were about to drift ever so gently against the shore.

'A clever guy, no doubt about it.' Fox's gaze ahead was vacant, deep in thought. His big strong hands kept the wheel in a tight lock, so the boat would meet the edge of land portside in a wide, slow manoeuvre. 'I just find it hard to believe a private company would operate on this scale in this sort of matter.'

Gammaldi looked at his friend's expressionless features; it was a rare sight to see the learned and worldly Lachlan Fox locked deep in puzzled thought. He decided to go in for the knock-out blow.

'Things just aren't black and white any more,' he quoted with a sigh of helplessness.

'Hey!' Fox snapped out of his thoughts with a rueful smile and punched his friend in the arm. 'I was pissed off when I said that,' he said, 'and I've since come to realise that things never were black and white. There are always grey areas, where basic ideologies get confused and rarely play out a fair deal. That's life.'

'You know what?' Gammaldi said, his chestnut eyes open wide as if he was finally coming to a revelation. 'I do believe you're having another mid-life crisis.'

It earned him another hit in the arm, this one harder, which aggravated a bruise from his session in Italy with the pirate.

'Again, I wonder why I saved your bacon,' Fox said with a laugh. 'Go on the deck and get ready to tie the boat to, you clown.'

Gammaldi exited the pilothouse with a good-humoured grunt. Fox watched as he got into position on the deck, picking up a rope that was tied to a heavy brass eyelet. The stocky little man shook his head at the chore and waited for the pending soft impact, little more than twenty metres away.

Something in the last conversation flicked a switch in Fox's mind, illuminating a dark corner he had been trying to shed light on for the past day. GSR and Wallace's motives, however philanthropic, began to clear. *Is what Wallace is doing so different from my ill-fated mission into Timor? Who else would intervene here? The UN? Fat chance.*

He left the deep thoughts for another time and called down to Sefreid that the landing was only seconds away. With a tingling of pride, Fox knew the action he was about to take was for all the right reasons, even if it meant the lives of a couple of local toughs guarding the site.

•

The white Airbus A400M touched down on a dirt airstrip outside Tabriz in a gigantic cloud of dust. The wide dirt runway was a joint effort of the Red Cross and United Nations three years earlier, enclosed in a fenced-in compound. A sprawling cluster of temporary buildings housed a medical centre for the local region, as well as supporting UN personnel who used Tabriz as one of the Middle East logistic centres.

The commander of the UN force was a brigadier with the British Medical Corps. He greeted the aircraft along with the six armed members of the Gurkha Regiment that provided security for the compound. The brigadier stood tall and broad-shouldered, dressed in desert fatigues that hung from his frame and flapped in the stiff breeze.

'Captain Farrell.' The brigadier offered his hand.

'Thank you for having us, sir,' Farrell replied, sizing up his countryman.

'Nonsense, Queen and country, lad,' replied the brigadier with seriousness.

'Sir, this is Major Antinov of the KRV, and Captain Zimmermann of GSG-9.' Farrell introduced the other members of the semi-EU Special Forces teams as they disembarked from the Airbus. They all shook hands and the brigadier led them to a long truck that had pulled up near the plane's cargo doors.

'Lieutenant Paulson of the Gurkhas here will take you to the outskirts of town.' The brigadier introduced the wiry little dark-skinned man with eyes like coal. 'There we have arranged a helicopter from the northern militia group to transport you to the site. You understand why I can't let you use our UN bird.'

'Of course, sir.' Farrell knew the arrangements would have been made by request of military command back home—this was certainly not a mission representing the UN. 'These northern militia are up to the task?'

'They are well equipped and backed, so don't worry about the reliability of the helicopter—a big MI-8 Hip. And the price we dished out means they will give you up to twenty-four hours and ask no questions.'

'I take it we can have faith in this group?' Antinov asked after he had ordered the men to move all equipment into the truck.

'Faith, Major Antinov, is all these people know,' the brigadier answered.

'And they have no idea who we are?' Zimmermann asked.

'These people ask few questions. Lieutenant Paulson has built up a rapport with this group and delivered a truckload of medical supplies to them last night—something far harder for them to obtain in this country than money or arms.'

The brigadier spoke a few words to Paulson before walking away. He turned back again with an afterthought. 'Good luck . . . with whatever it is you are doing,' he said with no trace of a smile.

'Thank you again, sir,' Farrell said with a casual salute. He climbed into the cargo hold of the truck with the rest of his team and pulled the back canvas down to hide their presence as they exited the compound and the city.

•

At the theterium site, Fox and Gammaldi were the last ashore. As with the incursion in Italy, Fox led one team, Sefreid another. The groups were identical to last time, but with one change: Geiger stayed on the boat because of his wounded arm and Gammaldi took his spot in Fox's team.

As before, the two teams kept in communication with encrypted radios, the throat mikes taped around their necks. Each member carried a twenty-kilogram backpack as well, except for Ridge who had the job of carrying a Stinger missile launcher and three rockets.

'Meet you in the middle,' Sefreid said, and charged off at a run with his team in tow.

'We'll be waiting for you,' Fox said, leadig his troops off at a fast-paced jog over the two-kilometre distance.

'You coping there, Fatso?' he asked of his friend, who was running beside him, with Gibbs and Beasley behind.

'I'll get by,' Gammaldi replied with a grin, even though pain registered in his joints at every stride over the rocky terrain.

The site of the theterium was a low double hill. The ground underfoot was barren from the high salinity near the lake and consisted of crumbling sedimentary rock and windswept sand. To the south were endless rolling hills, much like the one they were running around, and much smaller than the mountains that climbed to the north of the lake and stretched to Iran's northern border.

After five minutes, Fox's team reached some wide tyre tracks that marked the road leading to the encampment. Following the tracks, they came to a thicket of prickly shrubs and ducked behind them for cover. The sun was shining through inter-mittent cloud cover, but whilst its rays were bright and golden in patches, it failed to warm the winter's day.

'Sefreid, we have cover at the south end of the camp but no fix on any targets. Repeat, zero visual targets,' Fox called over the throat mike.

'Roger that. I have Ridge covering the area up here. We are moving in for a closer look,' Sefreid replied.

'Copy that. We're closing in too,' Fox said, then ordered Beasley to stay behind to guard the track.

'You're enjoying this, aren't you?' Gammaldi said as they continued running, carrying their MP5s ready for action.

'I miss the life a little,' Fox said with a sideways smile.

'Give me the comfort of a cockpit any day. I'm not fond of this grunt work.' Gammaldi came to a stop next to his friend as they closed on the last section of cover. There was an open expanse of about a hundred metres to the campsite, and to the right the mouth of a large cave opened up the western side of the hill.

Fox studied the scene, comparing it with the image he had memorised on the flight earlier. Two canvas tents stood opposite each other, joined by shadecloth; a water tanker sat close to one of the tents with an old Korean War-era Jeep beyond it. Three men sat in the shade between the tents, playing cards and eating lunch, oblivious to any pending threat.

'Fox to Sefreid. I have three figures between the tents.'

'Copy that, Fox, we have them too. We are almost at the water tanker,' Sefreid replied quietly.

Fox watched as Gibbs and Gammaldi climbed up the sloping rock of the hillside to cover the campsite and check the cave for any threats not visible from below. Sefreid's voice came over the radio as the pair disappeared from view.

'We have position at the north. Ready when you are, Fox.'

'Copy that, Sefreid. Waiting on Gibbs,' Fox replied.

'Don't you boys hold back on account of me,' Gibbs replied in her hammed-up southern drawl. 'I'm ready to play and can confirm that there are three targets in view.' Her voice was short of breath as she scrambled to the nearest vantage point looking over the campsite.

'This is Fox. I'm moving in.'

Fox sprang up from his position and ran straight towards the lunching guards with no concern for concealment. It took him five seconds to run half the distance before the guards noticed the armed figure charging at them. It took another two seconds for them to respond, staggering up from the table and reaching for their AK-47s leaning up against the tents. By the time they'd picked up the weapons, Fox was nearly upon them and Sefreid, Goldsmith and Pepper had emerged from behind the tanker a few paces behind the group.

'Drop your weapons!' Sefreid said in scratchy Arabic.

The three guards looked behind them and saw their equal number of armed men, weapons raised at head level. Pepper was waving his big M60 across the three guards, as if daring them to give him an excuse to fire. His wide grin and menacing stare showed he meant business. The guards dropped their rifles and raised their hands high in the air.

'Is there anybody else guarding this site?' Sefreid asked the men as Goldsmith moved forward and bound their hands behind their backs with plastic straps.

'No, just us,' said one of the guards.

'What is your mission here?' Sefreid demanded.

'We are paid to guard those caves,' said another guard, fearful for his life.

'Who hired you?' said Sefreid, already knowing whom the hirer represented.

'A Russian man who speaks like a local. Orakov is his name,' stammered the guard, his eyes fixed on the menacing men before him.

'Tents are clear,' Fox announced as he joined the group.

'Hi, everybody. This is Gammaldi. The caves are secure.' Gammaldi's voice came over the headsets.

'Thanks, Al, you clown,' Fox replied as he looked up at the hills and saw Gammaldi waving from the main cave entrance. South of the large opening was a smaller one, about the height of Gammaldi and just as wide.

'Is anybody expected here?' Sefreid asked of the talkative guard, standing inches away from his face to intimidate him further.

'No!' the man said quickly. 'We are to radio in any contact we have. We are paid month to month by Mr Orakov.'

Suddenly Fox heard a distant hum; at the same instant Geiger's voice came over the radio.

'Heads up! We have a heavy-lift 'copter coming in fast and low from the northeast!'

Sefreid backhanded the guard.

'Everybody find cover!' he bellowed over the radios, not that anyone needed any prompting.

The Hip emerged from around the caved hill so close to the ground that a large sandstorm followed in its wake. Gibbs and Gammaldi scrambled into the smaller of the two caves and trained their weapons on the emerging threat.

Fox raced for the cover of the water tanker as the sandstorm created by the Hip's rotor wash blanketed the campsite.

•

The Hip circled the camp once and saw the three Iranian guards running from the scene with their hands tied behind their backs. The pilot instinctively pulled the trigger on his toggle and the huge twin machine guns unleashed a torrent of fire against them.

'What the hell are you doing?' Antinov demanded. 'Just set us down, you idiots!' he barked. He stormed back into the main cabin, fists clenched and face red with anger at the trigger-happy pilot.

'So much for the covert landing, comrade,' Farrell yelled over the engine noise.

'Imbeciles!' Antinov raged as he picked up his compact length AK-74A, the newer addition to the Kalashnikov submachine gun family.

'Let's go, people!' Farrell called.

Jenkins opened the side door away from the camp and the SAS squad jumped out, instantly followed by the Russians.

The Hip did not touch the ground as it disgorged more than half of its occupants; it hovered a metre in the air for the few seconds the manoeuvre took, then flew off around the camp in a circling path to the cave entrance.

•

Fox and Sefreid lay side by side under the belly of the water tanker, watching the twelve men coming at them in two groups from five hundred metres away. The helicopter buzzed off to their side, again kicking up a cloud of sand that helped maintain their cover position behind the advancing ground troops.

'I don't like the look of all that firepower,' Fox said. The heavy machine guns and rockets on the Hip were hovering far too close for comfort.

'I agree. Ridge, can you take a shot at the Hip?' Sefreid yelled over the maelstrom erupting around them.

'I'm ready to take them down when you say,' Ridge replied.

'Gibbs! Gammaldi! Get clear from the caves. We're taking that 'copter down!' Sefreid bellowed.

•

In the smaller cave, Gibbs and Gammaldi had watched the drop off and Gibbs was now sighting the two squads of men running towards the campsite. She thought it odd the squads were armed so differently, although they wore the same desert pattern fatigues. The sight of the Hip heading straight for her position sent her edging back into the shadows of the cave. The Hip levelled and dropped another squad of troops by the base of the cave's main entrance. It was then that Sefreid's order to take cover came across the radio.

'Copy that, we're moving deeper into the cave. Take the shot!' Gibbs yelled.

She darted backwards and tripped over Gammaldi who was crouching behind her. The pair stumbled to their feet and had run fifteen strides into the cave when the explosion came.

•

Ridge rose from his cover position, bringing the Stinger up on his shoulder. It chimed as it locked on to the Hip's hot engine signature.

'Rangers, lead the way,' he said, squeezing the trigger.

The instant the launcher had belched the heat-seeking missile, Ridge tossed it and ran to back up Geiger at the boat.

•

Farrell saw the missile streak through the air but there was no time for a warning. Within seconds, the Hip exploded in a fireball, the warhead hitting the rear turbine and disintegrating the roof of the helicopter, the main fuselage sent to the ground twenty metres below in a shattered mess. His initial fear was for the German contingent, whom he had seen alight from the 'copter just moments before.

'Zimmermann, are you—?' His call over the radio headsets was cut off by the distinct *crack-crack* of an M16, followed by the staccato thrumming of an M60.

'The Americans are already here!' someone in his SAS squad exclaimed, identifying the weapons.

To Farrell's left, machine-gun fire churned up the ground around the running Russian team and they dropped for cover behind a rise of rocks. One of the Russians fell to the ground screaming as a 5.62 mm round passed through his thigh.

For the SAS men, the situation was better. They were able to take cover behind thickets of shrubbery and large rocks.

'Farrell, I have one down and we are pinned here.' Antinov's voice came evenly over the radio.

'I copy that,' Farrell replied. He raised his head over a boulder—to have it shot at. A piece of stone scratched him under the eye. 'The fire is coming from behind the tents. The trucks, I think.' Farrell ducked lower as more shots hit his rock shield.

•

'Zimmermann, what's your status?' bellowed Antinov. His men struggled to assemble a small field mortar whilst crouching for cover.

'I have a few wounded and we are being pinned down by fire from the caves,' Zimmermann replied through the sound of gunfire. 'We are going to fire rockets and move around the rear of the hill,' the German added matter-of-factly.

'Copy that, Zimmermann. We're preparing a mortar if that will be of use,' Antinov said. He looked over his shoulder at his men, who signed the job was done with a thumbs up.

'That should give them something to think about. Fire a shell into the smaller of the caves,' Zimmermann replied.

'It's on its way,' Antinov said, relaying the order to his men.

•

The GSR team was fighting a losing battle.

For Sefreid, Fox and Pepper, the cover of the truck was good only until the attacking force spotted them. Now the only thing keeping the attackers at bay was the constant barrage of fire, but they were quickly running out of ammo.

Goldsmith had crawled to the cover of a mound of rocks to spread the defensive front as far as possible. Beasley, Gibbs and Gammaldi were firing on the Germans, herding them away from the caves and the campsite.

In a brief pause in the gun battle, Fox heard the distinctive cough of a mortar round.

'Mortar fire! Get cover!' he yelled, covering his head with his arms where he lay face down in the sand.

•

Gammaldi heard Fox's call, but Gibbs did not move from where she lay taking pot shots at the Germans below. Gammaldi yanked one of his big beefy paws onto the scruff of her flak jacket and dragged her backwards into the depths of the cave.

The mortar round struck below and to the side of the cave entrance, embedding molten shrapnel deep into the soft stone walls. The smoke and deafening thunderclap of the blast had not cleared when a second shell exploded in the cave entrance, resulting in an instant rockfall. A deep rumbling sound reverberated through the air as the ancient rocky hill, protesting at the onslaught, belched a cloud of sandy rubble into the sky, causing the smaller cave to collapse in on itself.

•

In the ensuing silence, Fox looked up through sandy eyes to see Goldsmith rise from his rock cover. He fired his M16 in a fury, letting loose with a rocket-propelled grenade from the underslung M203 launcher. The grenade exploded far behind the attacking force.

'Al! Talk to me! Al! Gibbs!' Fox yelled through a faceful of sand as he also resumed firing at the attacking positions. From this angle, he could see only the sandy cloud from the cave-in and the dark plumes of smoke rising from the flaming carcass of the downed helicopter.

Before a response came, and before he could call again, Sefreid yelled from beside him: 'Incoming!'

•

Fox's world was thrown into turmoil. He could hear nothing, see nothing, and it felt as though his brain were spinning in his head. No pain was registering, and for a fleeting moment he thought he was at the end and resigned himself to it. He felt comfortable and light-headed, as if floating in a warm sea.

Then a jarring pain, hard and hot, pushed into his cheekbone and snapped him out of his fatalistic haze. He felt his body being dragged along the ground, then his MP5 was prised from his grasp—he did not realise he still had it until it was gone. He thought he heard voices and more gunshots, but he was too disoriented to respond.

A minute later, water was thrown onto his face and his vision cleared. He could make out Sefreid next to him, in a similar state, and the bulky shape of Pepper beyond. Raising his head, he saw four blurred figures in desert fatigues, material wrapped around their heads and faces, looking like local militia. Only they stood too straight, too alert. There was a common discipline that Special Forces men sensed in one another. And something else . . . Fox had trouble making sense of it as his head was still spinning, but then he realised. The guns. The men standing around him, and those who were now dragging Goldsmith over to them, weren't armed with old AK-47s. They held the latest editions of the Heckler & Koch family: MP5s like those used by the GSR team, as well as the smaller calibre MP7s.

A man of similar proportions to Fox, but maybe ten years older, stood over him. The soldier stared into Fox's bloodshot blue eyes, pointing his MP5 down at the unarmed man.

'I assume you are the leader?' he asked, keeping up his end of the staring contest. He had a Scottish accent. 'Who are you?'

Fox was somewhat relieved at recognising a Brit. 'What do you care who we are?' he replied. 'We're here to blow the site.'

The man broke his stare with Fox and looked at his companions. 'We've been sent to blow the site as well,' he said, keeping his gun trained on Fox.

'SAS, right?' Fox said.

'Something like that.'

Fox weighed up his options as the man handed him a flask of water to wash off his face. Sefreid groaned to life by Fox's side and he passed him the water.

'Look, the way I figure, we just smoked your means of escape.' Fox motioned to the flaming wreck of the Hip. 'Let's work together on this and share a ride back to Maragheh. From there, we go our separate ways—no questions asked.'

The man conferred with two of his companions in hushed tones. Finally he turned back to Fox. 'You can tend to your injured, and don't get in our way.'

He held out a hand to pull Fox to his feet. 'We'll be watching you,' he said into Fox's face.

•

'Al!' Fox called over the throat mike for the tenth time. He, Beasley, Pepper and Goldsmith were working to clear the rubble from the cave entrance.

'Yes, Lachlan,' Gammaldi replied finally, his voice groggy.

'Al!' Fox exclaimed, throwing a rock clear into the air. 'Where are you? Are you okay?'

'Oh, I'm fine. Lying on a beach drinking a cocktail with a beautiful woman lying next to me.'

'Is she okay?' Fox said, a little ashamed at not asking about Gibbs earlier.

'She's out cold. It's too dark to see in here, but I felt around and she seems okay. Her heart rate is normal,' Gammaldi replied with unusual seriousness.

'Hang tight, we won't be long,' Fox replied.

The four dug at the stones and rubble with renewed strength, Gammaldi egging them on with talk and commentary. He soon broke into song despite the protests of his rescuers.

'I've been work'n on the railroads . . .'

46

IRAN

With the help of Jenkins and the GSR men, Gammaldi and Gibbs were freed from the small cave after twenty minutes of sweating and grunting.

'Thank you, thank you,' Gammaldi said as he emerged from the small opening in the rocks, which was just big enough to crawl through. Fox helped him to his feet and he stood a little shakily. Pepper and Goldsmith pulled Gibbs out of the opening and supported her as she stood. Her short mousy blonde hair was caked with dried blood and dirt from where she'd been struck in the explosion. Both were covered from head to toe in sandy dust, like a pair of chimney sweeps.

'Remind me never to go caving again,' Gammaldi said.

Jenkins laughed. 'You're a funny lot, you Aussies,' he said. Then the big Norse descendant moved off to the larger cave. 'I'd better check how the others are doing.'

'So this is an EU mission to destroy the site?' Gammaldi said after taking a long pull from the offered water flask.

'Some kind of semi-EU team. It seems they don't want the Americans to emerge as a military superpower all over again,' Fox answered. He paced over to the larger cave.

'Mighty neighbourly of them to lend a hand,' Gammaldi said, following. He noticed the dried trickle of blood running out of Fox's ear and down his jaw. 'What happened to your ear?'

'Your singing,' Fox replied as they entered the larger cave. Gammaldi's reply was a mock hurt look.

'I had a close encounter with a flash-bang grenade from our friends here,' Fox added. He looked around the room and saw the explosives the GSR team had been carrying in their backpacks set up at various points around the cave. Two men Fox recognised as German from their speech were delicately assembling what looked like some kind of science-fiction space object. It was the size of a basketball, bulbous in the centre, with four cylindrical canisters sprouting from the sides. The whole object was made of gleaming polished stainless steel.

'What the hell is that?' asked Gammaldi as he wiped his face with a damp cloth.

'I have no idea,' Fox said. He moved closer to the object.

A no-nonsense soldier came over. 'Can I help you?' he asked in accented English. Fox pegged him as one of the GSG-9 troops Farrell had told them about.

'We're just looking around. What's that?' he asked, motioning to the unidentified object.

The man glanced over his shoulder and back at the two questioning men before answering. 'A type of fuel air explosive, capable of vaporising up to five hundred metres around the blast zone.'

Their curiosity satisfied, Fox and Gammaldi left the Germans to finish setting the explosives and moved out of the cave. Fox paused at the entrance as a glint on the ground caught his eye. On close inspection, he realised it must be theterium. He picked up the baseball-sized rock and rubbed it on his pants, shining the centuries of dust and dirt from the surface.

'That's the stuff?' Gammaldi asked. He looked over the ground for his own souvenir, but found none. Still, he could see the differing shade of rock set into the ground under their feet.

'That's the stuff,' Fox confirmed as he held the crystal up to the sun. He looked through it with one eye, the swirls of red and orange within the translucent yellow stone projecting onto his face. 'It's beautiful.'

Fox went to pass the theterium to Gammaldi, only to find him holding a small sliver he had found himself.

'Hey, this looks like an arrow head,' Gammaldi said as he held his own piece up to the sun.

'Come on, chief, let's get out of here,' Fox said, pocketing his theterium. They set off at a jog down the hillside.

•

Farrell and Sefreid were talking quietly while Antinov directed his men to put out the fire-engulfed hulk of the helicopter—a task that was almost complete. They were using a combination of the water in the tanker truck—which had now run dry—and shovels of sand and had reduced the wreckage to a steaming mound as tall as a man. Both pilots had been burnt beyond recognition in the white-hot fire and were unceremoniously left in their places.

A dark cloud of smoke hung in the afternoon sky, much to Antinov's frustration. He stormed over to his English counterpart. 'Comrade Farrell, any word from Zimmermann?' he asked, wiping sweat from his brow.

'No—but he's coming down now,' Farrell answered, pointing to the figure jogging down the hillside towards them.

'Sorry about the flash-bang,' Farrell said to Fox, as he and Gammaldi joined the Special Forces commanders.

'It was an experience,' Fox admitted with a smile.

'This is Al, a good friend of mine,' Fox said, and gestured to Antinov. 'I believe one of your men sent him a present in the form of a mortar shell, Major.'

'Yes, good to see you in one piece,' Antinov said, slapping Gammaldi on his much-bruised arm.

'It's good to be in one piece, let me tell you!' Gammaldi assured the men. They were all laughing as Zimmermann appeared.

'My men are setting the timing device for thirty minutes. May I suggest we evacuate the site?' the German said with a gleam in his eye.

The commanders nodded in consent and began organising their troops for the jog back to the boat.

•

The old jeep rattled to a stop near the smouldering helicopter wreck and Ridge and a Russian soldier climbed out.

'How'd it go?' Sefreid asked.

'Fine,' Ridge replied. 'Geiger and Beasley are babysitting three wounded EU dudes back at the boat.'

'Why do they always get the easy jobs?' Pepper asked mischievously as he, Gibbs and Goldsmith joined the group. Ridge left to retrieve the Stinger missile launcher he'd left at his previous position.

'Once we get back to the Ahman Research Centre,' Sefreid told the others, 'we'll fly our new friends to the UN medical compound in Tabriz for treatment.'

'Does the princess need a ride back to the boat?' Goldsmith asked Gibbs as she stretched the aches out of her neck.

Gibbs pointed up to the sky, not acknowledging Goldsmith's comment. 'What's that?'

Sefreid followed her hand to a section of the cloudy sky above the lake. 'A flock of birds—vultures, I'd wager. Been there since our little battle.'

Gibbs peered with her sharp eyes, unconvinced. 'Anybody got field glasses?' she asked the team.

'Even better,' Pepper replied and passed her the scope from her sniper's rifle, the only piece retrieved in working order from the cave-in.

'Oh, shit!' Gibbs said with quiet dread, looking into the sky through the scope. 'They're Falcons!'

The marines were coming in. Fast.

•

Near the top of the hill above the theterium deposit, an SAS sergeant lay rock still, looking through the scope of his sniper's rifle at dense shrub a kilometre away. He had been doing this for almost ten minutes, not daring to move a millimetre, even when an evil-looking desert spider had crept up the barrel of his gun. His patience paid off: the mass of shrubs moved forward ever so slowly.

With a smile, he squeezed his trigger. A cloud of blood filled the air where the other sniper's head had been.

'Gotcha,' he whispered, before saying over his radio set: 'Bird Eye to Farrell. It's confirmed. We have company.'

He scanned slowly for another target, soon finding one almost a kilometre away.

•

Farrell had a sixth sense something bad was about to happen. He turned to order a man to higher ground—only to see the young SAS soldier's head explode.

The assault was on.

'Take cover!' he yelled—too late. He spun around to see two more of his command fall to the ground in a hail of silenced sniper fire.

Three of his soldiers were killed instantly, leaving only himself, Jenkins and their sniper. The Russian who'd ridden with Ridge in the jeep was killed as he ran to group with his comrades, as were two of the Germans scrambling for cover back into the cave.

•

The GSR team dropped to the ground between the water tanker, jeep and sand-covered wreckage of the Hip as bullets whipped through the air around them.

Sefreid looked up from the sandy ground to see Ridge running towards them. He stared helplessly as Ridge snapped backwards and stood still in the air for what seemed like an eternity.

'No!' he yelled.

The bullets riddled his friend's chest and he crashed to the ground in a bloody explosion.

•

Farrell, Jenkins and Antinov lay on the far side of the sand-covered helicopter wreckage, away from the GSR team. They wasted no time in calling for situation reports from their men, who replied their positions were under heavy fire with very few targets to fire on in return.

The SAS sniper on the hilltop began acting as a spotter for those on the ground, but suddenly all radio communications went down.

'They're jamming the radios!' Farrell yelled as he unleashed a torrent of fire at some figures running towards the campsite.

'We have to move, sir!' Jenkins added, firing his MP7 at the same advancement.

'Let's go!' Farrell said.

They raced around the helicopter mound and came back to back with the GSR team, fighting for their lives.

•

Antinov watched his crack squad being shot down like rabid dogs beyond the water tanker. He couldn't let them die alone like that. He got to his feet to run to their aid, but Jenkins pounced and wrapped his arms around the Russian's legs.

'There's no point you dying as well!' the burly SAS sergeant boomed. He left Antinov stunned on the ground and stood and let rip with his MP7 in a vain attempt to help the Russians.

Antinov shook off his daze and joined Jenkins and Farrell in the firefight.

•

'This isn't looking good,' Sefreid said, pleased to see Farrell by his side.

'No,' was all Farrell said as he watched the last Russian fall. The man's final action had been to launch a shell from the mortar, which flew wildly, almost vertically, in the air.

'Any ideas?' Jenkins asked between clenched teeth, picking off another attacker who had ventured into his line of fire.

'None. Except that we're going to have to throw stones soon. I'm down to my last clip,' Sefreid said as he inserted it into his M16. A jolt in the back lurched him forward and knocked the wind out of him. Sefreid fought for breath, but fortunately the rounds had not penetrated his thick Kevlar flak jacket.

Farrell turned to see two attackers charging over the mound behind them, only to be shot down by Pepper's M60.

Pepper continued to fire over the mound until the others could cover that front. A fresh belt in his M60 fed into the big gun as he attacked a retreating squad moving in on the unguarded flank.

•

Fox and Gammaldi were side by side behind the jeep, which was taking a battering of bullets. They missed Pepper's heavy machine gun in their group, but as Goldsmith's M16 ran out of ammo he brought the underslung M203 into the attack, launching his remaining five grenades at known points of attack.

'Okay, I want to go home now,' Gammaldi said to Fox, as the attacking fire seemed to wane in strength. He'd given his MP5 to Gibbs and only had his pistol left.

'Just tap your heels together three times, Dorothy,' Fox replied.

•

On the old fishing boat, Geiger and Beasley listened to the raging gun battle, unsure who was winning. Sefreid's last command before the radios went off the air had been for them to hold their position at the boat; now the earpieces of the highly advanced radio systems whirred with static.

'It's the US marines all right,' Beasley said. 'I recognise their radio jamming package. It's one hell of a signature.' He pressed his earpiece deeper into his ear, as if listening to a Bach master-piece.

'What I don't get is, if they aren't using choppers for their assault and evac, how the hell are they going to get out of here?' Geiger asked with a puzzled expression. He locked eyes with Beasley as both came to the same answer.

Geiger grabbed the field glasses and scanned the horizon. About five hundred metres away, a vessel surged at full speed towards the site. Geiger hoped to hell the camouflage netting he had covered their boat with would keep it concealed.

They couldn't take any chances though, so he and Ridge assembled the injured men and fled into the desert.

•

The new arrival touched the bank around a headland, out of sight of the GSR boat.

'Set up the ramps!' Colonel Pugh barked at his resourcer troops, then switched radio bands to speak to the marines in battle.

'Scot, this is Pugh. We're in place.'

His call was answered and a squad of marines was promised his way. Then he heard the gunfire slow and eventually cease from the battle zone.

•

Through the ringing in his ears, Fox noticed the attacking fire dwindle. He raised himself from his position just enough to see two armed figures running away from the site.

'They're falling back!' he informed Sefreid and the others around him, and soon all fire in the battle stopped.

•

Pugh's team of experienced engineers set up folding aluminium ramps from the boat to shore. Each man in the newly formed and top secret Resourcer Regiment could have passed for a professional football player, all with thickset shoulders and necks.

Two men sat behind the steering wheels of a pair of Roadrunners—vehicles which were custom-built for Special Forces and had proved their worth in the first Gulf War and more recently in Afghanistan and the liberation of Iraq. Built for speeds of over one hundred kilometres per hour and adapted to carry heavy firepower, the Roadrunner was in its element in the desert. Resembling a dune buggy, it sat a driver in front position and a gunner behind controlling a hefty punch—a mini-gun on one side and an anti-tank rocket launcher on the other.

'Sergeant Miller, sir.' A squad of Scot's marines appeared from nowhere, the leader saluting Colonel Pugh.

Pugh looked at the men. They wore desert fatigues and face paint, but it was their irregular profiles that camouflaged them more than the colour schemes. Netting covered their clothing and equipment, and various desert shrubbery and tattered bits of cloth sprouted from their bodies.

'They're all yours, Sergeant,' Pugh said, waving his men to bring the Roadrunners to the marines. The big two-stroke engines hummed to life as the resourcers brought the vehicles to shore and handed over the controls.

'Good hunting,' Pugh said with a rough grin as the marines roared off in the direction of the theterium site. The colonel then barked a series of orders to his men, which were, strictly speaking, unnecessary as they were well drilled and briefed. That was how Colonel Pugh liked to run things: plan twice, execute once.

•

Crouched behind their scant cover, Fox and the others listened to the sound thundering through the afternoon air towards them.

'What do you suppose that is?' Fox asked the Special Forces commanders.

They were caked in sweat and grime and their faces bore ashen, desperate expressions. The situation was grim—ten of their number killed within ten minutes; three wounded, plus Geiger and Beasley out of the action as well. That left just fourteen lightly armed defenders against an unknown foe that comprised superior numbers packing superior firepower. The deep rumble of the approaching engines just made the situation seem more dire.

•

The Roadrunners had split up, speeding off around either side of the hill in a pincer movement. One vehicle spun to a stop far past the campsite, turning to train its weapons on the main cave. A voice called through a loudspeaker as the second Roadrunner neared the centre of the campsite.

'Drop your weapons and surrender. Resist and die!' The Midwest US accent echoed through the site as it struck the hillside and cave.

To accentuate the point, the Roadrunner closer to the campsite began to make a wide circuit of the defenders on the ground.

•

Fox looked again to the Special Forces commanders. Sefreid made a gesture as if leaving the decision up to his counterparts.

Farrell and Antinov spoke a few hushed words together, then turned to what was left of the defenders on the ground and nodded their agreement. The group silently agreed that surrendering to the marines would be a better fate than dying in a dusty nowhere.

The entire group looked up to the cave entrance above, where the German team were isolated, willing them to come to the same conclusion.

•

In the cave, Zimmermann had only one of his GSG-9 men and the two army engineers left under his command. From his vantage point, he could see the Roadrunner direct its formidable firepower towards the cave entrance.

'Can you take them?' he asked his last trooper, apparently unfazed by the marines' warning.

'I can—but the range is going to limit the effectiveness of the shots,' replied the German. He was lying in a corner of the cave and training his MP5 out at the vehicle.

'Then do it. If we can't get out of here, we have to at least stall them to the deadline,' Zimmermann said.

The GSG-9 trooper tensed his grip on the MP5 and opened fire.

•

Bullets peppered the Roadrunner in the centre of the campsite, most bouncing harmlessly off the interspersed armour plates, but some ricocheted into the semi-enclosed cabin. The driver set the vehicle into gear, but a bullet caught him under the eye and killed him instantly, leaving the gunner vulnerable.

With an electronic whirring, the Roadrunner's six-barrelled mini-gun came to life, spewing two thousand rounds per minute around the cave entrance, strafing the hillside with streaking orange tracers and shredding the cave's roof.

It had been sixteen minutes since the marines' attack began. For the third time that day, the site had fallen.

47

SPACE

The Dragon was defenceless. Floating idly in space, oblivious to predators, the giant weapon pointed at the pre-designated target below: Tehran. In less than twelve hours the deadline given to Iran to secede its westernmost slice of land would pass. By then, the Dragon would have built up enough charge to prime its magnets and strike again.

•

The Pegasus Mk4 anti-satellite missile flew through the thin atmosphere at incredible speed. Designed to lock onto the specific electronic resonance put out by the pre-programmed target satellite—in this case, the generic military communications output deployed by the Soviets in the 1980s—the missile rushed to complete its task.

Fifteen seconds to impact . . .

48

THE PENTAGON

Peter Larter sat in his office, perspiring as the seconds ticked
down to the Pegasus strike.

Vanzet was in the room with him, as well as the Joint Chief
responsible for the air force, who had his ear glued to a telephone
handset. The other electronically secure phone on Larter's desk
was on speaker, the connection open to the Situation Room in
the White House. A huge screen showing the missile nearing
the target held the audience captive. Along the bottom of the
screen, a digital counter clicked down the seconds remaining.

'Ten seconds, Bill,' Larter said into the speakerphone.

'I've got it on screen here,' McCorkell replied.

The remaining seconds went by in absolute silence.

49

SPACE

The Pegasus never faltered. It hit its target right on the mark, exploding its eighty-kilo warhead on impact.

50

THE PENTAGON

With a smile, Larter shook hands with Vanzet and offered to do the same with the Air Force Joint Chief. He declined the offer with a wave and remained glued to the phone handset.

Larter shared the jubilation over the speakerphone with a relieved McCorkell, then explained they now had to wait for confirmation of the Dragon's complete destruction.

Minutes of static silence ticked by, increasing in intensity.

The Air Force Joint Chief finished the call and turned to face his Chairman and Defence Secretary.

'We have bad news and, ah ... not so bad news,' he said steadily.

'Well?' Vanzet asked.

'Well, the not so bad news is we hit our target.' He paused. 'The bad news is, it's still up there.'

51

THE WHITE HOUSE

McCorkell clicked off the speakerphone, then stared at the inanimate device for a moment, before picking up the receiver. He asked the White House receptionist to put him through to the President.

'Bill, how'd we go?' asked the President.

'The Pegasus strike exploded on impact with the Dragon, sir, destroying the electronic control signature beaming back down to Earth—'

'Great news, Bill!' the President interrupted, then stopped himself. 'Wait. You said "destroying the control signature". Not the actual weapon?'

'That is correct, Mr President,' McCorkell said from the Situation Room. 'The Dragon remains in orbit, damaged and trailing debris, altering course in what we estimate will be eventual re-entry into the atmosphere.'

'Can it still be fired?' the President asked.

'It seems unlikely, sir. The Pentagon tells me the weapon cannot be re-tasked as its electronic command links have been cut off by the strike. But we cannot rule out the possibility that it is still functional to fire,' McCorkell allowed.

'Okay, keep me posted, Bill. Have the resourcers begun their extraction?'

'They are just beginning now. It seems Scot's marines met a defending force that gave them a brief firefight,' McCorkell said rather slowly.

'I'm sure it's nothing Scot's marines can't handle. I just hope he went easy on them!' the President said, causing McCorkell to cringe.

'So do I, Mr President,' McCorkell said sincerely. 'So do I.'

52

SPACE

The designers of the Dragon coilgun were no strangers to anti-satellite missiles, something the Russians had considered since the launch of their first Sputnik in the 1950s. To safeguard against such a strike, the Dragon's main data downlink was held fifty metres from the main body of the coilgun by a tether—a compound cable transferring data such as targeting and firing coordinates. So an anti-satellite strike would take out the downlink, not the weapon itself.

If the data downlink was destroyed, the Dragon changed to a pre-designated orbit to avoid or delay a second missile strike.

The Pegasus warhead had rocked the Dragon violently and sent it off course, but the Dragon's automated thrusters had quickly begun dispelling compressed air to shift it to its pre-determined evasive course.

While the structure of power had changed much since the 1980s, weapons and machines did not know the Cold War was over. Most had been reprogrammed, but many still pointed ominously towards their old nemeses. The Dragon was so secret, no one in its former mother country even knew of its existence, let alone the need to change the input commands.

There was only one target programmed into the Dragon in such circumstances; one dot on the globe that it had long ago been designed to destroy if it was itself attacked.

The capital city of its old enemy.

53

IRAN

Colonel Pugh's resourcer troops had set up their mining equipment by the time Major Mitchell Scot and his squad landed their Falcons at the site.

Watching the whole scene unfold from the air, Scot had commanded his forward deployed troops to victory, whilst giving thanks for the added firepower and versatility the Roadrunners had provided. Now, the leader of the marines force walked over to his second-in-command, who had led the men through the firefight on the ground.

'Lieutenant, there is a boat tied ashore about a click to the east,' Scot said. 'Take a squad in one of those Roadrunners and comb the area for any threats. Then destroy the boat.'

'Yes, sir,' the lieutenant replied and rounded up a squad of marines for the task.

Scot took a brisk walk around the campsite to observe the remainder of his men setting up a defensive perimeter. Six hours had been scheduled for the mining operation and the major knew his men would have no problem holding the position for that long. He had two platoons of his marines in the field, just over sixty battle-hardened warriors. That number had been reduced to an even fifty due to the unexpected resistance at the site.

Standing five eleven and with hair shaved down to his skull, Scot often drew a second glance because of his eyes. They were the lightest and most piercing grey imaginable, like the sheer brilliance of an Antarctic ice shelf. There was not a person alive who could match the major's harshness, his innate ability to strip someone down to their frailties with his icy glare.

Satisfied the area was secure, Scot moved off to check on the forces at the cave.

•

Fox and Gammaldi were the last to be pushed into the small cave.

The marine doing the pushing was a huge black woman, at least six foot two and close to a hundred kilos. Her head—or what they could see of it under the Kevlar helmet—was clean-shaven, and when she walked she had a limp. With a heavy boot, she aided Gammaldi through the small opening he had been freed from only thirty minutes before.

'Sleep tight,' she barked, before motioning a pair of marines to seal off the small hole made during the cave-in earlier.

•

'Well, Sergeant?' Scot asked, moving up the hill towards his trusted subordinate.

'They're a fuckin' EU outfit, sir,' the woman answered. 'And wait until you see what they've left us.'

The marine led her commander across to the main cave, which was swarming with Colonel Pugh's resourcer troops, several of whom were disconnecting the GSR plastic explosives.

'Scot. Take a look at this little beauty.' Colonel Pugh motioned over his shoulder to where a couple of beefy engineers were crouched around an explosive.

'What is it?' Scot asked of the experts, noting that there was a digital timer counting down, currently reading:

00:09:43

'We are not exactly sure, sir,' one of the resourcer engineers replied. 'But if I had to bet a month's pay, it's either a fuel air device or possibly . . .' The engineer looked to his colleague crouched next to him, who shrugged in agreement.

'Or possibly even nuclear,' the engineer admitted.

'Either way, this baby will leave a real mess of the site,' Pugh said.

'Can you shut it down?' Scot asked. If anyone was going to blow the site, it would be him. His means, his way.

Pugh looked down at his troops, then up again at Scot with a devilish smile.

'Give 'em two minutes,' he said confidently.

•

Ten minutes later, with all explosive material disarmed and removed, the resourcers' mining operation was underway.

Although nearly an hour behind schedule, the engineers were pleasantly surprised by two things: the theterium deposit was easily accessible and close to the surface; and the element was easily extracted from the ground using their specialised diamond-cutting tools.

Spanning the short distance between the cave and the boat tied to shore was a carbon fibre structure that would not have been out of place attached to the International Space Station. Made of chopstick-sized pieces that clicked together like a child's toy, the structure supported a series of fibreglass and Kevlar bins that were filled with the mined theterium. The bins each held a hundred litres and, when loaded, were pulled by an electric motor at the receiving end—in this case, the boat—where a team of resourcers stacked the bins in various areas, to even out the load.

The size of the boat limited the amount of theterium they could carry, but this was a planned constraint to fit in with the time frame. There was simply not enough time to mine all of the theterium and destroy the site before the pending battle of Iranian and Chechen forces.

They had just under five hours remaining.

•

Geiger and Beasley were satisfied with their hiding place. Nestled within a field of large rocks and boulders, they had found a small space that was covered with ages of rubble on three sides. At the front, they formed a fourth wall from plant foliage and smaller rocks, creating a den that concealed them from all but the closest inspection. The three wounded EU men lay propped against the rear of their enclosure, where

Beasley tended to them. Geiger pointed his M16 through an opening at a possible point of advance. They were almost a kilometre from the shore and a similar distance from the theterium site.

'I'm going to go out and find cover, to act as a forward point of defence,' Geiger said, getting up.

'No, wait,' Beasley called after him, making Geiger turn in his tracks. 'I'll go out. You have a much better chance of defending these men here,' he said.

'But you're our team's medic. You're needed here.' Geiger looked down at the wounded men, who were lying quietly, doped up with painkillers.

'Look, Eyal, I've done all I can for these men. They need a hospital—and soon.' Beasley stood in the small confines of their hideout and faced Geiger. 'Give them more methadone on the hour and hang tight with this,' he ordered, swapping his Franchi shotgun for Geiger's M16.

'I suppose that's an order,' Geiger said resignedly. Although he had much more combat experience than the ex-FBI man, Beasley ranked higher within the GSR force. Given the situation, Geiger could see the sense in the plan, but he was surprised by the former lawman's courage, a man whom he had pegged as prioritising self-preservation.

'If I see an opportunity to get us out of here, or any sign of the others, I'll let you know,' Beasley said and the pair locked hands in a friendly grip.

'Have fun,' Geiger said as Beasley dashed through the cover foliage and into the afternoon sun.

•

The SAS soldiers broke the darkness of the small cave with a few small flares. They had to speak loudly to be heard over the mining equipment blaring in the main cave opposite.

'If I could only tell you how handy these have been over the years,' Farrell said, holding his flare up to look about the cavern. It was long and narrow, barely high enough to stand at the highest point, and came to a small end almost a hundred metres from the covered entrance.

'I don't doubt it,' Sefreid replied in a grim voice.

While the pair spoke with Antinov, Fox took the offered mini-flare from Jenkins and began searching the cave.

'Did you have much of a look around here before?' Fox asked Gammaldi, who was following close behind.

'It was kind of dark for sightseeing,' Gammaldi replied, pausing to wipe a thick spider-web from his face.

'Seems like a dead end,' Fox stated as they crouched to peer into a fissure that funnelled the diameter of the cave down to nothing.

'Seems like our hosts want us to stay here for good,' Gammaldi said. He watched Fox's torso disappear into the tail end of the cave.

'Not exactly how I wanted to go out,' Fox said casually, his voice echoing comically in the narrow chamber. He emerged, his broad shoulders covered in silty dust.

'Well, we sure as hell can't excavate the cave-in again. Those marines wouldn't give us a second chance,' Gammaldi said, rubbing his buttocks from where the American woman had booted him into the cave.

Fox noticed his friend's actions. 'You know, you must have really done something wrong in a past life to have the biggest, meanest mother of a marine kick the only part of your body not already black and blue.'

Gammaldi gave his friend a mock smile.

'We'll find a way out. I know my fate isn't to die in the desert with the likes of you,' Fox said with a grin.

'I think I'm going to cry,' Gammaldi sniffed.

'Hey, look at that,' Fox said and motioned behind them. There was a hole in the base of the wall, probably just big enough to scramble through if you lay flat to the floor. Fox held the flare at arm's length for a closer inspection.

'See this?' he said, motioning to the fine silt on the floor of the opening.

'What am I seeing?' Gammaldi asked.

'There are drag marks here.' Fox waved his hand above the ground.

'And look . . . footprints!' he added, discovering the marks of several different sole patterns in the silt.

54

VENICE

'What!' Ivanovich screamed, spittle spraying Popov's face.

'The Dragon is altering course, sir, and is not responding to any commands. We must assume it has been attacked,' a shaky Popov repeated.

Ivanovich thought for a while, struggling to recall the day in the Kremlin when the Politburo had been briefed by Pushkin on the details of the coilgun. He faintly recalled something about the control systems of the Dragon being on a suspended tether, drawing an anti-satellite strike away from the main body of the weapon. The briefing came back to him, slowly but with increasing clarity.

'It can still be fired,' Ivanovich said, more a statement than a question.

'I believe so, yes,' Popov replied, raising an eyebrow at his commander's tone.

'How far off are we from building a second Dragon?' Ivanovich asked, again with a rhetorical air.

'Comrade President, we are still several months off. And we need to gain the fissionable material for the reactor, then launch . . .' Popov paused. 'It will probably take a year, maybe more. And that is if we take the theterium site,' he admitted.

'Do not worry about the theterium. We can take the site— if only for long enough to mine the element and retreat.'

Ivanovich walked to the balcony overlooking the Venetian lagoon and gazed at the sun lowering on the horizon. Things weren't going to plan. First his security leader, Orakov, had told him a force had defeated his soldiers at the farmhouse and rescued the captured Australian who could have led them to the second pod. And now this.

'Tell that imbecile Orakov to have my boat ready to sail at first light. We'll go to a more secure location, from where we can fire the Dragon if necessary.'

'But, sir, the weapon is altering course to the west at what may be a pre-programmed re-entry path over the Atlantic,' Popov said.

'Do not worry, Popov. I know exactly where the Dragon is heading,' Ivanovich said with a cryptic smile. 'It's not preparing for re-entry, merely re-tasking to a default target. And I think you will find it shall buy us the time necessary to launch another coilgun into orbit.'

55

IRAN

Gammaldi, with his stocky frame, had more trouble than Fox squeezing through the opening in the cave wall. The first thing they noticed in the chamber was that it was much noisier, because it backed right against the wall of the main cave.

'Well, I'll be . . .' said Fox, looking about the chamber. It was almost high enough for him to stand in and eight or so metres in diameter, with a smooth domed ceiling that danced with crude engravings visible in the dim red blaze of the mini-flare.

Gammaldi joined his friend to inspect the carvings up close—figures of running men etched into the soft stone. The figures came alive in the light, chasing after huge beasts that resembled long-extinct woolly mammoths.

'How old do you think they are?' Gammaldi asked.

'Pretty damn old,' Fox replied, letting his light shine in other areas of the cave. He took a step forward and something tripped him up.

His fall was broken by a string grid, like those he had seen countless times in *National Geographic* magazines in photographs of excavations. But he couldn't make out what he had fallen on. Gammaldi was helping him back to his feet when an object caught his eye. He rushed over to the edge of the grid and picked it up. It was a torch, the kind that doubled as a lantern. With a silent praise of fortune, Fox flicked the switch and the room lit up.

•

From his forward position, Beasley saw the Roadrunner park by their vacant boat. Four marines jumped from the steel frame and boarded her. After five minutes, they emerged and Beasley saw them give their leader an all-clear sign.

Then the Roadrunner came straight for him.

Beasley flattened himself against the rocky ground and the vehicle turned within a stone's throw of his position. It drove slowly back to the hill, out of consideration for the four marines clinging to the chassis, then turned again and drove out to the south.

They were driving a search pattern, Beasley realised. After fifteen minutes of watching, he thought he had the pattern down pat when a sudden change of course sent the vehicle straight at him again.

He sank deeper into his covered outpost, nestled among some tumbleweed to the south of where Geiger watched over the injured EU men.

•

Almost the entire group of captured EU and GSR forces had crowded into the small chamber, which they now knew to be a tomb. They gazed at the exposed skeleton set into the floor, painstakingly exposed not so long ago by a very patient person.

Fox knew who that person was, thanks to a leather-bound notebook found next to the excavation, which he'd tucked into the thigh pocket of his cargo pants. It was the plastic toolbox nearby, containing a pair of pointed hammers and various other small digging implements, that held everybody else's interest.

Using the lantern, they searched the chamber for another way to freedom, keeping as quiet as possible so the engineers next door wouldn't hear them.

In the wall adjoining the main cave, almost directly opposite the small hole they'd come through, was the dim outline of another gap, which, if excavated, would be big enough to crawl through.

After fifteen minutes of hushed silence and careful digging, Gammaldi and Sefreid had opened a hole the size of a small coin into the main cave.

Sefreid peered through and saw the US engineers methodically mining the theterium. He was astounded to see how far they had progressed in two hours. He gave up his position to allow Antinov to take in the sight, returning to help Fox and Gammaldi chip away at the opening.

'I count at least twelve in the cave,' Antinov said quietly, an unnecessary precaution as the sound of cutting and drilling was deafening now.

'They have already mined much of the element, enough to make many weapons,' Zimmermann added as he peered through the opening himself. The German commander had been silent since being sealed in the cave. Of his original command, only one GSG-9 member and an army engineer remained; the other had been crushed by falling stone when the Roadrunner attacked the main cave entrance earlier.

'Okay. We wait for an opportunity to break free and try to stop the bastards on the way out,' Farrell said, rejuvenated.

'Sounds good to me,' Sefreid concurred.

The stale air in the tomb chamber took on a new dimension as the Special Forces members rallied their resolve.

•

The Roadrunner sped past Beasley's position and literally brushed against his coverings, leaving him squinting through the dust cloud in the vehicle's wake. He watched in alarm as the craft entered the small field of boulders and circled the denser cluster in the centre. When it stopped and the four marines dismounted from the side pillions, he knew he had to do something.

Not wanting to fire and draw the heavy firepower of the Roadrunner's formidable armament, he knew he had to move.

Closer.

•

Geiger heard the big two-stroke engine of the Roadrunner long before he saw it.

One of the EU men, a Russian soldier shot in the neck by Gibbs, began making a sickly gargling sound. Geiger left his guard position and, with the aid of another, lesser-wounded Russian, tilted the soldier's head so that his mouth and throat drained of blood. He injected the man with another disposable phial of methadone and the pain in the soldier's face visibly subsided. His comrade applied more pressure onto the wound, thanking the ex-marine for his support.

'Just hang tight. We'll be home in no time,' Geiger reassured the soldiers.

The wounded GSG-9 trooper was less optimistic. 'We are all going to die here,' he said matter-of-factly.

Geiger could have knocked him cold for his untimely remarks. 'I was a marine once,' he retorted quietly, wary of being overheard by the hunting party. 'They certainly aren't in the business of killing helpless wounded men or leaving prisoners-of-war to die in the desert.'

'And there you have it, my American friend,' the German said, looking Geiger square in the eye. 'We are not at war. We are seen as terrorists, people in the way of their gain. And all the world knows where the Americans stand on that viewpoint.' He paused. 'And since none of us are meant to be here in the first place, no one will question our failure to return home.'

•

On the western horizon a pinprick emerged, not discernible to the naked eye and hardly visible with the most powerful of binoculars. It was a dust cloud, four kilometres across at its epicentre, using the darkening horizon to its advantage. It surged on at full speed, like an act of God heading directly for the hills that held the theterium. Its direction was no coincidence—within the clouds of sand were mechanical beasts being pushed to their limits in a race to the victory line.

The Chechen airborne armoured battalion. At this pace, their missiles would be in range within minutes.

56

THE WHITE HOUSE

McCorkell turned to the video conference screen where the face of Peter Larter came into clear focus.

'Bill, a half-time update,' Larter began.

'Thanks, Pete. I'm listening.' McCorkell rubbed the weariness out of his eyes.

'The resourcers are on schedule, despite the initial delay, as the theterium is proving easier to remove than expected.'

'That's great,' McCorkell said, a little flatly. 'What's happening with the survivors of the defensive force?'

'That's up to Scot's discretion. He's operational commander down there,' Larter replied. 'It's probably easier to leave the EU force in the desert than bring them out with us and have to explain—'

'EU?' McCorkell sat up straight and alert, as though one of his kidneys had just kicked in with an extra boost of energy.

'That's what he reported. You assumed they were the Chechens?'

'Well, I don't know what I assumed,' McCorkell said, turning his gaze to the carpet in thought. When he looked up to the screen again, after a long moment of silence, he saw Larter was on a phone call, listening intently. 'I'll be right down,' McCorkell heard him say.

'Bill, I'm moving down to the Ops Centre. Vanzet has just informed me the Chechens have left the camp in Iraq. They're already crossing the border,' Larter said as he stood.

'You'll pull the resourcers early?' McCorkell asked.

'Our marines can't hold the position against a force that size.'

'Do we have a visual of the site?' McCorkell asked, hoping for a satellite image.

Larter shook his head in response. 'Nothing great. Like everyone else in the world, they know our bird movements. We could have a real-time sat overhead in an hour or so if we re-task, but I'll have to run that by the boss. Either way it'll be too late. I'll keep you posted,' he promised as he moved out the door.

McCorkell motioned to an aide to switch off the link and picked up his coffee. It was his lucky mug, chipped but cherished over the past twenty-five years since he'd completed his doctorate in International Studies. It showed a blue picture of a four-seated rowboat, along with the year he had won the race between international universities. 'Oxford—again!' was stencilled under the image, and the names of those in the team. For McCorkell, it seemed like a lifetime ago: he'd lived through so much since those happy, carefree days. He sipped at the black liquid, enjoying its warmth.

57

IRAN

Geiger knew the marines were close, knew they would be using hand gestures to communicate and coordinate their movements. Whilst the position he knelt in was safe from a distance, he did not harbour any illusions that he and the EU men could remain hidden for long.

He flicked the safety off the pump-action shotgun and waited for the inevitable, hoping that Beasley was not too far away.

•

Scot switched the dial on his personal radio headset to communicate with his command. The message he'd just received from the Pentagon came as no big surprise, as one of his spotters had reported a growing dust cloud on the ever-darkening western horizon.

'Listen up, marines, this is Scot. We have under fifteen minutes to bug out of here. When the resourcers are all packed up, we fall back to the boat in defensive formation,' he ordered. He stopped at the cave entrance where the big female sergeant was standing. 'Squad leaders, acknowledge.'

One by one the leaders of each squad, mostly sergeants of various ranks, called in affirmative.

•

'Team two. Copy that, Scot,' Geiger heard a marine say, right outside his position.

•

Beasley could see how close the four marines were to his comrades, but smiled regardless. For the first time since the American force had arrived, he felt the adrenaline of having the upper hand. After a brief hesitation he yelled in his most commanding voice, 'Don't move!'

•

Every marine in the squad heard the yelled order, especially the two who sat in the idling Roadrunner. The M16 was levelled inches away from the driver's head and the pair raised their hands.

•

The lieutenant spun around and took in the situation—and also smiled. The figure holding the rifle to the driver's head did not display the drilled stance of a confident soldier, and he assumed the man to be alone in his foolish caper. If there were more, he and his men would have either found them or been attacked by now.

Leaving his M16 with the rest of his team, the lieutenant walked over to assess the unidentified figure.

•

Geiger could not see what was happening at the Roadrunner, but heard Beasley's shout. He saw one of the marines directly in front of him walk away and the backs of the others were now turned to him. He seized the opportunity.

•

The lieutenant walked towards the defiant man in fatigues and face paint. Over the radio headsets, he whispered for his men to hang tight. From ten metres away, he put his hand on his hip holster, resting on the butt of his pistol.

'Don't be a fool. You are heavily outnumbered!' he called to the man.

Beasley took a quick glance at the man advancing, then kept his eyes steady on the marines in front of him.

'Don't come closer or I'll shoot!' he said, unconvincingly.

The lieutenant slowed his advance, but kept edging forward. 'And then what?' he asked.

'And then I'll shoot!' Geiger boomed, emerging from the foliage behind the three marines. He pumped a shell into the shotgun breech to accentuate his point.

The lieutenant turned to assess the new threat, then drew his pistol and turned back to Beasley, raising the weapon with a straight arm only a metre from his face.

'Then it seems we are in quite the predicament, amigo,' the lieutenant said.

•

Beasley turned his head in slow motion and stared down the barrel of the pistol levelled at his head. He looked at the face of the man behind the pistol sights, which was as well camou-flaged as his netting-covered outline. The two of them were the same size, shared the same body language. Their eyes were almost identical.

'Chris?'

•

Colonel Pugh helped load the last tub of theterium aboard the boat. A dozen of his men began efficiently dismantling the incredible conveyer system, while the rest were packing up the mining equipment in the cave. The colonel had never mined anything as dense as the theterium; in just over two hours they'd mined over nine tonnes. The boat rode low in the water, the flat deck barely a metre from the surface, and he thanked his lucky stars there was no wind to contend with. Otherwise the lake could get dangerously choppy on the return voyage.

He had just stepped back ashore to expedite his miners when a warning call came over his radio headset. He turned to the west and saw a dozen smoking orange flames streaking through the sky towards him.

•

'Ben!' the lieutenant exclaimed.

The pair lowered their weapons and embraced tightly, then stepped back and looked each other over critically.

The Beasley brothers had shared but a few brief words when the warning call came over the marines' radios.

•

In the tomb there was deathly silence. Farrell whispered commentary to the others as he watched the miners packing up their gear.

He observed them pause briefly, some of them holding their radio earpieces closer in their ears, then they dropped their semi-disassembled power tools and scrambled to the cave exit.

'Okay, they're pulling out—in a hurry!' he said.

Together, he and Jenkins quickly kicked out the remainder of the ancient mud wall connecting them to the main cave.

'Must be lunch break,' Gammaldi said to Fox from the corner of his mouth, as the pair readied themselves.

'I think some unexpected visitors are dropping in,' Fox replied.

The SAS men moved through the opening, followed by Antinov and the Germans. After the GSR team, Fox and Gammaldi were the last to exit.

'After you,' Fox gestured with a slight bow.

'I'm never one to stand on ceremony,' Gammaldi replied as he ferreted through the opening.

•

Scot ignored the cacophony of calls over the radio from his marines as the missiles started striking the site. With the last of the theterium loaded on board and the remaining resourcers running to the relative safety of the boat, he quietly moved himself in the same direction, confident his marines could put up a fight long enough for the boat to be out of harm's way.

On his way, he picked up his signalman by the back of his flak jacket from where a near miss had thrown him to the ground.

'Order the strike now!' he boomed.

The shell-shocked corporal nodded in comprehension and fumbled the controls of the radio set as he raced after his commander, who was running towards the boat.

58

IRAN

The first wave of Chechen missiles struck forward of the perimeter established by the marines, spraying the area with debris and shrapnel.

•

The sudden explosions thundering outside took the EU/GSR alliance by surprise. There were no weapons in sight for them to use, so they decided to flee for their lives in the direction of the lake, hoping that the ensuing battle would distract the other forces from their move and that their boat would still be there, intact.

The three SAS men and Antinov were first to exit, dashing to the north along an unobstructed path around the mountain. The surviving Germans were next, making a run for it as more missiles tore up the encampment. That left just the GSR force, with Fox and Gammaldi behind, still working their way along the deep troughs that had been cut into the ground to remove the theterium.

'Okay, it's now or never!' called Sefreid as he surveyed the scene below. Two marines lay motionless in the centre of the camp by a crater where the water tanker had been. A few other bodies were visible in the seconds he allowed himself to scan the battleground, but the attacking force was blatant.

The box shapes trailing dust clouds were Chechen BMP armoured personnel carriers, surging towards the scene at full speed armed with seventy-three millimetre cannons. Four rocket-launching vehicles set up much further behind were bombarding the site, but fortunately none of the shells or missiles came too near the cave entrance.

Gibbs, Goldsmith and Pepper followed Sefreid out of the cave, running low to the ground to use what little cover was available.

•

Gammaldi gave Fox a helping hand out of the deep trench.

'Let's go!' he said, but Fox pulled him back into the trench. Bullets sprayed the air where they had been standing.

Gammaldi looked up to see a huge marine staring down at him, M16 raised. In a lightning move, Fox wrapped himself around the attacker's legs and pulled, bringing them both sprawling on top of Gammaldi in a life-or-death wrestling match.

Gammaldi, crushed, looked through squinting eyes at the face in front of his. He was shocked to see it was the huge black woman who had booted him into his early grave.

Fox gained enough balance to swing down in a judo chop on the woman's neck—a blow that would have momentarily paralysed a normal person, but it bounced off a rock hard muscular exoskeleton and seemed to inflame the marine's anger.

With surreal nimbleness that belied her bulk, the marine pounced at Fox, grabbing him by the ears and smashing her bulbous head into his face with incredible force. Leaving Fox to fall to the ground with a broken nose, the marine turned her attention to Gammaldi, who had managed to get to his feet behind her.

Again with feline reflexes she pounced, wrapping her mighty paws around Gammaldi's throat and pinning him against the wall of the trench, lifting him a foot clear of the ground. Like a vice slowly turning tighter and tighter, she squeezed his thick neck in an action that would soon crush his windpipe and turn his flesh to pulp.

With what energy remained in him, Gammaldi turned his hands away from the futile task of peeling the paws from his neck and reached to strangle the marine, only to find his arms falling pitifully short for the task. He improvised by digging his strong fingers into her bulging biceps. The move relaxed the death grip around his neck ever so slightly, buying him a few more seconds of air.

•

Zimmermann had halted in a nook not far from the cave entrance with his two remaining men and had let the GSR team pass their position. Now they doubled back to the other side of the cave entrance. There, partially covered by sandy rubble, was his explosive: a ten-kiloton nuclear bomb, one of a secret stockpile his nation had built up.

Following Zimmermann's orders, the German engineer reset the timer on the device:

00:30:00

00:29:59

00:29:58

•

Fox retched blood as he regained his composure. He saw the dire predicament of his best friend and looked about for the marine's M16 but couldn't find the slender black weapon on the trench floor. There were much bigger objects though.

The weight of the colossal battery-powered circular saw was staggering, but he hefted it in the air nonetheless. With a grunt, he charged at the beast that was literally squeezing the life out of his friend. As he moved, he depressed the switch that set the blade humming into action.

The marine turned her head at the noise and dropped Gammaldi to the floor like a rag doll. She swung her arm to fend off the attack and the diamond-edged cutting disc, designed to slice the hardest of elements, severed her arm just below the elbow in a clean cut. Screaming like an animal, she tried to reach her pistol with her good arm.

Not stopping his charging advance, Fox pushed the marine against the wall where she'd pinned Gammaldi only moments before. He drove the huge electric saw with all his force into her bulk, barely noticing the contact, the blade slicing through the Kevlar body armour and her torso as if it were made of plastic kitchen wrap. Only the cutting sound of the blade hitting the wall behind the marine made him release his grip and step back. With a dying grimace of defiance, the marine slid down the wall to the floor, the power saw still connected to her deflated carcass.

Fox helped his spluttering friend to his feet. 'Jesus!' Gammaldi gasped.

'No time for wisecracks. Let's go!'

Fox dragged Gammaldi out of the trench and they stumbled to the cave mouth to face the battle raging outside.

●

When the SAS men reached the boat, not only were they thankful to see it afloat and undamaged but they were delighted to be greeted by the exuberant faces of Ben Beasley and Eyal Geiger.

'Welcome aboard,' Beasley said as he helped the three men onto the already running craft.

'My men?' Antinov immediately asked upon setting foot on deck.

'In the hold below,' replied Geiger, and watched the Russian leader disappear down the forward hatch.

'Hold the boat!' Sefreid called as he neared, smiling like the Cheshire Cat at seeing his team unharmed.

The GSR members aboard, Jenkins turned his attention to shore. 'Where are the Germans?'

'They can't be far behind,' Sefreid replied. He moved to the pilothouse of the boat and stopped still at the door—an armed marine was standing before him.

'Richard Sefreid, may I introduce Lieutenant Chris Beasley, United States Marine Corps, my younger brother,' Ben Beasley said.

Sefreid stared at the pair incredulously.

•

The Chechen rockets stopped raining down on the campsite as the BMPs neared the target area.

The Roadrunner that had formed part of Lieutenant Beasley's squad fired two of its four Hellfire anti-tank missiles at the lead pair of Chechen BMPs, disintegrating both on impact. The northern Roadrunner fired three shots, destroying one target and crippling two others, prompting the remaining Chechen personnel carriers to scatter and disembark their troops to cover the last kilometre on foot.

The Chechen attackers used the cover of their BMPs to advance, their superior numbers and heavy firepower evening the battle against the well-positioned and well-equipped defending force.

•

A squad of marines ran past the cave entrance, heading north towards their own boat. Fox and Gammaldi hid in the same nook the Germans had occupied moments before and managed to go unnoticed.

'Come on. We're going this way!' Fox said, heading south away from the advancing Chechens.

'But the boat's that way!' Gammaldi said in protest, following anyway.

'So are a hundred marines in heavy battle,' Fox replied. 'We'll round the hill and take our chances.'

•

Major Scot stood on the deck of the boat watching the battle. The Roadrunners' anti-tank missiles and mini-guns were wreaking havoc on the Chechens' attacking ranks, but his men were heavily depleted and running out of ammunition.

The resourcer members were almost all accounted for, most taking cover in the cramped hold below, while a few manned the sparse collection of weapons they carried into the field for defence.

Colonel Pugh stomped from the pilothouse towards Major Scot, his face red with anger. 'We have to evac. Now!' he barked, as a shell exploded a hundred metres inland of their position.

'We can afford a few more minutes,' Scot said casually, turning his back on the colonel to look ashore again. He was searching for somebody in particular, someone whom he had specifically ordered to the boat but who was no longer answering his calls over the radio.

'Listen, son!' Pugh said, landing his rough hand on the younger man's shoulder and twisting him around. 'I don't think I need to bring rank into this. You know the importance of this mission as well as I. We're moving, now!' He released the marine and turned back to the pilothouse—only to find his way barred by a member of Scot's squad with a raised M16.

'We leave in three minutes, Colonel. I trust you can wait that long,' Scot said and jumped from the boat, two of his trusted marines in tow.

'Out of my way, boy!' Pugh screamed at the marine in front of him, expelling all the air from his mighty lungs.

The marine, a career sergeant who measured as rugged and tough as any of the resourcer men, did not even blink at the barking of the superior officer. 'Seems you are in quite a predicament, sir,' the marine sergeant said.

'I think not,' Pugh said calmly, as three of his resourcers came to stand with him, brandishing small firearms. More of his men came from below and a heavy wrench swung against the marine's Kevlar helmet. The sergeant fell to the ground like a sack of potatoes.

•

When the Germans arrived at the boat, Zimmermann's last GSG-9 trooper handed Ben Beasley a heavy square rucksack.

'I understand you are a signals expert,' the trooper said.

Beasley took the proffered rucksack and inspected it closely on the deck. It was the marines' radio-jamming equipment, it's netting-covered carry case splattered with blood, hinting at what had become of its rightful owner.

'All right! Gentlemen, it's time to give the marines a taste of their own medicine,' Beasley said as he twisted the dials and pressed some buttons.

The device could be set to jam all radio communications within five kilometres, certain bands or even specific frequencies. Beasley set the frequencies to be blocked out below 900.00 MHz. His own team's gear ran above that, and he was counting on the Chechens' older gear being at a lower frequency, like that of the NATO officers. He flicked the switch.

'Presto!' he said, as the radio earpieces of the GSR team came alive.

'I still have static,' Farrell said, fiddling with the volume dial on his radio's waist unit.

'I don't know the frequency the Chechens are using,' Beasley said, 'so I'm jamming all those below ours. Sorry, but I don't think it fair we just block out the marines.'

'You're right, of course. We have no need for the radios now anyway,' Farrell said.

Zimmermann turned to the others on deck outside the pilot-house. 'May I suggest we make a hasty retreat?'

•

'Fox, Gammaldi, this is Sefreid, do you copy?' Fox strained his still limited hearing at the sound in his earpiece.

'We copy,' Gammaldi replied as they slowed their run around the hillside.

'We're ready at the boat. Are you far off?' Sefreid asked, yelling over the raging gun battle.

'We're at the southern end of the hill. It'll take us about ten minutes!' Fox replied. An explosion rocked the ground fifty metres behind them, spraying the area with debris.

'I don't know if we can wait that long,' Sefreid replied, his voice full of despair.

Before Fox or Gammaldi could reply, an object crashed to the ground with incredible force in between them. They halted in their tracks, staring down at the ground.

'What was that? Are you all right?' Sefreid's voice came over the radio.

Fox crouched down and tentatively turned the object over. He recognised it instantly and remembered what the German had told him: 'A type of fuel air explosive'. It had been blown into the air by a nearby explosion, its heavy stainless steel casing undamaged from the ordeal. He turned it over; the digital display was cracked across its face, but there was no mistaking its message:

00:24:16

00:24:15

00:24:14

'Head off,' Fox replied to the GSR team. 'Move away and get the injured out of here. We'll follow the coast until we reach the research facility—after creating a little hell around here.'

Fox looked to Gammaldi with a foreboding frown, which his mate answered, understanding. They knew that if the boat waited for them, and managed to leave shore unscathed by the attackers, it would still be in the blast radius when the Germans' bomb went off.

The pair resumed running south around the hillside, away from the boat. Fox pointed ahead and he and Gammaldi watched with fascination as an attack took place between the two fighting forces.

'You're sure?' Sefreid asked.

Although Fox had just witnessed more lives lost, he allowed himself a slight smile as an opportunity presented itself.

'We're sure.'

•

Pugh ordered his boat underway, leaving Scot's marines ashore to fight alongside their comrades. 'This will be close,' he growled to his second-in-command as they stood in the pilothouse.

'We've had closer. Remember the Ural Mountains in '94? That battalion of Russian border guards dropped virtually on top of us!'

'Yeah,' Pugh replied. 'But we're not out of the fire yet.' He touched the wooden frame of the pilothouse superstitiously.

•

Antinov worked every knot he could out of the old diesel engine as the boat left the raging battle behind. On the stern deck, the GSR team sat in silence, most staring towards the site that had claimed one of their close-knit team and still held two men they had welcomed as their own.

'They'll make it,' Sefreid reassured his team.

'They're tough sons o' bitches,' Pepper remarked.

'Ridge deserved better,' Goldsmith said. Silence prevailed again.

Gibbs, who was watching the battle through her scope, gave a commentary on the situation. 'The marines are putting up one hell of a fight. The remaining Chechens are held back about three hundred metres, advancing only with the cover of their few remaining personnel carriers—those buggies have caused them hell,' she said.

'The Roadrunners are built for this kind of fighting,' Lieutenant Beasley said, staring at the battleground now fading into the distance.

'You wish you were there too?' Sefreid asked the marine.

Beasley shook his head. 'There were a few good men in Scot's unit, but most of them were out of control. Many were involved with revenge killings of civilians in Iraq. The JAG Corps sent me there undercover to observe their methods. They can fend for themselves now.'

'There were two Roadrunners, weren't there?' Gibbs asked, still scanning with her sniping scope.

'Yeah,' Chris Beasley replied.

'I only see one now,' Gibbs said.

'What's that over there?' Jenkins joined the group at the stern deck and pointed to shore.

'The boat that came ashore earlier!' Geiger replied, looking through field glasses.

'She's riding low—must be laden with theterium,' Gibbs said.

'We'd better do something about that,' Jenkins said, turning to gather a weapon.

'We may not have to,' replied Geiger.

•

As Colonel Pugh's boat turned about from shore in a wide arc, a seventy-three millimetre shell from a Chechen BMP splintered the pilothouse in spectacular fashion, instantly killing Pugh's second-in-command and shooting the commander himself into the air and overboard into the lake in a bloodied mess. Those on deck were shredded by shards of timber and metal, while those in the hold were concussed from the explosion.

The shell left the engine unscathed—which continued to increase revolutions and boat speed—but destroyed the piloting controls and locked the rudder in a mid-starboard position.

•

'Wow!' Jenkins said as the boat started in a wide turn that would soon run it aground.

'I don't think we need to worry about the theterium any more,' Sefreid said as he looked through Gibbs's scope.

'Except if the Chechens get it,' Jenkins said.

Zimmermann and Farrell came to the deck to find out what had transpired. The German looked like he was about to speak, but it was the marine, Chris Beasley, who took the opportunity.

'Scot ordered a Tomahawk strike when the Chechens' attack forced them to call the retreat,' he said quickly, ashamed at not having told the others earlier.

'When is the impact?' Farrell asked.

Chris Beasley checked his watch. 'Less than twenty minutes.'

The EU men exchanged triumphant smiles.

'That's one thing I love about you Yanks,' Farrell said. 'If you can't have it, you'll be damned if anyone else gets it!'

'I don't believe it!' Geiger said, staring through the field glasses to the northwest of the battleground and a few kilometres inland of the theterium site.

He'd sighted the face of Lachlan Fox, covered with dried blood and dust but still grinning. His brown hair was blowing about wildly in the wind and he looked like a madman invigorated by life on the edge as he sped from the gates of hell.

•

Fox and Gammaldi had watched one of the Roadrunners get peppered by a squad of Chechens that had snuck up from behind. The driver and gunner had returned fire with their mini-gun and some deft manoeuvring that left their attackers dead, but their vehicle out of control. By the time Fox and Gammaldi reached the pair of marines, the vehicle had rolled onto its side and they were hanging dead in their harnessed seats.

The two Australians unstrapped the bodies, which fell unceremoniously to the ground, then muscled the Roadrunner back onto its foam-filled tyres. Fox had tried to contact the GSR team again but they were too far out of range.

Now Fox sat in the forward driver's position, with Gammaldi in the gunner's seat behind, and they were flying over the undulating terrain at nearly a hundred kilometres per hour, the speeding vehicle often lifting clear into the air for seconds at a time.

Using the GPS screen strapped to the dash, Fox steered on the straightest possible course to Maragheh and the Ahman Research Centre.

•

Scot cursed as the radio turned to static. He marvelled that the poorly equipped Chechens had had the wherewithal to bring electronic jamming equipment with them. The attackers, he was pleased to see, had been reduced to perhaps a third their original size and were fighting from scattered positions in a haphazard way.

Scot ignored the pot shots taken at him as he ran up the hillside to the main cave where he'd left his most trusted sergeant. What he saw there made him pale with rage, and he almost missed the hole made at the back of the dark cave. With growing realisation, he added the escape of the EU team to his diminishing situation.

'We have to go, sir,' the corporal accompanying him said quietly.

Scot knew the three minutes he had given Pugh to wait were up and he left the darkness of the cave to make for the boat. From his vantage on the hillside, he saw the vessel moving off without him, its deck a smouldering mess. It was not headed north to the pre-planned evacuation point; instead, it was heading slowly inland.

•

Pugh swam to the rocky bank where he clung for a full minute to catch his breath. He swore black and blue that he would tear strips off Major Scot if the marine managed to live through this. He tried to pull himself up out of the water but the edge of the shore was just too high to raise his injured bulk effectively.

He turned to check his boat's position, confident that his men could get her underway again, but at that moment the heavily laden vessel crushed his body to a pulp against the shoreline as it ran aground.

•

Scot missed the collision, dodging to avoid the shots being fired at him. A bullet tore his ear almost clean off; it dangled from the lobe from the side of his head. He yanked the extremity from his body and tossed it to the ground.

'Kill 'em, kill 'em all!' he yelled, and sprayed a squad of oncoming Chechens with fully automatic fire from his M16.

The marines either side of him added to the blaze and the surviving Chechens fell back to form a small group of their own, no more than a dozen. The marines took cover in the main cave.

•

The two Tomahawks Scot had ordered ploughed into the theterium hill and encampment a second apart, collapsing the cave systems forever and rocking the ground with incredible force.

The theterium deposit reacted to the sudden heat and force as expected, and became a molten mass that sank into the sands of Iran before hardening into the water table not far below.

•

Major Scot lay crushed under a pile of rubble, staring towards the lake where the resourcers' boat had run ashore, unharmed by the strike and accessible. It was the last sight he would take in. He closed his eyes.

•

The German nuclear device—a simple fission explosive—detonated five seconds before the third Tomahawk struck. The Tomahawk vaporised harmlessly in the heat wave of the initial blast, which travelled for a five-kilometre radius before being sucked into the sky in the form of a giant mushroom cloud, taking with it hundreds of thousands of litres of water and tonnes of sand and rock.

The theterium site could never be utilised again.

•

The flash ripped through the dark evening sky. Every member of the EU/GSR team ran to the stern deck in time to see the mushroom cloud plume on the horizon. A few minutes after the water level retreated, a metre-high swell rocked against the boat.

•

Fox was checking the Roadrunner's open petrol tank when the sky lit up.

'She's empty all right—' He cut himself off, staring open-jawed at the explosion. Neither he nor Gammaldi doubted what they were seeing. The mushroom cloud was lit from within, the molten particles that made up its mass glowing like a billion fireflies.

'Do you think we're safe?' Gammaldi asked, watching the growing cloud.

'We've covered a good sixty kilometres. It seems like a small tactical nuke,' Fox said, surprising himself by his recall of information he'd learnt at the Academy.

'What do we do now?' Gammaldi asked, still entranced by the sight.

Fox was examining a map he had found in a steel box at the back of the Roadrunner. 'We walk to this train line and hop on a rail car heading north to Maragheh. If there isn't one, we walk the whole way. It's not far.'

'Hey, I'm on holidays, I've got nothing but time.' Gammaldi took the GPS system and walked off in the direction of the tracks.

Time . . . Fox thought, standing still.

'Actually, I don't think time is on our side yet,' he said.

'What do you mean?' Gammaldi asked, turning to eye him.

'By now the Dragon would have been armed with the pod we discovered,' Fox said. 'And the deadline's almost up.'

'Why wouldn't the Chechens have used it as security on the site to force the US or whoever to stay away?'

'There's the catch: it takes seven days to reload and charge,' Fox said.

'And that'll be . . .' Gammaldi looked at his watch.

'Less than eight hours from now,' Fox said, looking at his own.

'What the hell can we do?'

'Farrell interrogated a technician at the old control centre. He told him the controls were moved outside Chechnya to a safe location,' Fox said, his mind racing. 'Somewhere Ivanovich could retreat to.'

'The island in Venice?' Gammaldi said.

'No, that's too easily overwhelmed, he'd want something mobile.' Fox thought about it. 'It would have to be big—the controls require an enormous power supply.'

'A truck?' Gammaldi asked. 'A big semi with a generator?'

'Probably not. The antenna would be huge, far too tall to drive around or conceal. More like a battleship's mast really.'

Something clicked in Gammaldi's brain; Fox could see it in his face.

'What?' Fox said.

'Somewhere he'd hidden before,' Gammaldi said, the beginnings of a smirk on his face. 'Back at the island, there was a yacht with a satellite dish on the stern deck.'

'Lots of boats have sat dishes,' Fox said, playing devil's advocate.

'Yeah, but this sucker was the size of a VW.'

Fox looked at his friend. Over his shoulder the blooming mushroom cloud formed a surreal backdrop, lit by the setting sun.

'Care to see Venice again?' Gammaldi said.

'Al, again I . . . I'm amazed.' Fox shook his head in disbelief at the hypothesis his friend had put together during their hard run to the train tracks.

PART THREE

59

MARAGHEH, IRAN

Sefreid had organised for a truck to meet their boat at the dock they had left a mere eight hours ago. During the trip to the Amahn Research Centre, the worst of the injured were treated by a physician Eric Gunther had thoughtfully sent along. The weary GSR and EU team members passed the half-hour truck ride in reflective silence.

None of them doubted what they had seen. They knew there was only one type of weapon capable of such a display of destruction.

At the research centre the GSR pilots were waiting at the end of the runway, the engines of the Gulfstream running. Eric Gunther was nowhere to be seen.

'He's due back soon—had to go to Cairo for some sort of conference,' the captain of the Gulfstream informed Sefreid as he entered the cockpit.

'Okay, head off anyway. The UN medical compound at Tabriz. They'll be expecting us.'

Sefreid moved into the main cabin where his team, along with the surviving EU men, were strewn. 'You can use the UHF radio in the cockpit to notify Tabriz of our arrival,' he told Farrell.

'Thanks, Richard. I'll do that now,' Farrell replied and moved off to the cockpit.

'Should one of us stay behind for Fox and Al?' asked Gibbs.

Sefreid thought for a moment as the Gulfstream's engines began revving to take-off power. He recalled his last image of the pair as they'd escaped the carnage of heavy battle gloriously unscathed. They were two of the toughest and most dependable soldiers he had ever fought beside.

'I think they'll manage. We can come back and pick them up before we head for home.'

60

THE WHITE HOUSE

Images of the destroyed site came up on the screens in the Situation Room. A very surprised National Security Advisor and Chairman of the Joint Chiefs looked on.

'Tell me what I'm seeing, Don,' McCorkell ordered the highest-ranking member of the armed forces.

'I don't think the images need further interpreting,' Vanzet replied. 'The heat resonance, blast zone, and . . .' He motioned for an aide to switch the screens over to other images travelling via fibre-optic cable from the Pentagon. 'Fallout.'

'Could the radioactivity have been produced by the theterium? I mean, could the conventional explosion from our Tomahawk strike have reacted with the element?' McCorkell asked quickly.

'The final piece of evidence,' Vanzet said solemnly. 'Our readouts measure levels of weapons-grade uranium in the atmosphere, found only after a nuclear attack, which point to an interesting conclusion . . .'

'Which is?' McCorkell asked impatiently.

'The blast zone is consistent with a modern ten-kiloton tactical nuke common to any of the nuclear countries.' Vanzet paused. 'The levels of uranium are almost twice the amount needed by such a weapon.'

'Meaning?'

'Meaning the nuke used in this case was either an older variant built by one of these nations, or, more likely, a crude device built by another party involved. We won't know who unless we get soil samples from the site. Somebody wanted to make sure no one got their hands on the theterium. Ever.'

For all McCorkell's experience and expertise in military and intel affairs, he was dumbfounded. Never had he considered he would see a nuke used aggressively in his time in the House. Those days were meant to be long past. And, until further information was garnered from investigations, the report he was about to give the President was terribly vague.

61

IRAN

Fox and Gammaldi were throwing pebbles into a Kevlar helmet to pass the time when the piercing light of a locomotive shone towards them.

'Well, if it isn't the Orient Express, right on time,' Fox said. He got to his feet and dusted himself off.

'I hope you booked separate cabins this time. I simply couldn't put up with your snoring again,' Gammaldi said as he too patted the dirt and dust from his fatigues.

'Not to worry. First class all the way.'

The pair concentrated on the train as it moved closer, then slowed to climb the slight gradient of the track.

'Ready?' Fox asked as the diesel engine car passed their position. It was followed by almost two dozen boxcars and flatbeds laden with supplies, headed for the Iranian defence of the northern border.

'When you are!' Gammaldi called over the noise.

The pair sped up to match the train's speed. Fox grabbed onto a heavy strap tying down covered boxes and hoisted himself up, quickly righting himself and leaning back to aid his friend.

'Come on, slow coach!' he yelled as they locked hands to wrists.

Fox needed every ounce of strength to pull his mate aboard. They lay on their backs on what little of the deck was free, catching their breath in heaving bursts.

'Which way do you think the dining car is?' Gammaldi gasped.

62

THE WHITE HOUSE

McCorkell rang the President, who was at Camp David, from the Situation Room. He had to wait a full five minutes as the President was in a meeting with NATO heads of state, discussing the Middle East tensions.

'What say you, Bill? Good news, I trust,' greeted the President.

'Depends how you look at it, Mr President,' McCorkell said. 'Firstly, we failed to obtain the theterium. The resourcers and marines are presumed dead.'

'Dead, you say? A damn shame—fine, fine men.' The President paused, choosing his words carefully. 'Is the element accessible to anyone else?'

'No, sir, it has been wiped off the map. All signs point to the use of a crude nuclear device.' McCorkell let the gravity of this news settle in the silence that followed. When the

President spoke, it was not the explosive reaction McCorkell had expected from the man he knew so well.

'A crude nuclear weapon, you say? Who would dare use a nuke, do you think?'

'That is not clear yet, Mr President, and may prove difficult to find out conclusively,' McCorkell replied.

'Is it likely the blast was noticed by other nations?' the President asked.

'Not unless they were looking at the site from above, as there are no outside witnesses to the explosion.' McCorkell wondered where this line of questioning was leading, but continued nonetheless. 'The device was a small one—no more than ten kilotons—and as such, and because of the remote location, seismic tremors outside Iran will not be recorded to any determination of cause.'

'Excellent, excellent,' the President said quietly, before continuing quickly. 'We still have Baker in Tehran, who's been able to make good headway in the past week.'

He sounded a little too practised, McCorkell thought.

'I think it's possible he can persuade the Iranian government to keep a lid on this, in return for international support led by us to sanction the Chechen/Azerbaijan Alliance for their demolition of Bandar-e Anzali.'

'Convenient—but why would we want to keep a lid on somebody using a nuke?' McCorkell said, well and truly smelling a big fat rat.

'Because, Bill, the ramifications would be immense. Think about it,' the President recited. 'Imagine the public hysteria that would erupt if we went to the press saying someone, perhaps Chechnya, exploded The Bomb. We have to wait until we have indisputable proof of the culprit.'

McCorkell sat in silence on the other end of the secure telephone link, stunned by his Commander in Chief's considered words.

'Are we in agreement on this, Bill?' the President said, bringing the National Security Advisor back around.

'Sorry?' McCorkell said.

'Do you concur this would be the wisest course of action to take—for the sake of national security?' the President asked.

McCorkell thought about that for a full minute before replying. 'Under the circumstances, it seems to be an adequate course of action,' he allowed.

'Good to hear, Bill—because, you know, I couldn't have my National Security Advisor disagreeing with my own views on national security,' the President said. The subtext was clear.

'No. That would get in the way of a dictatorship,' McCorkell responded, his face flushing at the thinly veiled threat.

'Excuse me?'

'We've worked together too many damn years to dick each other around! You want some yes-man, go find one, but God help the planet!'

A stunned silence.

'You quoted Wilson in your first State of the Union, remember?' McCorkell said.

There was another pause before the President replied. 'Yeah, I did.'

'You quoted him as saying, "Is the present war a struggle for a just and secure peace, or only for a new balance of power? There must be not a balance of power, but a community of power; not organised rivalries, but an organised, common peace."' McCorkell paused to let the words sink in. 'Don't we still believe in that?'

'Now wait a second, Bill—'

'No, you wait a second, damn it!' McCorkell was squeezing the phone receiver hard. 'If you leave me in the dark on something—watch out. And if you get me involved in something I'm not aware of—'

'All right, Bill!' the President bellowed. 'There's nothing you need to know about, nothing you are involved in.' He paused for a long breath. 'Bill, you know I can't run this show without you.'

McCorkell recognised the sincerity in the President's voice and almost felt apologetic for his outburst—then thought again. The man on the other end of the phone line hadn't reached the top office without being a damn good politician, mastering all the necessary traits.

'Are you truly comfortable with this standpoint?' McCorkell asked his Commander in Chief. He had his own read on the President's standpoint. They'd started their first term in office together eager to make changes, but he'd watched over the past three years as the office had changed his friend.

'Yes, I think it's the only course of action now,' the President said.

'Okay,' McCorkell compromised. 'I'll tidy things up at this end, including making sure the Chechen Alliance find out their objective has been lost. If we can avert their attack on Iran and exploit our involvement in the process, it will make life a hell of a lot easier for Adam Baker.'

'Sounds like a solid plan,' the President said sincerely. 'Bill?'

'Yes, Mr President?' McCorkell had cooled down now.

'It's late and you've been on this thing nonstop for over a week. Take a day off. Don't go near a government building or I'll have the Secret Service deal with you.'

'I'm taking a few days, Mr President. If something comes up, I'll see you at the House,' McCorkell said, happy to have set things relatively straight.

'Bill?'

'Yes, Mr President.'

'What will you do on this little holiday?'

McCorkell sighed and put his feet up on the end of the long table in the Situation Room. Although late at night, the room still buzzed with activity as aides continued to monitor hot spots around the globe.

'Oh, I'll be around. You know me—I can never get far away from this place.' McCorkell thought for a moment. 'What will I do? Run in the mornings, as usual, perhaps even row the Potomac . . .'

63

IRAN

Fox and Gammaldi walked the short distance to the gates of the Amahn Research Centre. The GPS had helped them find the location in the darkness of nightfall.

A pair of sedate guards quickly snapped to attention when the two near-death-looking figures emerged from the middle of nowhere, demanding to see Eric Gunther.

'Who did you say you were?' one guard asked again, he and his partner warily drawing their pistols.

'I'm Lachlan Fox and this is Alister Gammaldi. We're with Cussler's Fantastic Flying Circus and we're here to see the good Dr Gunther,' Fox said, exasperated after the fifth request.

'I think I'm going to call the captain,' the second guard said to the first.

'What a good idea. Why didn't we think of that?' Gammaldi said mockingly to Fox.

'We are but circus performers . . .' Fox trailed off.

After a brief conversation over the phone in the squat concrete guardhouse, the guard exited. 'The captain of base security is on his way. It seems he may know who you are.'

The wait was a short one. A Humvee came rushing to the scene from the main building, lit up along the way by huge halogen floodlights scattered about the facility. The noise of the four-wheel drive was soon drowned out by the sound of a plane coming in to land: Eric Gunther's gleaming Lear jet.

•

The GSR Gulfstream touched down at the Tabriz medical compound where it was met by Lieutenant Paulson and his squad of Gurkhas, who rushed the wounded to surgery.

'I think you should take the time to have your injured seen to as well, Richard,' Farrell said, after he was sure the injured EU team members were being looked after.

Sefreid looked at his men: Geiger who had been nicked in the arm, Pepper sporting a nasty dog bite, and Goldsmith with gashes down his cheeks from the same source. Everyone had cuts, bruises and scrapes from the double ordeal of the farmhouse and the theterium site. Everyone was tired.

'I'm sure a professional change of gauzes and a few cold drinks wouldn't go astray,' Sefreid said and motioned for his team to move into the medical centre.

'You still haven't told me who you're working for,' Farrell said as the two commanders moved to a quiet corner of the surgery and drank from soft-drink cans. He wasn't too optimistic about getting a straight answer.

'Would you believe I'm here for the good of the world?' Sefreid said with a grin.

'Sure—but it doesn't answer my question,' Farrell prodded.

'Well, would you believe a genuine idealist with more *cojones* than Uncle Sam?' Sefreid said.

Farrell looked at his comrade in silence for a moment, taking in his deadpan expression.

'Forget I asked. I didn't really want to know anyway,' he said with a laugh. 'Just don't be a stranger. Drop me a line at Hereford if you ever find yourself in sunny England.'

Sefreid nodded and smiled, impressed that the SAS man felt he could trust him with his identity. 'Will do. It's been a pleasure to fight beside you and your boys.'

'Same here,' Farrell said as they shook hands. 'If you ever find yourself in a tough spot again, yell out—we might just be in the same neighbourhood.'

'Then I'm sure we'll bump into each other again,' Sefreid said confidently.

Farrell thought for a moment. 'Those two making their way on that contraption belonging to the marines—reckon they pulled through?' he asked.

'Fox and Gammaldi?' Sefreid grinned. 'It wouldn't surprise me if they were lying under palm fronds in some oasis being waited on by a tribe of beautiful desert nymphs.'

•

'You want to borrow my plane?' Gunther asked, looking proudly at the Lear jet.

'I assure you it's a matter of life and death. Not for us but potentially millions,' Fox said, hoping it would do the trick.

Gunther rubbed the five o'clock shadow on his chin thought-fully.

'Maybe you should call Wallace?' Gammaldi added.

'That won't be necessary. Not a scratch, you said?' Gunther gave them a crooked grin.

'We promise,' Fox replied, slapping Gammaldi on the arm in triumph as Gunther ordered a ground crew to top up the fuel tanks.

'Venice is a good three thousand kilometres from here and this old bird isn't like that snazzy Gulfstream of yours. She'll be lucky to get you there at maximum cruising speed,' Gunther said.

'She'll get us there gloriously,' Fox replied confidently. 'And before I forget, I brought you a souvenir.' He fished in his pockets. 'Here.'

Gunther took the offered baseball-sized rock and inspected it curiously, apparently surprised by its deceptive weight.

'It's an extraterrestrial element called theterium. I think your research team will have a field day analysing it—and who knows,' Fox smiled cryptically, 'you may even find it useful in your fusion accelerator.'

Gunther studied the dusty amber rock closely. 'Theterium?' he repeated, the name obviously meaning little to him. He looked back up at his gleaming jet. 'I normally fly myself about, but I have another man here who can do the job for you. I'm simply not up to the task tonight, I'm afraid,' he said.

'That won't be necessary. Al here is one of the finest pilots in the Australian Navy,' Fox replied.

Gammaldi looked a little stunned at being volunteered for the task.

'Oh?' Gunther attempted to hide his surprise. 'Okay then, I'd better show you the controls, I suppose,' and he led them off gallantly.

'Thanks a lot,' Gammaldi said quietly from the corner of his mouth.

'No problem,' Fox replied in the same fashion.

Gunther stopped at the bottom of the retractable staircase. 'You're sure you can handle this alone?' he said to Gammaldi.

Gammaldi looked from Gunther to Fox and back to Gunther, putting on his most charming face and voice. 'As Lachlan says, I'm one of the best. I can fly anything built for the skies.'

•

'Thanks again,' Gammaldi said, letting off the brakes and struggling to keep the 1984 model 55 Lear jet straight off the mark. The two tweaked Garrett engines pushed out nearly two thousand kilograms of thrust, hurtling the aircraft down the smooth runway with a satisfactory whine and into the dark northern sky.

'A plane's a plane,' Fox said as he tightened his seat belt.

'A plane's a plane in the air,' Gammaldi said, pulling back on the controls as he neared the two-kilometre mark on the runway, effortlessly lifting the jet's nose into flight. 'It's landing that's going to be the bitch.'

Fox tightened his seatbelt some more.

64

VENICE

Ivanovich's Chief of Intelligence awoke his boss from his prone position between two scantily clad women.

'What is it, Mishka?' Ivanovich asked, coming fully awake.

'If you will come to the briefing room?' Mishka said solemnly. 'News of the early incursion into Iran has come through.'

'Well tell me, man!' Ivanovich bellowed impatiently as he swung out of the bed and wrapped a heavy robe around his nakedness.

'The reports are somewhat troubling . . . a bit unclear. It is best you see for yourself,' the Chief of Intelligence said, trying to be diplomatic rather than the bearer of extremely bad news.

'Just say it, Mishka!' Ivanovich boomed.

'Well . . . we have reports that suggest the site has been wiped off the map.'

Ivanovich looked incredulous. 'Don't be a fool, man. It may have been attacked, yes—but wiped from the map? Impossible.'

Mishka could not match his commander's gaze as he accompanied him out of the room.

65

IRAN

Sefreid used the satellite telephone in the cockpit of the Gulfstream to call New York, where an anxious Tasman Wallace quickly came to the phone.

'Richard. You have time for the full rundown now?' Wallace asked.

'Yes, Dr Wallace. Again, sorry for the brevity of the call before, things have been hectic,' Sefreid said as he settled into the comfortable pilot's chair.

'I can only imagine. Although you have left me hanging on what became of the site. And have you heard from Fox and Gammaldi?' Wallace asked with paternal concern.

'No word yet, but we'll head back to the research centre once we're done here,' Sefreid replied. 'As for the theterium site, it's damn hard to believe, but the explosion was nuclear.'

'Nuclear?'

'Yep,' Sefreid said. 'We heard the initial hit, which was the Tomahawk strike, followed minutes later by a tactical-sized blast that was probably no more than ten kilotons.'

Wallace was silent on the other end of the telephone connection. Then, 'I'll find out what I can about that,' he said thoughtfully.

'Aside from those on our boat, and Fox and Al speeding from the scene, I believe it's impossible that anyone else could have escaped the blast zone,' Sefreid admitted.

'So we are the only witnesses on the ground—aside from the surviving EU members,' Wallace stated.

'And one marine—Beasley's brother.'

'Pardon?'

'Ben Beasley's brother was assigned to Scot's marines unit recently, on an investigation assignment for JAG,' Sefreid explained. 'Apparently, he was building a case on the unit for a whole heap of hell.'

'And now he's alive and well there with you?'

'Yes, he's with Ben now. They seem to get along famously,' Sefreid said.

'Then we have to assume he knows a little about us?' Wallace said.

'More than the EU team, who aren't displaying any interest.'

'Well, bring him home with you and I'll get his military records. I dare say he'll be listed as KIA by the Pentagon, written off as another Iraq casualty, so he may like the option of a new vocation,' Wallace said confidently.

'Will do,' Sefreid replied.

'I'm sorry about John Ridge,' Wallace added after a pause. 'I know you were close. Just remember what he died for. A damn good job was done all round . . .'

Wallace paused again and Sefreid heard a knock in the background.

'Really?' he heard Wallace say before he returned to the phone.

'We've just had a message from Gunther in Iran,' Wallace said disbelievingly. 'Lachlan and Al have just commandeered his jet and are en route to Italy.'

'What the hell are they doing going back there?' Sefreid asked.

'Apparently, they said something about saving millions of lives.'

Sefreid thought for a moment. 'I'll be damned . . . they're going after the Dragon controls!'

66

ITALY

Gammaldi landed the Lear jet in hair-raising fashion, over-running the end of the farmhouse's runway so that the aircraft's chrome nose ended up pushing against the tin wall of the motorbike garage, which squealed and bent in protest. Fox's knuckles were chalk white as he squeezed the armrests of the seat.

'Told you so,' Gammaldi said as he casually unclasped his seatbelt and looked through the windscreen to assess the damage.

'So much for not a scratch,' Fox said. He peered out the cockpit window to see if the farmhouse had been restocked with more guards in the last twenty-four hours. Evidently it hadn't.

'That was your assurance, not mine,' Gammaldi said as he shut the aircraft down and moved into the cabin.

'You got us here in one piece—that was the only assurance I was after,' Fox replied with a grin.

The two men loaded and readied the SOCOM pistols they had acquired from the marines they'd removed from the Roadrunner. The Heckler & Koch pistols were custom-made for Special Operations Command, and chambered for the awesome power of the .45 APC round.

'Now we just have to figure out how we get to the island,' Gammaldi said as they moved out of the craft and into the still dark early morning.

'Elementary, my friend, elementary.' Fox ran over to the nearby hangar. 'Go to the guard box to the right of the Lear,' he called out. 'There's a surprise for you on the roof.'

•

Fifteen minutes later, Fox and Gammaldi were on the timber jetty at the lagoon's edge.

'Ain't she beautiful,' Fox proclaimed as he clambered down into the raft. He had constructed it using the emergency inflatable life raft from the Lear jet, crudely attaching a working outboard motor from those stacked in the aircraft hangar. A plastic oar from the life raft was tied to the side of the engine and extended into the water—Fox hoped it would steer the craft by turning the motor around on its makeshift attachment.

'Beautiful, she ain't,' Gammaldi said. 'I just hope it stays together long enough so we can storm the island stronghold and save the world.'

'Do you have to be so morbid all the time?' Fox asked. 'You know you have a tendency to jinx things.'

'Okay, I won't comment on the state of these then.' Gammaldi held up the two AK-47s Fox had thrown onto the guardhouse roof during the earlier rescue.

'Don't tell me they're not loaded,' Fox said with dread as he set the outboard in motion. Satisfied it was well fastened, they set off at full throttle.

'Oh, they're loaded. I even found an extra pair of magazines in the guardhouse,' Gammaldi replied. 'But I doubt these antiques have ever been cleaned.'

'Great,' was all Fox said as he steered for the first channel marker.

•

At the first hint of sunrise, President Ivanovich's sixteen-metre motor yacht was loaded with his personal effects ready for departure.

The bulk of the security force had left an hour prior, destined for a point in the Adriatic Sea where the two vessels would meet to travel in tandem to a secure location in South America.

In the room adjoining the master bedroom on the yacht, Popov had worked through the night to set up the firing controls for the Dragon coilgun. They were wired into their own generator on deck, and he had connected the satellite dish on the stern deck, muscled from the island by a gang of burly guards. Tied to a chair in the corner sat the woman prisoner whom Popov had selected as his reward.

Ivanovich strode onto deck with Orakov and Mishka in tow. 'Let's get out of here,' he ordered and the crew untied the yacht and set the engines forward.

•

As Fox and Gammaldi drifted along the northwest coast of the island on a reconnaissance sweep, they observed the yacht preparing to sail, and three men boarding it. Fox had committed to memory the face of one man on the first flight to Italy to rescue Gammaldi—that of Sergei Ivanovich. Behind him was a man Gammaldi remembered well: Orakov.

'Well, at least we don't have to storm Alcatraz,' Gammaldi said.

'Yeah, now we have to chase, board and disable the controls of a vessel ten times the size of ours,' Fox said.

'You're convinced the firing controls are on board the yacht now?'

'I don't think that satellite dish is there just to pick up the Super Bowl,' Fox said. 'And if you figure these guys have recently found out their invasion of Iran is unnecessary, they'll not only be pissed, but on the move *fast*.'

'Heading underground?'

'I'm sure they have no other option,' Fox said. 'Until they gain another foothold of power through mass terrorism somewhere else.'

'Like using a loaded gun in space to intimidate any nation on Earth,' Gammaldi added.

'Exactly,' Fox said. He gave the outboard more throttle and chased after the yacht.

'Do we have a plan?' Gammaldi asked hopefully.

Fox just smiled.

•

For ten minutes, the small rubber craft managed to follow the motor yacht with relative ease. Fox took a wide arc to come around to the east of the yacht when it suddenly sped up another few knots.

'Have they seen us?' Gammaldi asked, alarmed.

'I don't think so. We'd surely know it if they did,' Fox replied. He again applied full throttle to the outboard, the ungainly rubber boat protesting at the speed, the engine bellowing blue smoke. The pair had to position their bodies with skill to keep the vessel steady.

'They must have been warming the engine. It's going to be now or never,' Fox said with slight unease.

'Ready when you are, mate.'

•

Gammaldi opened fire first: a short controlled burst that splintered the side edging of the yacht, followed by another that peppered the roof of the pilothouse.

In response, the yacht veered to starboard, away from the threat. Figures could be seen scurrying about the decks in the darkness.

'That got their attention,' Gammaldi said as he took over control of the ungainly vessel.

'Yep,' Fox said as he sighted his AK-47 and waited, finger poised on the trigger.

Within a few seconds, a powerful spotlight came to life and probed the waters in the direction of the gunfire—just as Fox had anticipated. With two shots from Fox's AK-47 they were in darkness again. Fox felled the guard manning the now defunct spotlight with another bullet, correcting his aim to account for the crooked sights of the old assault rifle.

'I do like evening the odds where possible,' he said.

He resumed the controls and zigzagged the craft in the water, losing some forward speed but avoiding the cacophony of automatic fire that lashed wildly in the water about them. The darkness that hid their craft would not last long as the first hues of light were spreading across the sky.

'This just might work,' Gammaldi said as the yacht started to round the famous glassworks island of Murano north of Venice.

'If they don't shoot us out of the water by the time we get close enough to board,' Fox replied. He let rip with a full burst of AK-47 fire, emptying his thirty-round magazine.

The yacht sped around the island without slowing, breaking into clear water to pass the cemetery island of San Michele, then heading straight for the rising buildings of picturesque Venice and its famous canals.

The leading edge of the sun broke the horizon behind the chase, revealing the ungainly craft in pursuit of the yacht to the half-dozen guards on board toting assault rifles.

'Look out!' Fox warned as he turned the craft hard, almost capsizing them in the process.

Several bullets found their mark, shredding sections of the inflated rubber craft. The life raft just managed to stay together.

As Fox brought the craft back around, Gammaldi fired his AK-47 on fully automatic. Not many of his shots hit the yacht as it disappeared into the canal system.

'Shit! We're too far behind to catch them now,' he said resignedly.

'Don't count us out of the race yet,' Fox said as he steered for a canal to the left of the one their quarry had taken. 'Navigating through the city is going to limit their speed. We can still catch them.'

'I'll hold my breath,' Gammaldi said.

They entered the canal, the three- and four-storey buildings either side forming canyon-like walls that echoed their full throttle outboard motor, much to the voiced annoyance of the locals awakened by it. A bend followed, where Fox bounced the craft off the side of a garbage barge; water filled their little craft, forcing Gammaldi to bail it out quickly. The spraying water soon had them soaked through, their craft becoming airborne as it sped over the wake of other traffic.

Then they came upon the Grand Canal. And collided with Ivanovich's yacht.

Fox jammed the end of the makeshift rudder under his arm and held his craft against the side of the yacht as he unleashed a torrent of fire at the deck. Gammaldi quickly joined in.

'Take the rudder!' Fox ordered.

He grabbed hold of the railing at shoulder-level and hoisted himself up, instantly finding himself in a rolling fistfight with a guard. After a minute Fox had the upper hand, and was aided by Gammaldi, who literally picked the incapacitated guard up off the deck and threw him overboard into the water of Venice's main canal.

A water bus of early-morning commuters droned by, the passengers staring agape at the unfolding drama.

A few shots came at them from the pilothouse, but in vain. Fox and Gammaldi took cover to rise again and empty their AK-47s until the wounded guards fell silent.

'You get control of the yacht and heave-to somewhere. I'll go below,' Fox said and disappeared before his friend could object.

•

Gammaldi waited by a timber door leading into the side of the pilothouse. He glanced through the glass: two crewmen were busy steering the yacht to safety, despite the ruckus outside. The man at the rudder wheel motioned for his comrade to go outside and check on the situation. Gammaldi waited out of sight as the man picked up an AK-47 and made for the door.

•

Fox bounded through the open stern hatch, lost his footing on the wet stairs and landed on his backside a rung from the floor. Bullets sprayed above his head—where he would have been standing. He returned fire, the .45 calibre SOCOM booming twice in the confines of the space below, and felled his attacker—a man with a rat-like beard.

Fox got to his feet and began searching the cabins.

•

The crewman stepped out onto the narrow side deck, leading with his assault rifle. Gammaldi waited until the man was clear of the doorway and out of sight from his comrade before making his move.

Grabbing the muzzle of the AK-47 with his left hand, Gammaldi swung a powerful uppercut at the crewman with his right, hitting the startled Chechen square under the chin with as much force as his rock-like fist and thick arm could muster. With a grunt, the man went overboard headfirst.

•

There were four doors leading off the companionway: two on his left, one to the right and another at the stern. Fox kicked in the closest door to find two women cowering in a corner of the master bedroom. They were strikingly beautiful and stared wide-eyed at the figure in desert fatigues stained with blood and grime, soaked to the bone from the canal water and brandishing a mean-looking pistol.

Fox looked about the room, bowed goodbye, and closed the door to continue his search.

•

Gammaldi spun into the doorway of the pilothouse, holding his pistol straight ahead with both hands. 'Hi there!' he said to the crewman at the controls, who nearly jumped out of his skin in surprise.

'You have three seconds to exit that door behind you,' Gammaldi said casually.

The man nodded, then paused, looking over Gammaldi's shoulder. He smiled.

•

Fox kicked open the opposing door to the bedroom and found his objective—a control panel with a pale, sickly looking man not much older than himself standing in front of it.

'Don't come any closer!' the man said in a wavering voice.
Then his eyes opened in recognition. He had seen this man
before. A man he'd left for dead . . .

'You!' Popov cried in disbelief. 'You . . . how . . . ?'

Fox looked at the man with a questioning frown. He certainly
hadn't seen him before, but he made the connection anyway.
'Let me guess. You've been to Christmas Island?' he said as
he stepped into the room.

'Don't come any closer!' the man said again. His hand was
on a key in the control panel. To one side it read 'Fire'; to the
other, 'Reset'.

Without delay Fox sighted his SOCOM pistol and fired.
The heavy round transformed the man's outstretched hand to
a bloody pulp, but he'd managed to turn the key anyway. A
red light blinked above the 'Fire' sign.

•

As Gammaldi turned he was smashed in the face with the butt
of an assault rifle.

He managed to move with the blow, which lessened its
impact, but failed to save him from being knocked to the
ground.

'We meet again,' Orakov said as he sank the stock of his
rifle into Gammaldi's stomach.

The crewman laughed maliciously and continued his navi-
gation of the Grand Canal, forced to steer around a group of
gondolas looking for early-morning fares.

•

As the man screamed in pain, Fox was knocked to the ground from behind by a heavy blow to the head.

He was on all fours and saw legs rush past him, then heard a struggle, presumably between the man at the controls and Fox's attacker. He used the distraction to roll onto his side and blindly fire his pistol in quick succession, hitting his attacker in the leg as another heavy blow struck his shoulder.

●

Gammaldi clenched his stomach, the force of the blow lessened by his Kevlar flak jacket. As Orakov moved around to attack from another angle, Gammaldi struck out with his leg and managed to trip the Russian over.

Orakov controlled his fall to land with all his weight atop the prone man, digging his elbow into Gammaldi's sternum. Gammaldi was stunned breathless, causing the watching crewman to laugh again.

●

Fox rose groggily to his feet and raised his SOCOM pistol again at Ivanovich, whom he now recognised. Ivanovich had dropped the fire extinguisher he'd been using as a club and was clutching at his wound.

'Sergei Ivanovich,' Fox said. 'President Terrorist of Shitsville.' He rested a hand on the doorframe to steady himself. On the control panel, a digital clock was counting down:

1:38

1:37

1:36

Ivanovich looked into the eyes of the man before him, clutching at the firing control panel to steady himself. His leg was pumping copious amounts of blood. 'Who are you? CIA? MI5? Special Forces?' Ivanovich asked as he moved slowly backwards.

'I'm just a guy who doesn't like to see innocent lives taken by arseholes like you—and you can stop moving now,' Fox said.

'I take it you're not American then.' Ivanovich looked with genuine intrigue at the man before him. 'Still, they'll get theirs in the end. You do know where the Dragon is now pointing, don't you?' Ivanovich said, inching away again.

'Tehran?' Fox said and glanced at the digital display.

1:29

1:28

'Washington.'

Ivanovich's grin was pure evil. He looked at the man in front of him, so dishevelled and weary, trying to work him out. Another inch back and he bumped into the woman tied to the chair. In a lightning move he twisted behind her, using her as a shield. He held a small two-shot pistol to her head.

•

Fox held the SOCOM level, aimed at Ivanovich's eye, while he shot another glance at the counter.

1:23

'You know that the theterium is gone,' Fox said. 'You've got nowhere to go.'

Ivanovich was starting to pale from the loss of blood. He pulled the gag from the woman's mouth and she let out a scream, tears running down her face as she struggled in his grip.

'Why don't I make you a deal, Mr . . .'

'Fox,' he replied, not wasting time.

1:15

'Walk away, Mr Fox, and you can take this woman with you.' Ivanovich squeezed his hand around the woman's neck, pressing the pistol harder against her head. 'Or I take her life. What's your name, woman?'

She did not answer, just kept crying, making gurgling sounds.

'Let Mr Fox know your name, darling. He doesn't have much time.'

For Fox, time seemed to stand still. He could reach the fire control key and let this woman be killed. Or he could wait for an opportunity to take a shot at Ivanovich, but the clock would beat them.

'Alissa,' the woman sobbed. 'Alissa Truscott. Please help me.' Her voice was hoarse. Desperate. She was thin and sick after months in captivity.

'Decisions, Mr Fox!' Ivanovich said, swaying from his wound.

Fox looked from Ivanovich to the controls.

0:49

He looked into the bloodshot eyes of Alissa Truscott. He could see her young beauty, but there was a lost innocence there too. She'd been to hell and back.

She pleaded with her expression, then saw the tear roll down Fox's cheek and closed her eyes.

•

Gammaldi used every ounce of strength he could muster to wrap his hands around Orakov's neck and squeeze off his air supply. The Chechen fought back, swinging wildly at Gammaldi but achieving nothing.

Gammaldi, still lying against the ground with Orakov atop him, tightened his grip until the man's eyes bulged and blood dribbled from the damaged tissues in his throat. After two minutes, Orakov was totally limp and Gammaldi tossed him aside like a rag doll.

Gammaldi got to his feet, heaving exhausted breaths, his face reddened with strain, and looked to the last crewman.

The man bolted out the door and jumped over the side of the boat.

•

0:27

Fox lunged at the fire control key and turned it, his other arm and the SOCOM outstretched towards Ivanovich.

Before he could fire, a pop rang out and Alissa Truscott went limp in Ivanovich's grasp. The Russian quickly turned his small pistol to fire at Fox.

Fox fired twice into Ivanovich's head and chest and the Russian slumped to the floor. He emptied the remainder of his .45 magazine into the firing controls, which caught fire with the last shot.

There was nothing he could do for Alissa Truscott, but he picked up her lifeless body and walked out, stepping over the extinguisher that had dented his head moments earlier.

He paused at the door of the main bedroom and looked in at the cowering women.

'You might want to jump overboard now,' he said.

•

By the time Fox reached the pilothouse, Gammaldi was bringing the yacht to a stop against the edge of St Mark's Square, Venice's famous open piazza at the southern end of the Grand Canal. Two scantily clad women emerged from the forward hatch and jumped over the side of the almost motionless vessel, smoke escaping from the hatch after them.

'Who the hell were they?' Gammaldi demanded, thinking he had missed out, but then he noticed Fox was carrying a body. He saw the look in his friend's eyes.

'Come on,' Fox replied as he stepped over the body of Orakov and onto the side deck.

Gammaldi set the engine to full speed ahead, then pulled the rudder wheel off and tossed it overboard. He and Fox leaped to shore as the boat moved off.

They watched the yacht head off into open water, trailing smoke. Soon the sirens of police boats cut through the morning as they chased after the blazing hulk. They could see Popov standing on the stern deck, shaking his good fist in anger.

Moments later the boat exploded spectacularly in the open expanse of St Mark's Canal.

Fox gently laid the body of Alissa Truscott on the pavement and placed his Kevlar vest over her face, for what little dignity it offered.

'You're leaving her here?'

'We can't walk the streets with a body,' Fox said. 'The authorities will look after her.'

The sound of more sirens was enough to urge Fox and Gammaldi into a run. They passed the early-morning traders setting up in the square, startling thousands of sedate pigeons into flight.

•

After several minutes of zigzagging through incredibly narrow cobbled laneways and crossing the Rialto Bridge, the weary pair came to an antique telephone booth outside a newsagency. Gammaldi entered the box, picked up the receiver and paused. 'You said the number was 1800 GSR HQ?'

'Yeah,' Fox said as he waved a bloodied hand to the stunned newsagent.

'Notice anything about this telephone?' It had an old-fashioned dial ringer.

'Just call the operator. They can figure it out,' Fox said.

'Okay . . .'

Gammaldi read the listed numbers on a laminated panel in front of him and dialled as quickly as the device would permit. The conversation that transpired became increasingly heated.

'She's not being very helpful,' Gammaldi said, putting his hand over the mouthpiece. 'She will only put us through if we know the number.'

'Shit!' Fox said in despair.

'Okay . . .' Gammaldi pinched the bridge of his nose in thought. 'We can do this.'

'All right . . .' Fox paused. 'Do the letters start on one?'

'I thought they started on two,' Gammaldi said.

'Shit!' Then Fox saw a cyclist riding towards him, talking jovially on a cell phone. 'I think the gods are smiling on us,' he said.

Fox stepped into the bike's path and plucked the phone from the stunned man. The cyclist looked like he was about to yell in protest until he noticed Fox's blood-soaked army clothes.

'Here we go! 1800 . . . 477 . . . 47.' Fox tossed the cell phone back to the man. '*Grazie*,' he said, using the one Italian word he knew. The man sped off.

Gammaldi relayed the numbers in Italian and passed the receiver to Fox.

A GSR operator answered the call.

'My name is Lachlan Fox and I urgently need to speak to Tasman Wallace,' Fox tried.

•

Fox and Gammaldi found the Continental Hotel after ten minutes of searching along the Grand Canal's many properties. As per Wallace's directions, the pair went to a side door where they were met by the manager, who gave them a cursory look over before shuffling them inside and leading them up an internal fire escape. Gammaldi profusely thanked the man in Italian, blessing his family for years to come, and the manager left them alone in their assigned room.

'I do believe this is the Honeymoon Suite,' Gammaldi said, as Fox discovered the minibar and produced a couple of beers.

'So long as it has a shower, I don't mind playing your husband,' Fox said, taking in the postcard view from the balcony.

'A shower?' Gammaldi echoed from the bathroom. 'It has two!'

•

After two long showers that almost ran the hotel's hot water system dry, the duo ate a full room-service breakfast and received fresh civilian clothes from the manager.

Gammaldi was enjoying an in-room massage to ease his battered body when the phone rang.

'Hello?' Fox answered.

'Lachlan, it's Tasman. I trust you've settled in?' Wallace said.

'Yes, thank you, we're feeling much more alive,' Fox replied, drinking another beer.

'Good to hear. I cannot tell you how glad I am to know the two of you are alive and well. And after all that you have done!' Wallace sounded extremely happy.

'Anyone would have done the same,' Fox said. 'Before I forget . . .' He picked up the small journal he had carried with him from the theterium site. 'I found a book at the site . . . belonging to Alissa Truscott.'

Wallace was silent on the other end of the phone line. When he finally spoke, his voice quavered. 'Then you know who she is?' he said. 'Do you know where she is now?'

'There was an unsealed letter addressed to you inside,' Fox explained quietly. 'I'll send it to you this afternoon. And . . .'

He took a few moments to muster the strength to tell Wallace about Alissa Truscott. Only once before had he been the bearer of such news: to the widow of John Birmingham. This was just as bad.

67

NEW YORK

Tasman Wallace walked to his bathroom, where he splashed water on his face. He entered his spacious lounge room and sat on the stool at his grand piano, and began to play. As he keyed the notes of Chopin, he gazed at the silver-framed photo atop the highly polished Steinway. It was of a person he had known for barely two years—two wonderful years. Someone who had literally turned up on his doorstep one day and introduced herself in such a dignified manner. Alissa Truscott.

His only child.

EPILOGUE

WASHINGTON

McCorkell was grinning from ear to ear, elated by the pain across his shoulders and the burning in his legs as he rowed with all his might. It was a feeling he hadn't had the luxury of indulging in for so long, and it took him back to his happy days at Oxford. As did the company of his old dorm mate and exercise partner.

The pair had rowed the Potomac leisurely at first, then broke into a sprint just to see if they still had it. Evidently they did—passing numerous other similar craft—but it was a pace their middle-aged bodies couldn't keep up for long. At the urging of McCorkell's companion, who was a few years older, they slowed to a lazy stroke.

'What's happening with the nuke situation?' the older man asked.

'Word hasn't got out yet, but it seems a French satellite picked up the blast so it will probably become public knowledge soon,' McCorkell replied.

'And what will the President do?'

'Explain it as an Iranian-based Al-Qaeda terrorist tactic to further inflame the growing tension of the Iranian–Chechen situation. That the Iraqi army attacked the Chechens, who were in their territory, further fuels the flames of suspicion. What's more, it will galvanise the world to back us in any further pre-emptive strikes against rogue states,' McCorkell said.

'What does that mean for Iran?'

'UN personnel will sweep in and snoop under every rock in the country. Maybe overthrow the governing council and get involved in making the country a democracy; appoint a UN body to hold provisional elections,' McCorkell explained. He pulled a water bottle from the bottom of the boat.

'Good old UN saves the day. They could do with the good press,' the man said.

'Exactly what the President said.'

'And what of the situation with the Dragon?' his rowing partner asked as he watched a local college team row past with ease.

'Last I heard, we're still searching—and certain people close to the President are urging the need to recover the weapon intact. Purely for study purposes, of course. Drink?' McCorkell offered.

'Thanks, Bill.'

Tasman Wallace took the bottle and drank, then pulled off his cap and splashed a little water over his mane of white hair. He handed the bottle back over his shoulder. 'Do you know who set off the nuke?'

McCorkell took a pull of the water.

'That, Tas, we may never know. But I have my ideas.'

VENICE

The afternoon sun warmed the city, which was abuzz with tourists taking in the sights and vying for positions in the city's gondolas. Fox and Gammaldi soaked up the atmosphere at an outside table of a restaurant, sharing a bottle of wine.

'What did you order for us?' Fox asked, topping up his friend's glass.

'A mixed plate of fresh pasta, followed by an osso bucco that will probably put my momma's to shame,' Gammaldi replied.

'Sounds great,' Fox said with a grin.

Gammaldi sat thoughtfully for a moment. 'Returning to the navy is going to seem a bit dull now.'

'There are plenty of options,' Fox said, swirling his wine in its glass. 'We should take Gunther's plane back tomorrow. I'm sure he'll be fretting by now.'

'And from there?'

Fox stirred from his thoughts. 'From there we can get the GSR boys to pick us up.' He looked into the face of his friend, the corners of a mischievous grin beginning.

'Why do I get the feeling you're roping me into something dangerous?' Gammaldi asked with raised eyebrows.

'Oh, I don't know. I can't imagine things will be this frantic all the time,' Fox said. He watched a pair of gorgeous Mediterranean women approach the busy restaurant.

'Why does that sound like another famous Fox quote that will come back to haunt us?' Gammaldi said. The two friends laughed harder than they had in ages.

'Excuse me? May we share the table?' one of the women Fox had seen approaching—a tall curvy brunette—asked in accented English.

Fox shared a quick glance with his friend, their eyes glinting in the setting sun.

'Please do.'

New York Herald
16 February 2006

CHECHEN CRISIS AVERTED

By L. Fox

The potential military conflict between Chechnya and Iran has been averted with the death of Chechnya's leader, President Sergei Ivanovich. President Ivanovich's body, and that of his chief military commander, were found in Venice, Italy. Authorities are investigating the deaths.

All military personnel on either side of the Azerbaijan–Iran border have withdrawn. Iran's forces have moved into the port city of Bandar-e Anzali to help with the continuing clean-up effort. Bandar-e Anzali, located on Iran's Caspian Sea coastline, was destroyed last month. The cause of the destruction remains unknown but it was most likely due to tremendous seismic activity in the region.

Eight thousand bodies have been retrieved so far and authorities hold little hope for the seventeen thousand people still missing.

In Chechnya, the UN has set up an interim government representing the diverse ethnic population, and has slated elections later this year for a 45-seat parliament. Five thousand peacekeeping soldiers from Canada, Australia, England and Spain are keeping the peace in the streets of Grozny. So far there have been no altercations and the population appears excited at the prospect of free democratic elections.

Lachlan Fox is an investigative journalist with the GSR news agency.

ACKNOWLEDGEMENTS

Being a first novel, there are many people I wish to thank for helping me get there.

To Nicole Wallace, my literary guinea pig and main protagonist. Thanks again for your support, generosity and tried and true patience. To the Beasleys, my driving force, inspiration and critical friends. To my family, for putting up with my conspiracy theories and backing my dreams.

To my friends who endured early drafts of *Fox Hunt* and were honest in their appraisals. Anne Looney and Louise Truscott were brilliant in helping get my work to a publishable standard – and thanks for the great title Louise! To my friends at *The Age* and Swinburne University for their time and encouragement. Special thanks to my expert panel of readers and supporters: Bill Green, Wendy Newton, Emily McDonald, Louise Zaetta, Steve Kynoch, John Birmingham, Stephen Javens, Tony Neiman, Bec and Janet Dickson . . . and of course my best mate from high school, Alister Gammaldi. Thanks Al for letting me cheat by not having to make up a 'buddy character', you've got it all mate.

To my contacts in the Australian Defence Force, serving and retired, my hat goes off to you all. Thanks for your expert commentary even if it was at the expense of my poetic licence. When I can get DARPA to make some Falcon parachutes, I'll send one to each of you. Be safe.

And finally, eternal thanks to my publishing team. My extraordinary agent, Pippa Masson, is knowledgeable, talented and supportive. Same goes for all the gals at Curtis Brown Australia. To all the staff at Hachette Livre Australia, thanks for your enthusiasm. Special thanks to: my wonderful and talented editor Vanessa Radnidge for spotting a diamond in the rough, publishing maven Lisa Highton for her generosity, my line editors Deonie Fiford and Nicola O'Shea for cutting out thousands of superfluous words, Louise Sherwin-Stark sales and marketing genius, Deb McInnes and Amy Hurrell publicity gurus. Last but not least, each and every sales rep out on the front line, cheers.